It felt like the most natural thing in the world when Bart pulled Pia closer.

This would not be their first kiss. . . . But this kiss would be different.

When their lips touched it was like the brush of a feather, so light, so gentle.

Almost as if by some primeval instinct, Pia's response was eager and willing. She wound her arms around his neck, and when she felt his mouth open on hers, she opened hers as well, trusting Bart completely.

This, she realized, was what it was like to love and be loved by a man, and she was powerless to stop herself. She wanted, more than anything, for him to continue, to go on until . . . until what? She didn't know, she just knew that there was more—and she wanted it.

Critics adore Sara Luck's blazingly hot Western romances!

RIMFIRE BRIDE

A pretty and courageous schoolteacher comes to Bismark and turns heads as a dress model in a shop window! And in the arms of the handsome single father who owns Rimfire Ranch, she discovers what home feels like. . . .

"Luck's devotion to historical accuracy shines again. . . . *Rimfire Bride* warms the heart."

—*RT Book Reviews*

"Exciting. . . . A must-read. Sara Luck is truly a talented storyteller. . . . You feel as if you are there in 1882."

—*My Book Addiction Reviews*

More praise for Sara Luck and her novels

TALLIE'S HERO

A *Publishers Weekly* Top 10 Romance for Fall 2012

The dangerous American West is no place for a genteel British novelist fleeing a scandal . . . but one plucky lady embraces the spirit of Wyoming—and captures the heart of her new hero, a daring rancher with big dreams of his own.

"The Wild West retains its appeal in *Tallie's Hero*."

—*Publishers Weekly*

"Steamy Western romance."

—*Fresh Fiction*

CLAIMING THE HEART

As the Texas and Pacific Railroad expands across the wild frontier, a spirited young woman experiences the triumphs and tumult of building a part of history . . . and loving a track man bound to a politically powerful family.

"Terrific. . . . An enjoyable nineteenth-century Americana tale."

—*Genre Go Round*

"Luck captures the true essence of the Texas frontier. . . . A fast-paced story with plenty of action and engaging characters."

—Romantic Times

SUSANNA'S CHOICE

Sara Luck's "promising debut" (*Romance Views Today*)!

In a dusty Nevada mining town, an aspiring newspaperwoman crosses paths with a wealthy entrepreneur from San Francisco, and everything changes—including her own uncertain destiny.

"An exciting read. . . . A passionate, adventure-filled historical romance."

—Shadowfire Press

"Heartwarming. . . . Sensual. . . . This one's a keeper!"

—Night Owl Reviews
(5 stars, A Night Owl Top Pick)

"A solid story line with a just-right soupçon of romantic tension."

—Publishers Weekly

"Everything a historical romance reader could want. . . . An exciting story with strong characters and vivid descriptions of Americana history."

—My Book Addiction Reviews

"Luck is an author to watch."

—RT Book Reviews

HEARTS UNBOUND

SARA LUCK

Pocket Books

New York   London   Toronto   Sydney   New Delhi

Pocket Books
A Division of Simon & Schuster, Inc.
1230 Avenue of the Americas
New York, NY 10020

This book is a work of fiction. Any references to historical events, real people, or real places are used fictitiously. Other names, characters, places, and events are products of the author's imagination, and any resemblance to actual events or places or persons, living or dead, is entirely coincidental.

First Pocket Books paperback edition August 2013

POCKET and colophon are registered trademarks of Simon & Schuster, Inc.

For information about special discounts for bulk purchases, please contact Simon & Schuster Special Sales at 1-866-506-1949 or business@simonandschuster.com.

The Simon & Schuster Speakers Bureau can bring authors to your live event. For more information or to book an event contact the Simon & Schuster Speakers Bureau at 1-866-248-3049 or visit our website at www.simonspeakers.com.

Manufactured in the United States of America

10 9 8 7 6 5 4 3 2 1

ISBN 978-1-4767-1316-8
ISBN 978-1-4767-1318-2 (ebook)

HEARTS
UNBOUND

ONE

Guernicako arbola da. Haritz bat, Euskal Herriak tradizionalak sinbolizatzen da," Pia Carranza said as she pointed to the spreading oak tree that sat inside an iron-rail fence behind her. She was surrounded by bright-eyed young girls in brown pigtails, and young boys with wind-tossed hair, all paying close attention as they listened to her teach her English-language class.

"This is the Tree of Guernica. Now, answer me in English," Pia said, addressing the half dozen children who were sitting on the grass around her. "Why is this tree different from any other tree in all of Spain?"

"Because it was under this tree that the noblemen of Biscay and the kings of Castile and Aragon guaranteed us our liberties," one of the boys replied excitedly. "And even though King Alfonso took our rights away from us, in our hearts we will always remember that among the Basques, each one is the equal of the richest, each one is the equal of the poorest, and no matter where in the world a Basque might go, we will always remember this tree and the promise of freedom."

"Very good, Matia!" Pia replied, rewarding the boy with a big smile. "That is exactly right!"

"Oh, oh, Miss Pia made a mistake," Matia said, giggling at his joke. "I am not Matia, I am Matthew."

"How silly of me. Of course you are Matthew."

Pia was twenty-one years old, a beautiful young woman with long, dark hair, high cheekbones, and brown eyes under long lashes. She had attended the parish school of Santa Maria de la Antigua until she was twelve years old. Then she left school to join her mother and her older sister, who worked in the parish bakery. Her father, Sabin Carranza, was in America working for Lander Segura as a sheep-herder.

When Father Ignacio, the parish priest, returned from his studies in England and the United States, he was determined to teach his parishioners to speak English. He wanted them to be able to com-municate with the many foreigners who were in Bilbao, the capital of their province of Bizkaia, but most turned a deaf ear to his prodding.

That was, all except for Pia Carranza. She had such an amazing facility for learning English that the priest relieved her from her duties at the bakery and had her teach English to the smaller children in the school.

Father Ignacio smiled at his protégé as she sat among the children, every one of them speak-ing English as if they had been born in California, Nevada, Oregon, or Idaho, the states with the largest Basque population. Here in Spain, because of the near insurmountable language barrier the *euskaldunak* faced, more often than not the boys were forced into the lonely life of a sheepherder, and the girls took jobs in boardinghouses. Father Ignacio was convinced that if these children should someday move to America, they would, by their knowledge of English, have many more opportunities.

When Pia saw the priest, she waved to him. "Come join us, Father. Ion—I mean John—is telling us about the new pelota court that is being built behind the plaza."

"Let me see your hand," Father Ignacio said as he turned Ion's hand over. "Ah, there they are. Every young Basque boy must develop tough calluses if he is to be a good handball player."

"Father, why can't girls play pelota?" a little girl asked.

"Because girls have much more serious work to do, Kistiñe. Who would feed the oxen or tend the chickens if the girls were always out hitting a silly ball up against a wall?"

"I'm Christina. That's what Miss Pia calls me, and I don't think it's fair that the boys get to play all the time and we have to work."

"It will make us better people if we work hard," Pia said as she hugged the child to her, "but for now our lesson is over. Why don't you run home and see what your *ama* wants you to do before it gets dark?"

"It's not *ama*, it's *mother*," Kistiñe said as the children rose to leave. "May we be excused, Father Ignacio?"

"Of course. I need to talk with Miss Pia."

When the children were gone, the priest withdrew an envelope from the pocket of his black cassock. "This came from Idaho, today. When are you going to tell your father you can speak English as well as I?"

Pia lowered her head. "I'm not sure he would be pleased."

"And why would you say that, my child? Any parent would be proud of his daughter when she is as educated as you are."

"That's just it, Father Ignacio. I am not educated in the ways that a woman should be. My sister can make the lightest bread in Guernica, and she can spin a fine thread from the sheep's wool. I can't even scour the floors without Elixabete coming behind me to do it again."

"But who can pluck the hedgehog and split the osier for the baskets and tie the vines in the vineyards? And who spent the summer in the hills with the sheep when she was not yet twelve years old?"

"Thank you, Father," Pia said as a smile crossed her face. "You've made me feel better."

"Isn't that what a priest is for? Now run along and share your father's news with your family."

Pia hurried to the bakery where Zuriñe Carranza and her daughter were working.

"*Ama*, Elixabete, Father Ignacio got a letter from *Aita*," Pia said as she entered the bakery where several women were working.

"Read it," Zuriñe said excitedly. "Read it quickly!"

Pia opened the envelope and removed the letter, which had been written in a neat, easy-to-read cursive script.

Dear family,

It has been a long time since last I saw my wife and my daughters.

Since our old neighbor, Lander Segura, sent for me to join him in America, he has been a good friend and a generous employer. I have saved my money and have now hived off a thousand head of sheep that I can call my own. Floria Segura grew weary of being so much alone in Mountain Home, where there were few Basque women, so Lander built a house some forty miles away in Boise, Idaho. He turned it into a boardinghouse for the herders, called the Bizkaia. Floria has been running the place all by herself, but Lander thinks it is too much work for one woman. He has offered me a half interest in the boardinghouse if you, my wife, will come and help her. You and our daughters will live among Basque at the Bizkaia House.

Segura's son Marko has a very responsible job at a bank. He has arranged for passage from Liverpool, England, for the three of you and a draft for some American money that will get you to Boise, Idaho, once you reach New York. (This is enclosed with this post. B.W.)

It is with happiness at the thought of seeing you that I close this letter.

Your husband and father, I remain Sabin Carranza

Note to Father Ignacio: This letter was written by Barton Wilson, M.D., a friend of Sabin Carranza's. I would like to suggest that you prepare instructions in English that could be attached to the traveling clothes of Mrs. Carranza and the children. I further recommend that they take the ferry from Ellis Island to Jersey City, where they will get train transportation to Idaho. Their trip will be on the Baltimore and Ohio, the Pennsylvania, the Chicago and Northwestern, the Union Pacific, and their last transfer will be in Nampa, Idaho, where they will take the Oregon Short Line to Boise. I know this may be confusing, but it will be helpful if they have written directions to help them with their itinerary.

Pia withdrew the three tickets and the draft from the envelope. When she did so, she looked toward her mother and saw tears streaming down her face.

"Oh, *Ama*, is something wrong?"

"Every night before I close my eyes, I pray that your father is in God's keeping and that he will soon be back in Guernica. I never dreamed that he would want us to come to California."

Pia smiled when she heard the word *California*. Because so many Basque had emigrated to look for gold, a lot of the older people used the word interchangeably with *America*. She did not correct her mother but embraced her.

"*Aita* is proud of his accomplishments. Listen to this part of the letter again: *a thousand sheep that I can call my own*, and *a half interest in a boardinghouse*. I think to own a thousand sheep and a boardinghouse must make *Aita* a rich man, and he wants to share the life he is living with us."

"Pia, you are so smart. Of course that is what he wants."

"And it's what I want, too," Elixabete said. "I am happy that we will be going to America soon. Did the letter say when we would be leaving?"

"It did not, but the tickets are for the *Lucania*." Pia looked at the date for the departure, and the color drained from her face as she fell into a nearby chair.

"What is it, Daughter?"

"The *Lucania* sails from Liverpool on September ninth."

Zuriñe's hand went to her face as she gasped. "How could he do this to us? How could he expect us to leave our home in nine days? I'm not going to go."

"Would you rather stay here and bake bread from morning till night?" Elixabete pleaded. "Pia, will you go with me, because I'm going to be on that ship when it sails."

"We'll all go together," Pia said. "*Aita* needs us."

ᥫ᭡ᥫ᭡

Boise, Idaho

The sign on the front door of the big brick house read:

FRANK E. WILSON, M.D.
BARTON F. WILSON, M.D.

"How did this happen?" Dr. Bart Wilson asked the man who was sitting on the treatment table. The lower part of his left leg was covered with blood, and Bart was cutting away the trousers just above the wound.

"It was the ignorant horse, Doc. He didn't see the barbed-wire fence and run right into it, catchin' my leg between the fence and the side of the horse. Ripped me up good, it did."

"Yes, I'd say it did." With the cloth cut away Bart was able to see the wound. The gash was quite deep, but hadn't severed the artery. He brought over a pan of hot, soapy water and a bottle of alcohol. After washing away the blood and the dirt with the soapy water, he took the cap from the alcohol bottle.

"What are you goin' to do with that?" the man asked.

"I'm going to disinfect your wound."

"Is it goin' to hurt?"

Burt chuckled. "Oh, yeah. It's going to hurt like hell. You want something to bite on?"

"No, go ahead. Pour away."

Bart turned up the bottle and started pouring.

"Damn! Damn! That hurts!"

"I told you it would." Now, with the wound cleaned and disinfected, Bart put a square patch over it, then began wrapping it with gauze. When he had the wound well wrapped, he held the gauze in place with pressure-sensitive tape.

"There you go, Mr. Barnes. You're all patched up now. That'll be five dollars."

"What about my trousers?" Barnes asked.

"What do you mean?"

"You tore up my pants, Doc. If you had just took 'em off 'stead of cuttin' 'em off, I coulda washed 'em clean. But you cut 'em up."

"I'm sorry about that, Mr. Barnes, but had I taken them off, there would have been the danger of further contamination."

"Yeah, but now I ain't got but one more pair of trousers, an' if I was to pay you five dollars for your doctorin', why, I wouldn't likely have enough money to buy me another pair."

Bart drummed his fingers on the treatment table for a moment, then sighed. "All right, Mr. Barnes, we'll call it even."

"Yeah, well, it seems only right." Barnes hopped down from the treatment table and walked around a bit as if testing the job.

"How does it feel?"

"It feels good, Doc. It feels real good. You done a fine job."

"Try and keep it clean," Bart said as Barnes left the office.

No sooner did the man leave than the senior Dr. Wilson came into the room. Frank was a sophisticated man, always wearing a starched white shirt, a brocade vest, and gold watch chain. He wore a neatly trimmed mustache that didn't extend beyond the edges of his mouth, and his hair was streaked with more gray than brown.

Bart was taller than his father—well over six feet tall, with a flat stomach and broad shoulders. He had piercing blue eyes and light brown hair, and while he wasn't disheveled, he made no effort to maintain as dapper an appearance as did his father.

"Did I hear right? Did you let that cowboy leave without paying?" Frank asked, his displeasure obvious in the tone of his voice.

"He said I cut up his trousers."

"That was his problem, not ours. This isn't Saint Alphonsus, and we aren't the Sisters of the Holy Cross. People who come here pay for their medical care."

"Tell me, Pop, if he couldn't afford to pay us, was I just supposed to let him get gangrene?"

"You're supposed to exercise a little common sense. Last week you treated a miner on credit, knowing full well he's never going to pay. And for all I know, you only collect food and drink from about half the Basques you treat."

"That's not true, the Basques always pay. Maybe not right away, but they always pay."

"This is a doctor's office, not a bank for credit. You love being the hail-fellow-well-met, don't you? You like to drink with your low-class friends and play games with the Basque. You live a high-dollar life, Bart, and where do you think that money comes from? If you don't hold up your end of the practice, why should I keep you as a partner?"

"Yeah, why should you?" Bart replied in a short, clipped voice. He started toward the door.

"Where are you going? Office hours aren't over yet."

"They are for me."

Guernica

Pia's world had been turned upside down. Never had it occurred to her that her father would send for his wife and daughters to come to Idaho.

Basque men had been leaving to go to South America—Argentina, Chile, Uruguay—since the First Carlist War in the 1830s, and after gold was discovered in California, many ventured into North America, hoping to make their fortune. But all left with the idea that once they earned enough money, they would return to their homeland.

The women stayed behind to take care of the *etcheonda*, the house. Once established, this physical place became the sturdy trunk from which the branches of the family tree emerged. The laws of succession, without regard to gender, had been in place since ancient times and were rooted in the social character of the people.

Pia looked up at the sturdy stone house that was the only home she had ever known. Wisteria vines twined up the doorway, covering a tablet embedded above the archway. With a stick, she pushed back the vines and read PAUSE AND REFLECT UPON YOUR LAST HOUR—YOU WILL NOT REGRET IT. 1610. This house had been in the Carranza family for almost three centuries.

As the eldest child of the eldest child, the *etch-eonda* would pass to Elixabete when her father passed away. In the interim, Elixabete had arranged for their cousin Bernardo and his family to occupy the house. There was no question that the house, which had a personality of its own, would stay in the Carranza family.

Tears gathered in Pia's eyes as she walked down the hill toward Guernica. As she passed the house that was the closest to hers, she felt some resentment. It was the Segura *etcheonda*, and because of Lander Segura she was being forced to leave her homeland. Because of Lander Segura she had not seen her father for thirteen years.

Mr. Segura had been their first neighbor before he left Guernica, becoming one of the first Basques in Nevada to build a large flock of sheep. Thirteen years ago, he had sent for the oldest three of his five sons to come herd sheep, and he had asked Sabin Carranza to come as well. Her father had agreed, telling his family he would be back in no more than five years. But then four years later, Lander had sent for his wife and his two younger sons. Nevada was getting too many sheep, and Idaho was the new promised land. Lander needed the rest of the Carranza family to help with the sheep, and now to run a boardinghouse.

Sabin Carranza was still in America, and Pia didn't like it. She didn't like it at all.

She walked down to Guernica, studying every little detail, noticing things that had always been there. The strings of red peppers, dried beans, garlic, and maize that hung from the red and green balconies of the houses were swaying in the wind. The colors of the houses, ocher and lemon and pink and yellow and red, made Pia think of fruit in a basket. Would Boise have anything that could compare to this? Would this boardinghouse her father now half-owned be a place that brought joy and happiness to its residents, or would it be filled with transient people who had no story, no history?

She continued down the street, hoping to fix forever the images and memory of this place; its sights and sounds and aromas.

There was the fruit shop where Mr. Borotra and old Mrs. Uribe were haggling over the price of a basket of plums, the plums washed and shining purple.

In the window of the wine shop, acrid goatskins and bota bags were waiting to be filled with Spanish wines from the great casks.

In front of a drinking shop, two older men were sitting at a small, square table exchanging in loud voices tales of the places they had been, and the sights they had seen in their long lives.

Just beyond the shop windows displaying colorful berets, scarves, and yellow oilskins, several young boys were playing pelota. She watched as they bounced the ball off the brick wall, shouting enthusiastically of their accomplishments and groaning in their defeats.

Though it had not been her intended destination when she left the house, or perhaps it had been, she found herself standing in front of the Tree of Guernica. As she had tried to impress upon her students such a short while ago, this tree was the most revered symbol in all of Bizkaia. The blood coursing through her veins had compelled her to return to this very spot, where Basques had stood since before the time of Christ.

Quietly, Pia began to sing:

Gernikako Arbola
Da bedeinkatua
Euskaldunen artean
Guztiz maitatua.

"Sing it in English."

Pia had been so lost in her thoughts that she had not heard Father Ignacio come up behind her.

"I can't."

"Yes, you can. I've heard you sing it with the children."

Father Ignacio began the national song and Pia joined him.

The tree of Guernica is blessed
Among the Basques; absolutely loved.
Give and deliver the fruit unto the world.
We adore you holy tree.

"See the meaning is the same if you sing it in Euskera or in English. And you, my child, are the same if you are in Bizkaia or Boise. You will always be an *euskaldun*, no matter where you go."

"Oh, Father, is it a sin not to want to honor your father's wishes?"

Father Ignacio laughed. "Well, it makes a difference which Father you mean. If it is God the Father, then, yes, you should honor his wishes, but if it is Sabin Carranza, well—that's different. But I think it is God the Father's wish that you go to Idaho."

Pia's brow furrowed as she looked toward the priest.

"I mean it. I have never had anyone learn English the way you have. Don't you think that could be a gift from God? Why did He give you such a gift if He didn't mean for you to use it?"

Pia smiled. "I learned English because I had an outstanding teacher."

Father Ignacio nodded his head. "Would it be prideful if I agreed with you?"

Both laughed, and Pia's melancholy began to lessen.

He took Pia's hand and led her to the iron fence that surrounded the Tree of Guernica.

"You will not leave your home, because for the Basque, home is the family. As long as you are with your family, you will never actually leave home. Right now, your family has been your mother and sister, but soon you will be reacquainted with your father. And, when you get married, your home will be even bigger as you will love and cherish your husband, and the children you will have. No, Pia, do not be sad. The best is still ahead of you."

"I will miss you, Father, and I will miss this place."

"Of course you will, but you are going to take it with you here," he said, pointing to his head, "and here." He put his hand over his heart. "But now I have a special gift for you. Hold out your hand."

Pia did as he directed, and from his closed hand over hers, she felt something. When he took his hand away, she saw an acorn.

"The Tree of Guernica. Keep this with you, and you will always have a part of the place where you were born. And should you find you cannot come back, plant this acorn and nourish it until it grows into a tree itself. The Tree of Guernica is an idea, my dear, a belief in the rule of law and in freedom, and what better place to experience that than in the United States?"

Father Ignacio insisted upon taking the Carranzas to Bilbao, where they would board an ore ship bound for Liverpool. He pulled up in front of the house in a two-wheeled cart pulled by a team of cream-colored oxen. When she saw the cart, Pia lowered her head. She had thought they would take the steam tram the twenty miles to the city, but perhaps the slow, laborious trip in the cart would be best.

As the sign read: PAUSE AND REFLECT UPON YOUR LAST HOUR—YOU WILL NOT REGRET IT.

Pia had always thought that statement chiseled in stone above the door referred to the end of life, but perhaps it could mean her last hour in the house as well.

"Come in, Father. *Ama* and Elixabete are going through the house one last time, making certain they have not overlooked a single dust mote. They wouldn't want Augustina and Bernardo to think they were poor housekeepers. May I offer you the last of the goat's milk and a crust of bread?"

"I would like that."

The priest took a seat at a large table covered with a red-squared oilcloth. This kitchen, as in most Basque households, was the center of family life. The blue-and-white-tiled walls, the buffet filled with the plates and pewter, a huge fireplace with a stone oven in the chimney, the wooden floors now ashen from years of scrubbing—everything was shining with cleanliness, even the crucifix that hung above the mantel. Pia fixed all of this in her mind, as Father Ignacio patted her hand gently.

"Oh, Father, I didn't hear the bells on the oxen," Zuriñe said as she came into the kitchen. "I would have been ready. Do you know it's been thirteen years since I last saw my husband? Do you think he will remember me?"

The priest smiled beneficently. "Of course he will. Have you ever known a Basque man to forget his wife? In the eyes of God and in the eyes of a Basque, you are married until death do you part."

"I know. It's just that I pray for Sabin every night. I should not doubt that he is safe and well."

As Pia listened to the conversation, she put herself in the place of her mother. Why hadn't she realized that her mother was experiencing as much angst as Pia was, but for a completely different reason? Pia hated to leave. Zuriñe couldn't wait to get there.

Pia decided in that moment, for the sake of her mother, she would embrace this new adventure with gusto.

When Father Ignacio stepped to the holy-water stoup that hung by the door, he took the fresh sprig of boxwood and dipped it in the water. One by one he blessed Pia's mother, Elixabete, and Pia and prayed for safe passage.

And then he blessed the house.

"Heavenly Father, bless this house that has stood the test of time and keep it ever in the hearts and minds of those who have lived here, so that wherever they may be, this house and this place shall forever be with them, in the name of the Father, the Son, and the Holy Ghost. Amen."

As Pia crossed herself and uttered the amen, a calm that passeth all understanding came over her. She could leave now, secure in the belief that a part of her would always be here . . . and a part of here would always be with her.

Boise, Idaho

"Here's Manly, all saddled up for you, Doc," Julen Alonzo said, leading the bay Arabian from the back of the Boise Stables.

"Thanks, Julen. Are you still saving all your money?"

"*Bai.* I'm going to go back home and buy my own piece of land someday."

"You are a good man and a hard worker. I'm sure you'll do whatever you set out to do."

"Will you be back this afternoon?"

"I don't think so. I may not come back," Bart said, swinging into the saddle.

"Oh, no, Dr. Wilson. You have to come back. You're the only friend the Basques have in this town."

"Julen, you know that's not true. But just so someone knows, I'm going up to Silver City to visit my grandpa. I'll be back by the end of the week."

Bart smiled as he kicked Manly and started

toward the Boise River. How had it happened that he had become the go-between for the entire Basque community? Maybe it was because he didn't look at a sheepherder as some second-class citizen, and they didn't look at him as a derelict, the way his father did.

Silver City was close to seventy miles from Boise, and until one got to Murphy, a little settlement just across the Snake River, there were no towns of any sort. Bart considered stopping at a sheep outfit's home ranch, but he decided he would prefer being alone. Just after he crossed the Snake, he found a spot that was grassy and free of rocks. Removing Manly's saddle, he ground-tethered his horse to a greasewood bush. Gathering up some sagebrush branches, he soon had a fire going, but he didn't know why he needed one. Retrieving a bottle of bourbon from his saddlebag, he sat down leaning against his saddle.

"Here's to the great Dr. Wilson."

Bart took a long drink, enjoying the burn of the straight whiskey in his throat. The altercation between him and his father was not unusual. This time it was over money, but it could well have been that he didn't stitch up a wound with small enough stitches, or that he was using too many supplies. But the thing he hated most was when his father said he played too many games with the Basques, or that he gambled too much, or that he saw too many women, or that he drank too much.

Sometimes Bart wondered why he was a doctor—or at least, why he was a doctor in Boise, Idaho. When he'd graduated from Washington University Medical School in St. Louis, Bart had wanted to go to Chicago to work alongside Jane Addams and Ellen Starr at Hull House. This was a settlement house modeled after those in England, whose purpose was to have a mingling of social classes, especially among recent immigrants. He embraced the words of Samuel Barnett, the founder of Toynbee Hall, who had said, "to learn as much as to teach; to receive as much as to give."

Frank Wilson didn't understand how much the "dirty Bascos" or the "Celestials" had to teach. In the beginning, Bart had tried to tell him, but it soon became apparent that his father would never get beyond the idiosyncratic ways of either culture.

Bart enjoyed having the Basques and the Chinese not only as his patients, but as his friends. But he also realized that his friendship and charity wasn't all for altruistic reasons. If he was being truthful with himself, he knew his friendships were a way to aggravate his father.

That, and drinking and carousing with women.

He took another swallow from his bottle and settled back on the ground, his head resting on his saddle as he watched the sun set over the mountains.

Bart reached Silver City just before noon the next day. He had no idea why his grandfather Eli Wilson still lived here. At one time War Eagle Mountain had been the site of some of the richest gold and silver mines in the country, but when the Bank of California shut off credit in '75, the money had dried up and everyone thought the big bonanzas were over.

Eli had left his wife and son right after the War Between the States. Lottie was a Southerner whose family had fought for the South, and Eli was a Northerner who had fought for the North. She had never forgiven him. And he had never divorced her.

Eli joined his brother, Ike, who had a placer operation on Jordan Creek. When Ike died from an infected foot that developed gangrene, Eli inherited the claim. He worked the claim until it played out, and he was planning to return to southeast Missouri to make amends with his wife and son. But before he could leave, the ores on Florida Mountain were discovered. From that strike Eli Wilson had become a rich man.

Bart rode down Washington Street until he got to Avalanche, where he turned to go to his grandfather's house, a little cabin that looked no different from any of the other modest homes of the dying town.

When he reached the house, his grandfather was out front, working up a patch of ground behind a wooden fence. Tall, with white hair, Eli was neither clean shaven nor bearded. He wore a perpetual white stubble that he shaved about once a week. At the moment his hair was shaggy, and he was wearing denim trousers and a faded shirt.

Bart smiled when he saw him. If Eli had been walking the streets of Boise in such attire, passersby would have been so moved to pity that they might have offered to buy him a meal.

There was absolutely nothing dapper about him, and this distinct difference between Bart's father and his grandfather had made Bart's grandfather a hero of his.

Bart dismounted, tying Manly's reins to the fence.

"Comin' to borrow money, visit, or did ya run away from your pa again?" Eli asked as he continued to turn over the dirt.

"Do you have another fork?"

"Around back."

When Bart went to get the fork, he saw a gray-haired woman hanging clothes on the line. "There's my favorite woman!"

"Bart!" the woman replied, dropping a handful of clothespins. "Your granddaddy's goin' to be so happy to see you!"

"What about you, Aunt Suzie? I haven't had a good bite to eat since I left Boise and I'm sure enough hungry."

"Well, I can fix that in a heartbeat." Suzie embraced Bart. "I took some fresh bread out of the oven not thirty minutes ago. How would some butter and honey meltin' down into some hot bread sound?"

"That's why I rode all this way."

"You get on out of here while I finish hangin' up my basket, and I'll take care of you. Eli's around here somewhere."

"I saw him. Where's the extra fork?"

"In the lean-to."

"I'll never understand that woman. She wants a turnip bed," Eli said when Bart returned with the fork and climbed over the fence to join his grandfather.

Neither man said anything for a while as they worked.

"You didn't say. Is it money or Frank?"

"I've got plenty of money."

"He can be an ornery cuss when he wants to be," Eli said, shaking his head. "He gets that from his mother, you know. She's the one that raised him, not me."

The two men didn't say another word for the next half hour as they continued to turn the dirt. Bart knew that his grandfather was like that, and he was comfortable with it. Finally the little square was all turned.

"If you two are ready to eat, it's on the table," Suzie said, stepping out on the little front porch.

"I'm ready," Bart said.

He couldn't help but compare this cabin, which was one good-size open room that served as the kitchen, dining room, and living room all in one, with the big house in which his parents lived. There was a small annex where Eli and Suzie slept, and a loft that was reached by a stepladder, and that was it. There was no bathroom and no running water, but they did have electricity.

When they were seated, Aunt Suzie brought out the bread and honey. She'd also fried up a piece of ham and had some black-eyed peas.

"You know Aunt Suzie's a Southerner, too," Eli said.

"I know," Bart said.

Suzie Yarborough wasn't really Bart's aunt, though he had called her that for as long as he could remember. Suzie was the woman Eli had lived with for over twenty years. They were never married because Eli was still married to Bart's grandmother, who lived on a cotton plantation in New Madrid, Missouri.

"Have you heard anything from Missouri?" Eli asked as he carved into a piece of ham.

"Her brother died a while back, but she seems to be doing all right, now."

"Does that mean Lottie's running Trailback all by herself?"

"She's got some good people working for her, but, yes, she's running the plantation all by herself."

"It's a shame she's such a stubborn woman. She could be out here enjoying her son and you and your sister, but, no, because I fought for the Union, she'll never do it."

"I know she's grateful you pay the taxes on Trailback," Bart said.

"What did you and her son get into it about this time?"

"I don't think he likes the way I do business. He thinks I do too many charity cases."

"I may have made a mistake with your pa. When I hit it big, I thought I could make it up to him by givin' him a good education and anything else he ever wanted. But he's not got what his uppity friends call empathy. Now, you, Bart, you're a good man and I'm proud of you."

"Thank you. I appreciate that coming from you, sir."

"Don't give up on your pa. He and I have butted heads for many years. That's probably the biggest disappointment of my life," Eli said.

Suzie took Eli's hand in hers and began stroking it, which indicated to Bart that the two often discussed this subject.

"I don't want to see that same thing happen with you and your father, do you hear?"

"I hear what you're saying, Grandpa. Just coming out here and being with you has helped."

"How much money do you think your charity work costs the practice?"

"Really, not that much. Most of them pay something over time. It could be a chicken or a lamb or a gallon of milk or something like that."

"Do you ever get any turnips?" Eli asked.

"I don't think so, but I suppose I could ask for them," Bart said as he smiled at Suzie.

Eli reached into his pocket and drew out a money clip. He began counting out the bills in his pocket, and it was close to five hundred dollars. He slid all the cash over to Bart.

"Here, put this money in the kitty when you treat someone who can't pay. That ought to take care of Frank, don't you think?"

"Grandpa, you don't have to do this. I have money."

"I know you do, but what good is it going to do an old man like me? Look around you. Suzie and I are as happy as anybody in this whole country, and the only thing she needs to make her happy is a turnip patch. Now take the money and put it to a good use."

"Yes, sir." Bart picked up the money and put it in his pocket. He wanted to tell his grandfather how dangerous it was to carry around that much cash, but he held his tongue. Eli Wilson didn't need a lecture from Bart about how to conduct his business.

TWO

Bilbao, Province of Bizkaia, Spain

At last, the little cart with the screeching wheels reached Bilbao. Father Ignacio had been right to travel so slowly. He knew the family needed an envelope—a way to say good-bye to bucolic, little Guernica, and its quiet dignity, before they were thrust into the capital city's hubbub of activity.

This wasn't Pia's first trip to the busy port, which straddled the tidal river Nervion as it flowed between low-lying hills, the left bank apparently composed almost entirely of iron ore.

Everywhere Pia looked she saw a constant whir of activity. In all directions railways, tramways, and overhead wires carried ore from the quarries directly to the holds of the many vessels that lay at anchor in the river awaiting their cargo.

"What is that horrible smell?" Elixabete asked as she wrinkled up her nose.

"It's sulfur," Father Ignacio said.

Tall chimneys were belching voluminous clouds of smoke, and everywhere Pia looked she saw red iron-ore dust. The ships' holds were filled with it, the roads were covered with it, but what was most distressing was that even the animals were red from the dust.

The cart rolled by blast furnaces, smelting works, and shipyards. A ship named the *Vizcaya*, one of three warships built here for the Spanish navy, lay at anchor in the river. On the other side the scenery was more agreeable, with neat houses and shops lining the bank, where more ships were secured with hawsers to a long, white wall that ran alongside the river.

"What's the name of our ship?" Father Ignacio asked.

"The *Emma Louise*. That will take us to Liverpool, where we will board the *Lucania*," Pia said.

Soon the ox cart pulled up beside the ship, and the priest hugged each of them before they embarked.

"Pia, I have a gift for you. I want you to take my copy of *Gero*. Even though it was written over two hundred and fifty years ago, you will enjoy Axular."

"Thank you, Father. Thank you for everything." Pia kissed the priest before she followed her mother and Elixabete onto the *Emma Louise*.

This ore ship made regular runs between Bilbao and the Liverpool cannon foundry. The owner had converted a small space to accommodate eight people, and on this ship the first leg of the long journey to Idaho would begin.

After four days at sea, they arrived in Liverpool.

"Now what do we do?" Zuriñe asked.

Pia noticed a quiver in her mother's voice that she had never before heard. She thought about how it must have been thirteen years ago, when her father and the three Segura boys had left for America. At the time, none of them could understand a word of English. Pia said a silent prayer: *Thank you, Father Ignacio.*

"I believe our ship is the RMS *Lucania*," Pia said. "I suppose all we have to do is ask someone where we can find it."

After half a dozen inquiries, they were finally directed to the ship. When they found it, the gangplank was down and a uniformed guard was standing nearby.

"Sir, we have passage on this ship," Pia said with more confidence than she felt. "Is it boarding now?"

"I'll need to see your tickets."

When the guard saw the tickets, he stared at the three women. "This says you are Spaniards."

"We are Basques," Pia said with great pride.

"Lady, I don't care who you say you are, you're not English. You have to get cleared by the women's emigration authority before you can step foot on this ship. It's that long building over there." He pointed in the general direction where dozens of buildings that looked like warehouses stood.

"Thank you. You've been most kind. Come, Mother, Elixabete." Pia purposefully addressed them in English, hoping to give the illusion that they were all educated.

Once they got to the corrugated tin buildings, it was easy to find the right one. A figure of a woman with a large trunk was painted on the side of the building.

When they stepped inside, they got into a slow-moving line of women who were inching toward a table where a woman dressed in a uniform was seated. In front of her was a sign asking if the emigrant could read. It was printed in four languages: English, French, German, and Spanish.

They were instructed to enter a large, open dormitory with a line of bunks down either side. No one said anything as the women stood in small clusters in the center of the room. The silence was soon shattered when the woman in the uniform blew a loud whistle.

"Ladies!" she called. "The RMS *Lucania* will leave for America in two days." She held up two fingers. "Kindly follow all instructions, and cooperate with the officials."

When she left, the women were looking at each other with puzzled expressions, trying to find someone in the group who could translate what she had said. Pia repeated the message in both Spanish and Euskera, for the benefit of any who might be within hearing distance.

"What instructions?" Elixabete asked. "What do we have to do, other than wait for the ship to leave?"

Over the next two days, they found out what was expected of them. Steamship-company employees, both male and female, brought in metal tubs and began filling them with water. They poured an unknown liquid into the water, which Pia noticed was called sodium hypochlorite.

"Ladies, we're going to have to ask you to disrobe," one of the men said. He then began unbuttoning his own shirt, indicating that the women should do that, too.

Not one woman stepped forward, their faces blank as they stared at the man.

The man sat down on the floor and folded his arms over his chest. "You suit yourselves. The longer you wait, the colder the water will get, but let me make it clear: every one of you will do this before you step foot on the *Lucania*. Our ship will not be infested with your lice and fleas."

Pia looked around to see if anyone else would come forward. When no one did, she stepped up to the first tub, a look of defiance in her eyes as she stared at the man. When she began undressing, her clothing falling into a heap on the floor, she heard an audible gasp from the women in the room.

"Hail Mary, full of grace, the Lord is with thee."

The words were spoken in Euskera. Pia could not turn and face her mother and sister as she stood naked in front of everyone.

The man stood, a lascivious grin on his face. "I didn't expect the first one to be the prettiest. Here, let me help you."

"Sir, I understand why you have to do this. I do not understand why it is necessary to have men present while this indignity is being forced upon us."

"Ah, she's not only pretty, but she speaks English. Step into the water."

As soon as Pia got into the tub, she sat down, drawing her legs up about her chest. When she did so, a heavyset woman poured a bucket of water over her head.

"Here, use this to scrub your body, and don't forget your scalp."

Pia did as she was told, and one by one the other women began to take their places in the line of tubs. When Pia was told she could get out, she found her clothing and her satchel had been removed for fumigation. With a dripping body, she padded across the room to another man who was handing out bath sheets. She took the towel, not meeting his eyes.

For the rest of the day, their belongings were kept from them. Another group of men entered the room, and it was announced that each passenger would have a thorough medical examination to see if she was fit to make the crossing. By the time their clothes were returned, all sense of dignity had been stripped from the group of émigrés.

That night as Pia lay on her top bunk, in the darkness, she listened for the quiet breathing or even snoring that would indicate her mother and sister were sleeping. But she heard nothing. As she rolled over, she could smell the vile soap used to wash her hair. With tears streaming down her cheeks she thought of Guernica. Basques were survivors.

The next morning, before sunup, the woman with the whistle was back. She blew it, awakening the women.

"You'll be boarding the RMS *Lucania* within an hour. Do not leave anything behind."

This time when the woman left, everyone began to talk at once, albeit in many different languages. Again, Pia translated and began to quickly put her things together, hoping that by example she could convey what was expected to those who couldn't understand.

Leaving the dormitory, they were handed a dry

crust of bread, as someone pointed in the direction
of the ship.

When they reached Princes Dock, they saw the
RMS *Lucania* lying at anchor alongside. At the
moment the pumps were working, and two streams
of water were pouring out of the bilge discharge
pipes.

"Oh, my," Zuriñe said as she looked up at the
towering superstructure. At that moment, the ship's
horn emitted a long, loud bleat, causing her to jump.
Then she laughed nervously. "I guess we'll have to
get used to that."

"Those holding boarding passes should board
now!" someone shouted through a megaphone.

"They've called us to board," Pia said as she took
her mother's arm and started toward the ship's
purser who was examining the tickets.

Checking the boarding manifest, he nodded.
"Steerage passengers will be in the forward bay.
Your bunk numbers are 308, 309, and 310." The
purser wrote the numbers on a piece of paper and
handed it to Pia. "Go that way." He pointed to the
gangway marked THIRD CLASS. "Women to the left,
men to the right."

When the three women reached the numbers
assigned to them, they saw that their bunks were
stacked in the forwardmost section of the bay,
which, though it didn't give them any privacy in the
large, open room, was better than being out in the
middle of the bay.

On each bunk was a burlap mattress stuffed with
straw. There was also a life preserver that would

double as a pillow. Hanging from the end of each bunk was an empty pail.

"I wonder what this is?" Elixabete asked, picking up one of the pails.

"Surely they don't expect us to relieve ourselves in that," Zuriñe said.

"Oh, my," Pia said, reading from a piece of paper that was posted on the bulkhead beside the bunks.

"What's wrong?" Elixabete asked.

"I just found out what the pail is for. It says here that the food pail must be cleaned after each meal and must be maintained in a state of cleanliness."

"The food pail?" Elixabete picked the pail up again. "You mean we're to take our meals from pails?"

Pia raised her eyebrows, but didn't answer.

"I will not be fed like I'm some animal! They can't treat us this way."

"You'll get sick if you don't eat," Zuriñe said.

"But, *Ama*, eat from a pail? No, I won't do it. I thought the ore boat was terrible, but this is worse."

"We'll make the best of it," Zuriñe said as she laid her satchel on the lowest bunk and then climbed in beside it.

Three days out of Liverpool, the *Lucania* encountered heavy seas. It pitched and yawed, and Pia could hear loose items rolling about on the deck above. Because the sea was splashing in through the air vents, and the beds were getting soaked as a result, the slats had to be closed, rendering the air close and foul.

Pia felt that she had to get out of this crowded

bay, filled with sick women and crying children. Though her mother showed no willingness to do so, Pia was able to talk Elixabete into going up on the promenade deck with her. Topside, the deck was awash with water, and the storm-tossed sea was a sickly green under a dull-gray sky.

Pia and Elixabete stood at the railing, fighting nausea.

Their choice was to stand out on the deck, drenched to the skin by sea spray and the torrents of rain, or to go back inside, chilled to the bone, and try to find rest on the hard straw mattresses. But rest was hard to come by, what with the noise of hundreds of people packed into the small space, and the odor of people unable to change clothes, and not a breath of air in the closed compartment.

Finally the sea calmed and the sky brightened, and the steerage promenade deck, with its fresh air and delightful view, became a pleasant place to be. With the tossing of the ship stilled, appetite returned, and Pia, her mother, and even her sister took their pails to the pantry, where a fat, rather jolly cook's helper ladled out food. As all the food was put together in the single pail, every meal became a stew of sorts, whether intended to be or not.

There was no dining saloon for the passengers, so as soon as the Carranzas received their food, they had to return to the bay, then climb into bed and attempt to eat without soiling their bedclothes with the gravies, sauces, and stews. Washing the eating pails also proved difficult, as there was never enough freshwater. More often than not, the pails were merely rinsed in salt water.

As the voyage continued and they accommodated themselves to the food and the gentler roll of the ship, Pia and Elixabete actually began to appreciate their time out on the promenade deck. They enjoyed watching the emigrants of other nationalities, and because they and their mother were the only Basques present, they could make observations in their own language without danger of being overheard.

"You can tell everything about them by how they are dressed," Pia said.

"Tell me about those two men," Elixabete said, pointing.

"They are Polish. See their gray suits and the baggy pants with the high-heeled boots? They are coming to America to raise wheat and potatoes, and to make sausage."

Elixabete laughed. "Let me try."

She saw some men wearing red flannel shirts and fur caps. "They are Norwegians, and they have come to America to fish for whales," Elixabete said, getting into the game.

"Frenchmen who have come to make wine."

"Achh, French wine. The French cannot make wine without the Basque vineyards."

"That is true," Pia said with a little laugh. "Oh, those are Italians." Pia pointed to a group of people who were all talking at the same time. "They will open restaurants and tell everyone they meet that there is no place so glorious as Rome."

"And what are people saying of us?"

"They are saying, 'There are the Basque, there are no women more beautiful, no men braver, or smarter, and no children more delightful than Basque children. I have heard that all Basque go to Idaho. Idaho must be a wonderful place, to have so many Basque.'"

The two sisters laughed.

"Pia," Elixabete said. "What do you remember about *Aita*?"

"I must confess, Elixabete, I don't remember much about him. I remember him as tall, but I was only eight years old when he left, and all adults were tall. I remember him as being stern, and I know I was very frightened of him."

Elixabete chuckled. "I am older than you, so I remember better. He is a stern man, yes, but he is not a cruel man. I remember listening to *Aita* and *Ama* talking before he left. Mr. Segura had sent a letter asking that *Aita* bring the older boys to Nevada to help with the sheep."

"And then they moved to Idaho."

"Yes, and Mrs. Segura and Luken and Nikola moved there, too."

Pia smiled. "I missed them when they left. Do you remember how they used to pester us all the time?"

"Of course I remember. I wonder if they are all married by now. But I guess we'll find out soon enough since we'll be working for Mrs. Segura."

"Not *for* Mrs. Segura, *with* Mrs. Segura," Pia said. "Remember, in the letter, *Aita* said that he owns half of the boardinghouse."

"Yes, that's right, isn't it? I remember that Papa told *Ama* that if he found that he could make a better life for his family, he would send for us. If he could not, he would return home. He has sent for us, so it must be because he has succeeded."

"I am sad about leaving Guernica." Pia smiled. "But I am most anxious to see this new country."

"I'm a little hungry. I think it may be about time for our meal. Let's go back for *Ama* so we can eat."

Pia laughed. "Is this my sister who said that she wouldn't eat from a pail? And now you're hungry?"

"The food is good. And do you want to know what makes the food good?"

"What?"

"We didn't have to cook it."

"Yes, we're living the life of leisure," Pia said. "Just you, *Ama*, me, and about a thousand other steerage immigrants."

Elixabete laughed, then hooked her arm through her sister's arm. "Come, if we're early enough, we won't have to stand in line so long."

Boise

"Julen, you are driving carriages now?" Bart asked. Earlier in the evening he had arranged for a carriage to pick him up, and when it arrived, he saw that it was being driven by his Basque friend.

"Bai!" Julen said happily. "Mr. Moore said I can do this after I finish with the work in the stable."

"You work too hard, Julen. Promise me that you won't ever go to medical school. I don't think I could handle the competition."

Julen laughed, then stopped the four-in-hand carriage in front of the large Queen Anne–style house that was overgrown with ivy. "Here you are, Dr. Wilson, 1109 Warm Springs Avenue. If Mr. Moore asks why you're late, don't you blame me. I wouldn't want to make my boss mad at me."

"So many of Boise's *fine* people show up at these things that I don't think he'll even know I've been absent," Bart said, drawing out the word *fine* to show his disdain. "The best thing about being a doctor is you always have a good excuse for skipping this kind of nonsense."

"Maybe the banker won't miss you, but you know Miss Laura and a whole lot of other women will know you haven't shown up."

"Laura's decided I'm not her cup of tea, so she's moved on to Don Cunningham."

"Have a good time, tonight, Dr. Wilson," Julen said as Bart stepped down from the carriage.

"Riiiight, I just know I will," Bart said sarcastically.

Julen chuckled, then snapped the whip, and the horses pulled the carriage away.

Bart turned and looked toward Christopher Moore's house. Every window was ablaze with light, and from somewhere inside he heard a loud burst of laughter.

"All I have to do is be nice to a few people," he said under his breath. "How hard can that be?"

Bart took a deep breath and squared away his shoulders, then walked on up toward the house.

Bart was let into the vestibule by a white-jacketed Asian who led him into the main room, where the guests were congregated. Looking around, he saw the governor and the mayor and several other prominent citizens of Boise. He finally located the one person whose presence demanded that he be in attendance—his father, Frank Wilson.

"Fong Wee, didn't I tell you to stay off your foot for a while?" Bart said as he grabbed a drink off a tray from a passing waiter.

"I much better. I get herbs from Wong Gow. Now my ankle not hurt."

"Not Wong Gow—it was Dr. Wilson who made you better," Bart said as he patted Fong Wee on the back. "If it swells up again, you come and see me, do you understand?"

"Ah so, yes, I will do," Fong Wee said as he bowed his head in Bart's direction.

With drink in hand, Bart headed for the sunporch, where a bevy of young, and pretty, women were congregated.

"Look at your son over there, Dr. Wilson," Calvin Cobb said. Cobb was editor and publisher of the *Idaho Statesman*. "Miss Hasbrouck, Miss Horrie, Miss Newman, and my goodness, even Mrs. Davidson. All those young ladies buzzing around him like honeybees in clover."

"Yes," Frank Wilson replied, the response more of a grunt than a word. "If he would pay half as much attention to his practice as he does to socializing, he'd be a much better doctor."

"You mischaracterize him, sir," Cobb said. "The Basque people all swear by him. They think he's a fine doctor."

"I don't demean his medical skills. I have to admit he's a skilled physician, but there's so much more to being a doctor than just ability. A man has to project a certain demeanor, a decorum that is in keeping with the profession, and that he certainly doesn't do."

There was a burst of laughter from those gathered around Bart.

"He does seem to be an entertaining person though," Cobb said.

"Yes, doesn't he?" Frank lifted his drink to his lips as he stared at Bart, and his son's entourage.

"Here we have the most important men in Boise— if not the state, considering the governor is here— all gathered in conclave," Bart was saying to the women around him. "I think they are about to issue an encyclical that all you need to have the doors of society open to you is live on Warm Springs Avenue or Grove Street, and all you need to open the gates of heaven is to be an Episcopalian."

The women who were clustered around Bart laughed out loud.

"Oh, Bart, you say the funniest things," Lily Newman said. "Why, you aren't like a doctor at all."

"You've been talking to my father, haven't you?" Bart asked.

"No, I haven't. Why would you say such a thing?"

"Because that's exactly what my father thinks about me." Bart imitated his father's voice: "Boy, you are more a gadabout than a doctor."

The ladies laughed at his mimicry.

"You may be a gadabout, but you're the most

handsome gadabout in all of Boise," Lizzie Has-brouck said as she leaned forward and planted a kiss on Bart's cheek.

"Ladies, you make me blush!" Bart said sternly, then, with a big smile he added, "But keep it up." He lifted his hand to pat Lizzie on the cheek.

As the house servants moved through the guests, carrying trays of savory hors d'oeuvres and tidbits, it was announced that this would be the last time refreshments would be served until after the entertainment. The chamber orchestra that Catherine Moore had brought from Denver could be heard tuning their instruments in the alcove just below the tower that was an architectural feature of the house.

"You simply must sit by me at the entertainment," Jennie Horrie said.

"You can sit between us," Clara said, grabbing Bart's arm.

"Now don't be so possessive, ladies. I, of course, will be sitting with my husband, so I will bid the good doctor adieu." Louisa Davidson took Bart's free hand in hers and clasped it tightly.

Bart felt Mrs. Davidson passing him a piece of paper. He discreetly folded his hand over the paper.

"Well, ladies, shall we find a place at the entertainment?"

Louisa Davidson, with an enigmatic smile, turned to join her husband, who was approaching the group standing in the sunroom.

"Dr. Wilson! Dr. Wilson!" someone called, the shout arresting everyone's attention. Looking toward the front door, Bart saw his father approaching a uniformed police officer.

"What do you suppose that is?" Clara asked.

"I don't know, but it can't be good," Bart said. "I suppose I'd better go, too."

"Here he is," Bart's father said as Bart approached. The policeman was joined by Christopher Moore, the host of the party, Governor Steunenberg, and Mayor Alexander, who had been attracted by curiosity.

"Bart, Officer Ferrell has an emergency, and you'll have to go with him," Frank said.

"How far is it?" Bart asked. "Do I need to get my horse?"

"No, this time it's here in town, and I've got the patrol wagon," Officer Ferrell said.

Bart followed the policeman outside, then climbed into the second seat of the blue spring wagon, with the words BOISE POLICE DEPARTMENT painted in yellow on the side.

"What's the emergency?"

"It's Mrs. Way," the police officer said. "She's acting all crazy."

"Is she drunk?"

"Her husband doesn't seem to think so."

"All right, take me by the office so I can get my bag. And we'd better get there as fast as we can."

The driver urged the horses into a gallop and they moved quickly through the city, stopping to retrieve Bart's medicine bag before hurrying on to the residence of Mr. Ambrose Way. Several people were gathered around outside the house when they arrived.

"Make way, make way!" Officer Ferrell shouted, opening up a path for them as they hurried up the walk. Upon entering the house, they found several people already inside, including Mr. Way, who was standing by the fireplace, leaning on the mantel, as if totally detached from the scene.

Mrs. Way was sitting on the lounge, clearly agitated.

"Hello, Mrs. Way," Bart said, sitting beside her. Lifting her arm, he put a blood-pressure cuff around her arm, pumped it up, then began to take her pulse. Her pulse was weak and slow, and her blood pressure was low.

"I don't know why all theshe people are here," Mrs. Way said, slurring the words. "Do you know why all theshe people are here?"

Bart looked at her eyes and saw that both pupils were greatly dilated. "They're here because they're concerned about you," Bart said. "How much morphine did you take?"

"Jush a little. It makes me feel good. I don't know why all theshe people are here."

Bart continued to check her vital signs, and when he was convinced she was stabilizing, he turned to Mr. Way.

"Do you think you can get her into a warm bath, and then into bed? I don't think she's had enough morphine to kill her, but she's going to feel mighty rough when she wakes up. If she starts shaking, get her into the bathtub again, and then coax her to try to sleep again. But don't let her have anything to eat or drink until about noon tomorrow."

"I can do that, Doc. I don't know why she does this," Mr. Way said, shaking his head.

"It's a bad habit," Bart said. "Mrs. Way, can you hear me?"

"Uh-huh . . . you're the nice one. So pretty." She

started reaching for Bart, trying to pull him to her.

"You'd feel better if you can go to sleep. Why don't you let your husband give you a nice warm bath and then put you in bed?"

"Can't do that. Snakes in my bed."

"If Officer Farrell and I get rid of all the snakes, will you go to bed?"

"If you promise."

"I promise."

An hour later, with Mrs. Way sleeping peacefully in her bed, Bart and Officer Ferrell left the Way residence.

"I'm sorry I had to pull you away from your party, Doc, but Ambrose was scared to death. You want to go back to the Moore house?" Officer Ferrell asked.

"You did the right thing, and, no, I don't need to go back. I just want to go home."

"Earl, let's get him home," the policeman said. "And, Doc, I hope this is your last call tonight."

A few moments later Bart said good-night to the two men, then walked through the back of the dark house and up the stairs to his apartment. There, he turned on a lamp, poured himself a glass of whiskey, then sat in his rocking chair. That was when he remembered the note he had received from Mrs. Davidson. Pulling it out, he unfolded it and held it in the light of the lamp.

My husband will be in Winnemucca on business all next week.

"Humph." He balled up the paper and tossed it into his wastebasket. It was clearly an invitation for an assignation, and though Bart found Mrs. Davidson attractive, he didn't need a confrontation with an angry husband. Not when he was fending off attention from a dozen women—all of whom were the daughters of Boise's most prominent families.

Society. Which was worse? The life Mrs. Davidson lived or the life Mrs. Way lived?

Ellis Island—September 21, 1897

The *Lucania* joined another vessel that was already docked at Ellis Island, disgorging its passengers down the ramps. Pia estimated that several thousand people were waiting to be processed into the United States.

"I think you should have these," Pia said, handing her mother and sister each pieces of paper with the words *Dr. Barton Wilson, Sabin Carranza, Boise, Idaho,* written on them. "This is just in case we get separated. Father Ignacio said we may be asked for a sponsor, and if we are asked, we will say Dr. Wilson."

"Oh, Pia, we must stay together," Zuriñe said.

"We will try."

When they entered the building, their suitcases were marked and taken from them. All the immigrants were directed toward a high flight of stairs leading to what was called the Great Hall. A doctor stood at the top of the stairs, observing. If he found someone to be short of breath or limping or looking dazed, then the person was directed to one wire-enclosed pen; those that passed the doctor's scrutiny were placed in a different pen.

Each immigrant was interviewed. The questions

that had been asked in England were repeated—where you were going, if you had a sponsor or family member already in the country and if that person was meeting you, if you had enough money to reach your destination. The answers to the questions had been written on the manifest, and if there was a discrepancy in the answers, the person was sent to yet another holding pen.

From there they were interrogated to ascertain if the immigrant was mentally competent. The first tests were puzzles and mimicry tests that did not require knowledge of the language to complete. Then various medical tests were administered, and if some abnormality was discovered, a chalk mark was placed on the person's clothing.

As Pia had suspected, the three Carranzas were separated. Because of her ability to communicate, she was processed much more quickly than her mother and sister, so she was sent to the "stairs of separation" after only three hours. She waited an anxious two more hours before she saw Elixabete coming down the stairs marked FOR NEW JERSEY.

"Where is *Ama*?" Elixabete asked.

"I've not seen her, so perhaps that is good. From what I have been able to overhear, all the people in that line are being sent to a hospital here, or else they are being sent back to their home country."

"Oh," Elixabete said. "That can't happen to *Ama*!"

Just then the two girls saw their mother at the top of the stairs.

"Ruuu—ubru—uu!"

Pia yelled the *irrintzi*, its rising pitch echoing throughout the building. This was the traditional ululation that Basques had used for generations to call to the sheep in the mountains. The sound of the yell rose above the din of hundreds of people crowding toward the stairway.

Elixabete grabbed Pia's arm, a distressed look on her face. "Sister, why did you do that? These people will think you're crazy and you'll be deported!"

Pia smiled broadly. "We are Basques and I am proud of who we are. Anyway, the *irrintzi* got *Ama*'s attention. Here she comes now."

Ellis Island had money-changing and railroad-ticket offices in the building. After Pia cashed her bank draft, she got in the line that said TO THE WEST, where she bought tickets that would take them all the way to Idaho.

"I'm afraid America is a very big country," Pia said when she returned to Zuriñe and Elixabete. "First we will go to Chicago, and then to a place called Omaha. We change trains there and go to Granger, Wyoming. From there we go to Nampa, Idaho, which must be close to Boise."

"Oh, dear," Zuriñe said. "Your father didn't tell us about all of this."

THREE

The Carranzas spent a sleepless night in Jersey City, where the immigrant transport barge had brought them. Pia had considered trying to find some accommodation for them to spend the night, but Zuriñe had insisted they should stay in the train station. She said she didn't want to risk missing the train, but Pia knew she was being frugal.

"Western Flyer for Chicago leaving on track twelve in ten minutes!" a man called through a large megaphone. *"Last call, Western Flyer for Chicago, leaving on track twelve in ten minutes!"*

"Come, that's our train! It's time to go see *Aita*," Pia said as she picked up her leather satchel and headed for a sign that read TO TRAINS.

Out in the car shed, at least a dozen trains were backed in under an overhanging roof, and the atmosphere was redolent with coal smoke. The sounds were absolutely cacophonous with clanging bells and occasional whistles.

They found track twelve, where a train was already backed up against the car stop. A long, narrow concrete walkway separated this train from the one next to it. As they started up the pathway, the trains to either side of them seemed to breathe little wisps of steam from the various pipes and fittings, making them appear more alive than inanimate.

Uniformed men stood between the tracks, and as the three continued on, one of the men asked, "Do you have tickets?"

"Yes," Pia said to the man, then to her mother and sister, *"Sarrerak."*

Zuriñe and Elixabete produced their tickets.

"The immigrant car," the man said, pointing to a car located near the back of the train. To Pia it seemed he spoke the words contemptuously, as if there were something unclean about riding in an immigrant car.

"What did he say?" Zuriñe asked.

Pia raised her eyebrows, but she smiled. "It looks like we're in steerage again." She locked arms with her mother, and the two looked like children hurrying to an adventure.

Elixabete followed along behind, moving at a more sedate pace.

When they entered the car, dozens of people were already filling the high-backed, unpadded benches. Pia chose the first one that seemed to have enough room for the three of them and their satchels. She sat down, sliding over so she was next to the window as Zuriñe and then Elixabete took their places.

After about thirty minutes, the train pulled out with jerks and clanks. It seemed that they traveled for a long way before they quit seeing buildings on both sides of the train and finally moved into the countryside.

"How long do you think this trip will be?" Zuriñe asked.

Pia pulled out her ticket and began looking at all the pieces of paper. "I think it will take us six days and five nights."

"You must be wrong, Pia. It didn't take us much longer than that to cross the ocean," Zuriñe said.

"We shall see. Father Ignacio says this country is as big as an ocean."

"Oh, my."

Boise

"Hey, listen to this," Don Walton said, reading aloud from the newspaper. "'The Intermountain Fair will be graced with the arrival of the Queen of the Fair. Her pul . . . pul . . .' Hey, Doc, what's this here word?" Walton showed the word to Bart.

"Pulchritude," Bart said.

"What's that mean?"

"It means she's beautiful."

"Well, why don't they just say she's purty?"

Bart chuckled. "I think newspaper reporters enjoy using words to make people think."

Walton continued to read. "'Her pul . . .' uh . . ."

"Pulchritude," Bart offered.

"Yeah, that, 'is unmatched, as Miss Bessie Vollmer is fair of form and limb and graced with a wealth of lux . . .'" Again Walton showed the article to Bart.

"Luxuriant."

"'Luxuriant golden hair,'" Walton said as he finished the article.

"Damn," Tim O'Leary said. "That sure makes her sound fine, don't it?"

"I tell you who's a purty woman, Doc, and that's your sister," Walton said. "Only, she ain't never goin' to get herself a man the way she is. I don't mean anything bad by it, you understand. But she bein' so . . . so . . ."

"Strident?" Bart suggested.

"*Strident?* What's that mean?"

"It means she expresses her convictions rather forcefully."

"Yeah, about the women votin' stuff and all. It's almost like she's trying to run a good man away. She can't get a husband that way."

"Marjane is a proud, intelligent, dedicated woman. Right now, I don't think getting a husband is a very high priority for her."

"Don't be tellin' us that, Doc. Ever' woman wants a man," O'Leary said. "Just look at you. I'll be layin' odds how soon you've got this beauty queen right where you want her."

Bart chuckled. "You know it's against the law to gamble in Boise. You just read that to me."

"It ain't gamblin' when you can't lose. There won't none of the rest of us have a chance with that queen," Walton said.

"I tell you one damn thing, there ain't nobody in Boise who can catch a girl's eye quicker 'n ole Doc Wilson, and you can take my words to the bank," Tim O'Leary said.

Don Walton was a teamster with the Boise Freight

Line. Tim O'Leary worked for the same freight line but as a mechanic, rather than a driver. Bart, Tim, and Don were standing at the bar in the Naked Honest Truth Saloon, an establishment owned and run by James Lawrence who, in his advertisements, promised to *make drunkards, paupers, and beggars to be supported by the sober, industrious, and respectable portion of the community. Those who wish to acquire any of the evils above are requested to meet me at my bar, where I will, for a few cents, furnish them with the means of doing so.*

"James, my good friend," Bart said, holding his empty glass out across the bar to request a refill, "what do you think of these men—my friends, mind you—accusing me of being a lothario?"

"Well, Doc, I'm not sure what being a lothario means, but if it means the women all seem to cotton to ya, well, I reckon I'd have to go along with 'em on that."

"Doc's not goin' to mess around with some Queen of the Fair," a young woman at the far end of the bar said as she moved toward the three men. She was dressed in the rather risqué attire that indicated her profession as a bar girl. "Some fancy woman like that, why, she wouldn't be the doc's style. Isn't that right, honey?" The woman ran her hand through Bart's clipped brown hair.

"Listen to Fannie here," Walton said. "Are you tryin' to tell us that you're Doc's style?"

Striking a pose, Fannie Clark thrust her hip out as she smiled up at Bart, fluttering her eyelashes.

Bart knew she was only twenty-four years old, the same age as Marjane. He thought she was an attractive woman, though the indulgence of her vocation was beginning to take its toll.

"I'm more his style than some highfalutin beauty queen." Though she was looking directly at Bart, she stretched her arm across the bar toward James, spreading her fingers open as if asking for a glass.

Bart laughed. "Bearing in mind, my dear, that you posed your question as a qualitative assessment, I'm inclined to agree with you." Bart put a coin on the table. "James, I do believe the young lady wants a drink."

"Yes, sir," James said.

While Fanny was standing at the bar beside Bart, Walton and O'Leary were occupying the time of the other two girls who worked at the saloon.

"No, that's the truth, I swear it is," Walton said. "Tell 'em, Doc."

"Tell them what?" Bart asked.

"Tell Pearl and Sal that you're rich."

"I'm not rich."

"See, I told you," Pearl said. "If he's rich, why does he spend so much time in here? This ain't the kind of place rich folks go to."

Bart chuckled. "Well, tell me, Pearl, just what kind of places do rich folks visit?"

"Rich people spend all their time over on Grove Street going to afternoon teas and garden parties and the like," Pearl said.

"Well, there you go, Pearl. Doc lives on Grove Street."

"Do you?"

"My address is Grove Street, but my quarters are

over the carriage house, and my stairway leads to the alleyway."

Pearl got a smug look on her face. "That just makes coming and going more convenient." She elbowed Bart in the ribs and winked at him.

"Have you ever heard of Eli Wilson?" Walton asked.

"You mean the old codger that lives up in Silver? They tell me he's richer than Croesus," Pearl said.

"Eli *Wilson*," Walton said. "Dr. Bart *Wilson*." He made a grand gesture toward Bart. "Do you get a connection?"

Pearl turned her head and wrinkled her brow. "Are you sayin' our Doc here is kin to that man?"

"That's what I'm a tellin'."

"Well, Doc, is it true?"

"I'm not telling you that, Don is," Bart replied.

"Yes, sir, he's his grandpa," Walton said. "I seen him with ya when he comes into town."

"Blimey! You are rich! How come you don't act like it?" Pearl asked.

"Because I'm not rich, my grandfather is."

"Well, that's the same thing."

"I don't think so. And neither do my father, nor my grandfather, for that matter."

"Well, what good is it to have a rich grandpa if he don't give his money to you?" Fannie asked, jumping back into the conversation.

Bart laughed. "He worked hard for his money, so I say he can do whatever he wants with it."

"Mister, if you're so damned rich, what are you doin' talkin' to a whore?"

The speaker was standing at the opposite end

of the bar, staring into a half-empty glass. He was wearing a low-crowned, black hat, black shirt and trousers. His face was pockmarked, and he had about a week's growth of scraggly beard.

"Milt Garrison, you got no reason to be callin' my girls whores," the bartender said.

"Are you sayin' they ain't whores?"

"What I'm sayin' is, you've got no business talkin' like that. What kind of gentleman would say such a thing?"

"Well, there you go," Garrison said with a sneer. "I ain't no gentleman."

"You aren't any kind of a man, either," Bart said. "A real man wouldn't insult a lady for no apparent reason."

"A lady?" Garrison replied with a snarl.

"A lady," Bart said, holding Garrison in a cold stare.

If Garrison had any thought of challenging Bart, he held it back. Instead, he stood there, a vein in his temple twitching noticeably, then, with an unsteady hand he tossed the rest of his drink down and left the saloon.

Somewhere between Granger, Wyoming, and Nampa, Idaho

It was nearly midnight, and Zuriñe and Elixabete were sitting in one seat, sleeping comfortably, and Pia was in the seat facing them. The immigrant car was crowded, and while Elixabete and her mother could lean against each other, Pia was sharing a seat with a portly, older woman who appeared as if, and smelled as if, she might be wearing every bit of clothing she owned. The woman had the seat nearest the window, which meant she could lean against it. Pia had nothing, so she sat straight upright as she had done for the last five days, while the train roared through the night.

She listened to the rhythmic click of the wheels passing over the rail joints and stared into the dark interior of the car. She took comfort that this was the last night on the train. Tomorrow they would reach Boise. Tomorrow she would sleep.

Nampa, Idaho

"Wake up, Pia, wake up!" Elixabete said.

Both Elixabete and Zuriñe were shaking Pia, trying to rouse her from her exhausted sleep on the waiting-room bench.

"Our last train—it is ready to leave," Zuriñe said.

When Pia looked toward the train Elixabete was approaching, Pia tried to stop her. "No, no. Boise is to the east of Nampa. That can't be our train. It's facing the wrong way."

"For the first time in America, I can teach my sister. We met Boni, an *euskaldun*, who was bringing lambs to ship to market. He told us our train would back all the way to Boise, so this is the right one."

"That seems strange. I wonder why?"

"Because this is a special track that only goes to Boise and there is no way to turn it around," Elixabete said. "They call it the Stub."

"Whatever they call it, I'm glad it's the last train we'll have to ride."

త్యౖ

As they found seats, the long trip almost over, Pia saw a tense expression on her mother's face.

"*Ama*, are you nervous? Are you concerned about seeing *Aita* after so long?"

"I was a much younger woman when your father left. And when I was younger, he thought I was pretty. Now, I am old." Zuriñe reached up to touch her hair, which, while still dark, was laced with gray. "When he sees me again, sees that I am not young anymore, what will he think?"

"He'll think, there is the most beautiful woman I have ever seen," Pia said.

"And he will be right, *Ama*," Elixabete added. "You are still a very beautiful woman. And *Aita* will be very happy to see you."

"I think your father—he will have to learn to know us again. It will take time." Zuriñe stared out the window, a plaintive look on her face.

Pia, too, felt apprehension. What if Idaho was not a good place to be? She placed her hand in her pocket and clutched at her talisman—her acorn from the Guernica Tree. Taking a deep breath, she calmed herself.

Boise

The young boy on the examination table had been given enough chloroform to anesthetize him while Bart set his broken arm. Bart had put a splint on the arm and was just finishing the application of the plaster-of-paris cast.

"You're sure he'll be all right, Doctor?" the boy's anxious mother asked.

"He'll be fine," Bart said. "It was a clean break, no wound to get infected. He'll have something to show off to the other boys."

"Ha! That's how he got here in the first place; he was trying to walk along the top of the fence."

"Breaking a bone is just a part of growing up," Bart said. "Don't be too hard on him."

"Mama?" the boy said groggily. "Do I have to go see Dr. Bart?"

"You're already here. And Dr. Bart has already fixed you up as good as new."

"Sit up, Kenny, let me get a sling on your arm," Bart said.

Kenny sat up and Bart tied the sling around him, then cradled his arm. "Your arm is going to hurt for a few days so I want you to take it easy for a while," Bart said.

"Mama, does that mean I don't have to go to school?"

"Oh, no, young man. It's your arm that's hurting—not your mind," his mother said.

"She's right, but I don't want you climbing any more fences for a while," Bart said as he walked with them to the front door. "And whatever you do, don't kiss any girls."

Kenny made a face, forgetting about his arm. "Kiss a girl! That's nasty."

"I don't think Dr. Wilson agrees with you," the mother said. "Come along now. And thank you, Bart, for everything."

"You're welcome. We'll see you again when it's time to take that cast off."

Bart walked back into the office he shared with his father. The senior Dr. Wilson had just seen a patient and was writing a report in his receipt book. He looked up when Bart came in.

"How's the boy?"

"He's going to be fine. It was a simple fracture."

Frank nodded. "Did you ask Mrs. Kern to pay you anything?"

"She will."

"Uh-huh," Frank replied, though he didn't sound convinced.

"Pop, Kenny was my last patient so I'm going to take Mr. Egana some sodium salicylate. He's been running a fever."

"Egana? He's that old Basco over at the Bizkaia, isn't he?"

"He is Basque and that's where he lives, yes."

"If he's an old man, have him take the sodium salicylate with some sassafras tea. Have you thought about that?"

"Yes, sir, I have," Bart answered, fighting hard to keep from making another comment.

"Oh, because of Marjane's birthday, I'm closing the office for the rest of the afternoon. Don't forget that your mother is expecting you."

"I won't," Bart said, picking up the medicine for Mr. Egana and leaving the office.

"Boise!" the conductor said, walking through the car. "This is the capital of Idaho. Boise."

When Pia looked at her mother, she saw that she

was gripping the arm of her chair. Pia reached over and took her hand. "We're here, *Ama*. This is Boise."

"I suppose we are."

"Yes, at long last." Pia let out a deep breath.

"We're here!" Elixabete said, hurrying to get her bag. "I'm so happy!"

Pia and her mother exchanged glances but said nothing more. Picking up their satchels, they followed Elixabete.

The Oregon Short Line depot was in front of them when they stepped off the car onto the platform. It was a much more substantial building than Pia would have expected in this out-of-the-way corner of the West, where the train had to back in to get here. Constructed of sandstone, it was decorated with bracketed eaves, swooping dormers, and a domed tower in the middle. Pia thought it was a most attractive first impression for the town.

"I think the first thing we should do is inquire as to where the Bizkaia boardinghouse is," Zuriñe said. "Pia, you will have to do that."

"Yes," Pia agreed.

"Look at the mountains, how beautiful they are!" Elixabete said. "It's just like Guernica!"

"It is pretty," Pia said as she looked toward the nearby mountains, some of them so high that their tops were obscured by the clouds. "But I'm not ready to say it's just like Guernica."

"Yet," Elixabete said. "Just you wait. You're going to love it here."

Even though there was as much activity in Boise as there was in Bilbao, Pia was struck by the cleanliness of the city. Electric trolley cars ran on tracks laid in the middle of a street that was parallel to the railroad. In addition, half a dozen wagons and carriages were in motion, the hollow clop of the horses' steel-shod hooves sounding loudly on the cement pavement, which was swept clean. Apple trees and plum trees and pear trees were everywhere, their branches laden with heavy fruit. And flowers were blooming in abundance.

All of this was a good sign. Maybe Elixabete was right. Maybe she could learn to love it here.

"Newspaper! Get your *Statesman* here! Newspaper!" The boy hawking the newspaper looked no older than twelve. He had several of the papers clasped under one arm, while he waved a paper above his head so the headlines could be read.

"*Ama*, I'm going to ask this boy where the Bizkaia House is. I'm sure he will know," Pia said as she moved toward the newsboy.

"Bizkaia House? Are you looking for the Bizkaia House?" a man asked. What made the question so surprising was that he asked it in Euskera, so that both Zuriñe and Elixabete understood him.

"Yes! You are an *euskaldun*?" Zuriñe asked.

"*Bai*, but here, we are called Bascos. My name is Julen Alonzo, and I live at the Bizkaia House."

"I am Zuriñe Carranza, and these are my daughters, Elixabete and Pia."

"You are the family of Sabin Carranza?"

"Yes, do you know my husband?"

"Of course, he is now Lander Segura's partner. Did he not tell you he owns a boardinghouse?"

"He did. That's why we're here. We're going to help Floria run her place. Is she well?" Zuriñe asked.

"She is, but she'll be happy to have you," Julen said. "I see her always work, work, work. I have a wagon, and as soon as I pick up my employer's freight, I'll take you to the Bizkaia House if you'd like."

"We'd like that very much," Zuriñe said. "Come, girls. We shall ride up to the front door of our new home."

The drive from the depot to the Bizkaia House took but a few minutes. When they arrived, Pia was disappointed with the look of the house. The large two-story building was made of white-painted clapboard with a tin roof. The windows were evenly spaced across the front, giving the place the personality of a sheep barn. The only distinguishing feature was a painted sign across the gable end, saying BIZKAIA HOUSE, BASQUES WELCOME.

"This is it, ladies, the best boardinghouse in Boise." Julen jumped down from the wagon, and after helping the women, he grabbed their bags and showed them into the house.

"Mrs. Segura!" Julen called loudly. "We have new arrivals."

Floria Segura came from the back of the house. So, too, did an older man, who had to be one of the Segura boys, and another man who didn't look Basque.

"Zuriñe!" Floria embraced her friend, and both women began to cry and talk at once. "I wish Mr. Carranza was here. He has missed you, my friend. For thirteen years I know he has thought of no woman but you. He is a good and honest man, and my Lander is happy to have him as his partner and first neighbor. And now I can say I, too, am pleased you and your little girls have arrived."

"They aren't so little anymore," Zuriñe said, turning to her daughters. "Elixabete is the age of your Luken, and here is Pia, who comes just ahead of your Nikola."

"They look like fine girls," Floria said, looking over Elixabete and Pia, much as if she were purchasing a team of oxen. "They are both strong, are they? Are they good workers?"

"I can say that they are. Elixabete maybe more than Pia, but Pia is a smart girl. She has learned the English very well."

"Like my Marko and Dabi here," Floria said, turning to one of the men standing behind her. "Dabi can speak English, but Marko—he's so smart he doesn't herd the sheep. He's a banker just like an American."

"You have to be so proud of him," Zuriñe said. "Of all your boys."

"Yes. Can you imagine what honest and smart babies they would have together? Your girls look like they can breed well."

When Floria made this comment, all the *euskaldunak* began laughing and speaking at once.

Pia's cheeks flushed with embarrassment as she turned away from the group. To hide her mortification, she feigned a need to recover something from her bag. When she knelt to unclasp the buckle, a man who had not joined in the laughter knelt beside her, moving the other two bags out of the way.

When she looked at him, she felt the intensity of his gaze.

"I'm afraid I'm very tired," Pia said in Euskera, fighting to keep tears at bay. "Why aren't you laughing at Mrs. Segura's joke? It is a joke, you know."

"I'm sorry, I don't understand you. I don't speak Euskera."

Pia jerked her head up. "You don't?"

The man, one of the most handsome men she had ever seen, began to laugh—not a harsh laugh or a mocking laugh, but a gentle laugh. "No, and I'm not an Amerikanuak. I'm not even Boise bred."

"If you aren't Basque and you don't speak Euskera, why are you here?"

The man shrugged his shoulders. "Would you believe me if I said I like to play pelota?" He stuck out his hand. "My name is Bart Wilson."

"Bart Wilson? Dr. Bart Wilson?" Pia asked as she offered her own hand for the handshake.

"Now I'm befuddled. I am a doctor, but how did you know that? Surely my reputation doesn't precede me."

She could feel his strength and a warmth that she had never before experienced. She knew she should withdraw her hand but she did not.

"I am Pia Carranza. From Guernica."

"You're Sabin's little girl? Does he know his little girl can speak English so well?"

Pia shook her head.

"Then, it will be your surprise for him. I think Dabi is taking some supplies out to the sheep camps sometime this month, so it won't be long before you'll see your father." Then Bart did something uncharacteristic. He raised her hand to his lips and kissed it.

For the second time in less than an hour, Pia lowered her head in embarrassment.

"Welcome to America, Pia Carranza. I'm going to enjoy getting to know you." Bart stood, pulling Pia up beside him. "I don't know what was said over there, but I think it's been forgotten now."

He headed for the door, but before he left, he checked to see if the striking, brown-eyed woman was watching him. And he was not disappointed. He flashed a big smile and waved. Not until that moment did she turn and rejoin her countrymen.

Walking down the sidewalk, Bart had a bounce to his step. Old Mr. Egana was just about to have the most attention that any doctor could ever bestow on a patient.

And then Bart laughed out loud.

What would Marjane think?

FOUR

When Bart left the Bizkaia House at Eighth and Idaho, he had only a short walk to the corner of Eighth and Grove, where he lived in the apartment behind his parents' home. The house was a three-story, French-style brick with a mansard roof. The upper two stories were where his parents and his sister lived, while the first floor was used for the doctor's office he shared with his father.

It had originally been built by the banker Christopher Moore, and no detail had been left undone. When Moore had decided to build his house on Warm Springs Avenue, he sold this house to Captain Joseph DeLamar, a partner of Bart's grandfather's.

Long after others had abandoned their claims, Captain DeLamar had convinced Eli that there was silver on Florida Mountain. Joseph and Eli bought up many of the old claims and together poured money into the project, bringing some of the abandoned claims back to life.

It was a wise business decision, the public assay

reports saying the two men had taken more than $8 million off Florida Mountain since 1888. Captain DeLamar had bought the house on Grove for a schoolteacher in Silver City whom he intended to marry. When she refused, he left Idaho never to return, giving the house to his partner.

Eli was adamant that he would not leave Silver City, so Frank Wilson reluctantly agreed to move into the house, making it both his home and his office. Bart's mother, Anna, had been much opposed to the idea, but after Bart joined the practice, she agreed to move to the big house.

Bart took the steps to his apartment two at a time, whistling a little tune. He was in a surprisingly good mood considering he was expected to spend the evening with his parents and his sister.

He loved Martha Jane, who because of his childish shortening of her name had been known as Marjane her whole life. As a twenty-four-year-old woman, she had accomplished a lot. She had worked tirelessly for the successful campaign to give Idaho women the right to vote, and while he was proud of her participation in the suffrage movement, he didn't approve of her temperance advocacy.

"Hold your tongue, Bart. Remember it's her birthday," Bart repeated as he quickly took off his day wear and put on an informal evening suit.

When he left his apartment, he walked through the kitchen garden, with its carefully tended herbs and vegetables. He stepped onto the porch, where the old alley cat was curled up on the swing.

"How's Plaid Cat?" Bart asked as he petted the cat before opening the door to the kitchen.

"Ah, Mr. Bart, you come!"

"Of course, I'm here, Chee. Marjane may think it's because of her birthday, but really I came because I'm hungry. What's on the menu tonight?"

"Green," Mr. Chee said.

"Green?"

"You'll see. Miss Anna—she wants everything green."

"I can hardly wait for that." Bart moved toward the back stairs and went up to the living quarters.

At the head of the stairs, Bart stepped out into a central hall where a huge crystal chandelier hung over a highly polished round table. The front stairway, the millwork, and all the floors were made of walnut brought in from the Midwest. Wainscoting covered the bottom third of the high-ceilinged room, while wallpaper with a bird motif reached to the picture rail and the crown molding.

One wall had a huge oval mirror with a gilt edge that reflected a painting of a man on the opposite wall. The man, wearing a Confederate uniform, was Alexander Bussey, Bart's great-grandfather. Colonel Bussey had brought his daughter and her son to Trailback Plantation in New Madrid, Missouri, after Eli had joined the Union Army. When the war was over, Eli had tried to convince Lottie to start over, to move West with Frank, but Lottie refused to leave Trailback.

Bart believed his father displayed this painting of Eli's father-in-law just to spite the old man. Though, in truth, it was an empty gesture; Eli Wilson had never once set foot in this house.

❧❧❧

"Where have you been?" Anna Wilson asked. "I was beginning to think you'd forgotten."

"As you can see, I'm here." Bart kissed his mother. "Happy Marjane's birthday."

Anna chuckled. "Don't tell me that, tell Marjane."

"I'm scared of Marjane," Bart teased.

"Hush, don't talk like that about your sister. Just accept that she is passionate in her beliefs."

"I know, and I'm teasing. The truth is, I'm proud of what Marjane does—well, most of it."

Anna rolled her eyes and shook her head. "Not tonight. I don't want to hear the word *temperance* even mentioned. Do I have your solemn oath you won't say one word about it?"

Bart flashed a disarming smile. "Me? What would I ever say that would upset my sister?"

"Come on. She's in the parlor."

When Bart went into the parlor, he saw his sister looking out the window. Marjane was three years younger than Bart. She was pretty, but she purposely tried to downplay her attractiveness by keeping her long, blond hair tied back in a severe bun, and always dressing in gray or black. She did this, she explained, because she wanted people to pay attention to her as a person first, and a woman second.

"Happy birthday, Sis." Crossing the room, he kissed her on the cheek she presented him.

"Oh, Bart, thank you for the wonderful birthday present. You knew I wanted all three volumes of the *History of Woman Suffrage*," she said excitedly. "And to think, you got them signed by Susan B. Anthony!"

"I'm sorry I didn't get the other two authors to

sign, but I didn't think I'd have time to send them out and get them back before your birthday."

"Who needs Elizabeth Stanton and Matilda Gage when you can have Susan B. Anthony? She's the most important one."

"I thought you might like that."

"You know we'll be marching in the parade," Marjane said.

"What parade? And who is we?"

"Why, the queen's parade for the Intermountain Fair of course. And *we* is the Columbian Club, but now we have an official title: the Idaho Chapter of the National American Woman Suffrage Association. Doesn't that sound important?" She pointed to a placard. "What do you think of my sign?"

IDAHO WOMEN HAVE WON THE RIGHT TO VOTE
SHOW THE REST OF THE NATION
EXERCISE IT NOW
IDAHO'S NAWSA CHAPTER

"What are you going to do with it?"

"What do you mean, what am I going to do with it? I'm going to carry it in the parade."

"What does the parade have to do with women voting?"

"Bart, you can be so exasperating. Abigail Scott Duniway is going to march in support of Clara Campbell. Clara's running for Ada County treasurer, and if we can get every woman to vote for her, she'll win. But we have to remind them that they can vote, too." Marjane sighed in frustration. "Do you know some women don't even want to vote?"

Bart chuckled. "You'll get them all in line, and I think your sign looks nice."

"Do you really mean that? Or are you just trying to make me feel good?"

"Yes."

"Yes, what?"

"Yes, I really mean that, and, yes, I'm trying to make you feel good."

Marjane laughed and smacked her brother on the arm. "Don't you know a doctor's not supposed to be that frank?"

"What if I told you I don't want to be a doctor?"

"Nonsense, of course you want to be a doctor," Anna said. "That's why you went to medical school."

"Is it?"

"What do you mean, is it?" Anna asked.

"I thought I went to medical school because that's what Pop wanted. And that's why Grandpa paid for it."

"Bart, you're a good doctor. All the Basques love you. I've heard them talking about you," Marjane said.

"Ha! How often are you around Basques? And when you are, how do you know what they're saying? You don't understand Euskera."

"When I say I've heard them talking about you, I mean when they're talking to me. Once they find out I'm your sister, they can't say enough good things about you. There's a man at the bank who says he's Basque, and he says he knows you very well. Though I must say, he doesn't look, sound, or act Basque."

"How is a Basque supposed to look, sound, or act?"

"They don't dress like any kind of normal person,

you can barely understand them when they talk, and they are all so reserved. But this man acts like an American. I'm sure he is just teasing me."

"No, he's Basque, all right. That's Marko Segura. He speaks English as well as you or I, and he's college educated."

"If he can do that, why don't the others learn English?" Anna asked.

"For most of them that come here, the only work they can get is sheepherding, and that's because it's a job that not even Indians will take. How would you like to spend ten or eleven months of the year following a band of sheep—never getting into town, never seeing your family?"

"I just don't understand why they do that. It's such a dirty job," Anna said. "I know you like them, but, Bart, you shouldn't spend so much time with them. It's not good for your career. People will think you can't get respectable patients."

Bart took a deep breath as he clenched his fists, trying hard not to say something that he would regret.

"You are coming to the parade, aren't you?" Marjane said, defusing the conversation. "I'll be marching with the other suffragettes, and you know people are going to be yelling and throwing eggs at us. I'd like to know that at least one person in the crowd is on my side."

"I'll be there, Sis, and I'll be on your side. Hoorah for the women and their right to vote."

"The women of Idaho already have the right to vote, but most of them don't want to vote," a new voice said. "Why do you keep agitating?" Frank Wilson walked over to kiss his daughter on the fore-head. "Happy birthday."

"Thanks, Pop. And I do this because the four states that have granted suffrage for women have to show the whole country that women will really get out and vote, or everything the movement has done will be for naught," Marjane answered. "I believe the time will come when there'll be more women voting than men."

"That'll never happen," Frank insisted. "The only reason these biddies want women to vote now is so they can take away our whiskey. They think every woman they know would vote in favor of this temperance foolishness."

"Can we suspend this argument long enough to celebrate Marjane's birthday?" Anna asked. "Mr. Chee has prepared a fabulous meal for us."

Anna stepped into the butler's pantry and pushed a button over the dumbwaiter, signaling Mr. Chee that she was ready for the meal to be served.

"Isn't the table beautiful, Marjane?" Anna asked. "I decided the green theme would work best."

Bart smiled as he pulled the chair back for his sister to be seated. A row of silver-plated boxes were lined up down the center of the table, each containing maidenhair ferns and creeping cedar. A green napkin lay on each plate, a dinner roll tucked into the fold.

Anna found the call bell under her feet, and within minutes Mr. Chee entered with the soup course—cream of celery.

Because this was a family dinner, a few of the courses were omitted, but Bart was fascinated with

Mr. Chee's creative genius, incorporating some green into every dish, whether it be green peas with the venison or walnuts and celery mixed with green mayonnaise and tomato jelly to serve with the fowl. But his favorite was the cheese course. The cook had colored small balls of cream cheese green to imitate birds' eggs. These were placed in a nest of shredded lettuce.

"I can't believe you were able to do this, Chee. I'm waiting for the birthday cake to see what you've come up with."

Mr. Chee smiled and bowed but did not speak.

When he had left the room, Anna turned to Bart. "I can't believe you did that, Barton. It is humiliating both to me and to Mr. Chee. Never, ever, speak to the help."

"I wasn't criticizing, I intended to compliment him."

"They prefer to do their work without any comments."

Just then Mr. Chee entered the room carrying a large tray with pistachio ice cream molded into a ring and a cake with green icing. The cake had twenty-four burning candles.

"Mr. Chee, you've outdone yourself. I couldn't have asked for a better birthday dinner," Marjane said as she smiled conspiratorially at her brother.

"I'll second that," Bart said. "If there's any of this left over, I'll take it home with me."

Mr. Chee smiled broadly while Marjane blew out the candles.

Anna Wilson lowered her head. How had she gone so wrong in raising her children?

The Bizkaia House was the largest of three *osta-tuak* in Boise. It had accommodations for twenty-five boarders, most of whom fell into one of three categories: young men from the Basque country in Europe who were either single or had left their families and come to America alone, old men who could no longer work, or transient Basques moving from one location to another.

Most were herders whose work was dictated by the cycle of the sheep. Lambing came in early spring, and then they trailed the sheep to the high-country grazing, where the men stayed with the band until fall. When they brought them down to winter pasture, the bands were joined together and the lambs and wethers were separated out to be shipped East for market. Then the ewes were bred again, and when the lambs were born, the sheep-herder's cycle began again.

After the animals were shipped to market, many of the herders were laid off until they were needed again to help with the lambing. During this time, the boarding-houses became their "home away from home." They served as an address to receive their occasional piece of mail, a place to keep their town clothes, and, most of all, a place where they could speak their own language and feel secure and accepted.

A few Basques had "town jobs" and were residents year-round. The camp tenders who replenished the herders' supplies made frequent trips in and out of town and often lived at a boardinghouse as well.

"Because this is your first night at the Bizkaia House, I won't make you work," Floria Segura said as she ushered the Carranzas to one of the three long tables that would seat twelve. "And besides, the men will be anxious to hear any news from home."

"Nothing has changed," Zuriñe said. "There won't be much to tell."

"You don't understand. When these men spend so many months alone, all they do is dream about home, about the wives they left behind, and they will enjoy hearing another woman's voice reassuring them that everything is exactly the way they left it."

"I can understand that," Pia said. "On the train when I couldn't sleep, I thought about Guernica."

Just then about a half dozen men began to come into the big room. As Floria had predicted, most sat at the long table where the Carranzas were sitting.

Pia recognized several of the men. The old man Mr. Egana took the place at the head of the table; Julen, the driver of the wagon who had helped them at the depot, sat across from them; and Dabi, the son they had met in the afternoon, slid onto the bench beside Zuriñe.

Pia noticed that one man sat apart. The others were dressed in denim pants and flannel shirts, but this man was wearing a suit. She knew instantly that was the "smart one," Marko Segura.

"Pia, Elixabete," a young man said when he came into the room. "Do you remember me?"

"Of course we do, you're Luken," Elixabete said.

"Wrong one, I'm Nikola."

"How you have changed! You were just a baby

when you left," Zuriñe said as she stood to greet Nikola.

"Not a baby—I was ten, but now I work as hard as five men."

"Nikola might exaggerate a little, but we'll give him a little slack. He just got in from the range," Dabi said.

"Oh, is Sabin here?" Zuriñe asked anxiously.

"No, but if we had known you were here, I would have stayed on the winter range and let him come into town," Nikola said.

"He'll know soon. I want to stay for the fair—the first Intermountain Fair to be held in Idaho—and when it's over, I'll be taking supplies out to the range. When I return, I'll bring him back," Dabi said.

"We can hardly wait to see him," Pia said, but when she glanced toward her mother, she recognized the anxious look she had observed earlier.

"Here it is," Floria said as she came into the dining room carrying a big pot. "Dabi, get the trivet so I can set it down."

The huge pot was set in the middle of the table, and heavy white bowls were handed to each diner.

"I'll bet you haven't had any chorizo since you left Bizkaia, my friends, so for your first night at the Bizkaia House, we have chorizo and beans," Floria said, "with a little lamb, of course." She began ladling the food into the dishes.

Then, Marko joined the others at the table.

Pia smiled at him, but neither spoke.

During the meal, just as Floria had predicted, many questions were asked of the newcomers. Some were political, but most were about landmarks that all would recognize. At one point Pia shared her acorn, and it was passed around reverently.

The meal and the conversation stretched into several hours while everyone sat on the hard benches. Pia stifled several yawns before Floria stood to speak.

"These women have had a long day, and you'll have lots of time to talk to them again. Come, let's clear the table, and I'll show you to your sleeping rooms."

All the men rose and entered a room off to the side, which Pia hadn't noticed before. When the door opened, she saw that it had a bar and several tables where the men would play cards.

Pia and Elixabete began removing the dishes and followed Floria and Zuriñe into the kitchen.

"The family sleeps back here," Floria said as she led them to a small room off the kitchen. "But the boys sleep upstairs when we don't have guests. You might be more comfortable up there, at least until everyone returns."

When they entered, Pia saw a double bed and a chest.

"When all the herders return, we'll move you girls to the cellar, unless you'd want to stay with your parents?"

"We'd rather be in the cellar," Pia said quickly.

Floria shrugged her shoulders. "You haven't seen the cellar, but you will. You girls will take over the washing—just the sheets, though. The men take their own clothes to the Chinese, so you don't have to do that, but you will have to wash their socks. And you'll scrub the floors—not every week but at least once a month. Zuriñe, I expect you'll help me in the kitchen, and when we're full up with men, I'll need you girls to help there as well. I can't tell you how glad I am that you've come."

"How did you ever do all this work by yourself?" Pia asked.

Floria smiled. "I've had help, but as soon as a pretty little Basque girl gets here, what happens? She up and marries a good Basque man and I lose her. That's why Lander let Sabin buy half of this place. Because he figures if you own part of it, you won't run off and get married."

Before going to bed, Pia stepped out to the outhouse. She had not taken a lantern, and her unexpected presence caused the dogs in the pens behind the boardinghouse to bark. And even now as she lay in the bed beside Elixabete, she could hear the incessant barking.

Finally she heard the door to the kitchen open, and immediately the barking ceased. No words were spoken that she heard. It was as if the dog and his master had a symbiotic relationship—an understanding between man and animal that came from many days of living together with no contact with other humans.

This new life was going to be different, and it was going to be hard. She yearned for her idyllic days back in Guernica, and she vowed she would return as soon as she could save enough money to buy her passage home.

∞

The sun was shining through the window of Bart's bedroom and he knew it was later than he usually awakened. When he looked at the clock, it was close to 11:00 a.m.

"Damn," Bart said as he rolled out of bed to dress quick. "There'll be hell to pay this morning."

He entered the house through the kitchen, where Mr. Chee was preparing lunch.

"I have fresh coffee, just for you, Dr. Bart." The cook poured a big cup and handed it to him.

"Thanks, Chee. Keep the pot going all day. I'm going to need it."

"Yes, sir, I can do that."

Bart opened the door to the office, hoping his father was busy and that he would not notice the time Bart arrived, but that was not to be.

"Why did you come in at all today?" Frank asked when he saw his son. "You didn't even bother to shave."

"I'm sorry."

"Your mother was terribly upset last night, the way you encouraged Marjane to defy her, and then you didn't have the common courtesy to join us in the parlor for a decent conversation. The doctor—the town drunk. That's not the reputation you should be cultivating. Now get out of this office before I fire you."

Bart glared at his father. He had just received a tongue-lashing for something he didn't deserve. He could have told his father that, yes, he had spent the better part of the night on Levi's Alley, but it wasn't for his own pleasure. Some buckaroo fresh off the range, and drunk beyond reason, had broken into

Paulina Whitworth's place, and when she refused to entertain him, he had beaten her badly.

Bart did have a reputation and he was proud of it. This Dr. Wilson would help anyone, no matter if the person lived in the right place or even paid.

He turned and stormed out the same way he had come, banging the kitchen door, causing the cat to jump from his place on the swing.

Taking a few deep breaths, he gained control. Was it God's unwritten law that fathers and sons couldn't get along? In his experience this relationship was just history repeating itself. After all, Frank and Eli had not spoken to one another for years.

At first, he headed for the livery to get Manly and head for Silver City, but he decided he couldn't run away every time he and his father had words. The logical thing to do would be to separate his practice from his father's, but he had to decide if he really wanted to be a doctor at all.

Then he thought about Paulina Whitworth and Christobol Egana. Boise might not be Chicago, and he might not be working with Jane Addams, but Boise certainly had a population that needed him. He decided, for his mother's sake, he would give the partnership a little longer before he did something he might regret.

But what was he going to do with the rest of his afternoon?

Without another thought he headed for the Bizkaia. Perhaps he might catch a glimpse of that shy, pretty Basque girl who'd arrived yesterday.

FIVE

Pia pushed on the heavy dining-room table, but couldn't move it by herself. "Elixabete, help me move this."

"Can I give you a hand?"

Pia was surprised to hear the words in English, but she knew immediately who it was. "Dr. Wilson!" Her hand went instinctively to the kerchief she had tied around her head to keep her hair from falling while she was on her hands and knees scrubbing the floor. "I thought my sister was still here."

"I don't see her, but let me move the table. Where do you want it?"

"I just want it out of the way. If you will, please push it up against the wall."

Bart moved the table, and Pia moved her pail and her scrub brush.

"I don't think this has been done for a while," Pia said, wiping perspiration from her brow. When she did, she left a swipe of dirt.

Bart took out a handkerchief from his pocket and without thinking began to clean her face. He stopped and looked into her liquid brown eyes that seemed to be holding back tears.

"Pia, is something wrong?"

"No, nothing is wrong. It's just that what you just did is the nicest thing anyone has done for me since I left Guernica."

Bart pulled the cloth away and with his other hand cupped her cheek. He had an undeniable urge to kiss her, but he sensed that she was vulnerable, and were he to do that, she would retreat. He didn't know what had been said the day before when everyone had laughed, but somehow, he knew that she was the butt of the joke. He would not do anything to frighten her, a woman who seemed so fragile, yet he knew that she had a strength that few women in his acquaintance could claim.

Bart pulled back. "Do you want me to move the other table?"

Pia stared at him as if she didn't know what to say. "Yes . . . yes, that would be nice." She dropped to the floor and began scrubbing with vigor.

Just then another woman came into the room. Bart surmised that she was Pia's sister, although they didn't look alike. While Pia's hair was so dark a brown that it was close to black, this woman's hair was lighter brown and she had blue eyes. She also had a much huskier frame than the delicate Pia.

Bart extended his hand to the woman. "You must be Pia's sister. Welcome to Boise."

"Ez dut ulertzen."

"She doesn't understand English," Pia said as she stood. "This is my sister, Elixabete."

Then in Euskera, Pia explained who Bart was.

A big smile crossed Elixabete's face when she understood that he had written the letters for their father. *"Eskerrik asko."*

"You're welcome," Bart said, recognizing her words as "thank you."

"How is it that you speak English so well and your sister doesn't at all?"

"I don't know. We had the same opportunity. Our parish priest studied in England, and it was his belief that we should all learn to speak English."

"That explains it," Bart said.

"What is that?"

"Your accent. It makes you sound so cultured."

The expression on Pia's face changed. "And you don't think I am?"

"No, no. I love your accent. It's just that most Basques who learn English have a different accent. Dabi has a mixture of Euskera, English, and Spanish, and Marko speaks like I do. In America, English accents sound cultured—that's all."

Tilting her head to one side, Pia smiled. "Well, this cultured lady must get back to work. I've been told that because we own the place, we will want to do this."

Bart laughed. "I hadn't heard there was a change of ownership, but I'm glad."

"I sort of told a lie, I guess. It's my father who's half owner, not us."

"It doesn't matter. It just means you'll not feel you have to find a husband so quickly, and you'll stay around longer."

Pia cocked her head and squinted her eyes as she examined Bart. She had thought he was an attractive man when she had first seen him. His clipped brown hair, blue eyes, and now his shadow of a beard were unbelievably attractive. Without thinking she reached out to touch his cheek. The rough texture was suddenly scintillating, and she moved closer to him.

Elixabete said something rather sharply, and Pia dropped her hand immediately as she lowered her eyes. "If you've come to see Mr. Egana, he's in the bar, I believe."

"Oh, yes. I'll check on him," Bart said, having forgotten all about his patient.

Pia dropped to her knees and began scrubbing again while Elixabete stood over her, shaking her finger. Even though he couldn't understand a word that was being said, he felt sorry for Pia. A woman who was as intelligent as Pia should be working with her mind, not on her hands and knees.

When he stepped into the bar, Mr. Egana was sitting at a table playing a form of solitaire using a Spanish deck of cards.

"How are you, my friend?" Bart asked.

Mr. Egana's eyes lit up as he motioned for Bart to join him.

Yes, this was why he practiced medicine.

Bart stayed longer than he had intended. Mr. Egana tried to teach him *escoba*, a card game that needed more explanation than either Bart's Euskera or Mr. Egana's English would allow. When Bart thought Pia would be finished with her scrubbing, he stepped out into the dining room.

She was struggling with the tables again, and

Bart took one end without asking, moving them easily.

"I hope I didn't get you in any kind of trouble with your sister."

Pia took a deep breath. "Elixabete doesn't understand. We've both had very little contact with outsiders, and talking to one is new to both of us."

"I suppose I'm the outsider."

"Yes, you are."

"Can an outsider ever become an insider?"

Pia paused for a moment. "I don't think so."

"Miss Carranza, you have just thrown down the gauntlet."

"I'm not sure I know what that means," Pia said, a quizzical look on her face.

"It means you have given me a challenge. I'm good at pelota, I love chorizo, I know how to play *mus*, and now Mr. Egana is trying to teach me *escoba*. What more do I have to do to be an insider?"

With an unwavering gaze, she looked into his eyes. "Marry someone," she said, her voice barely a whisper.

Bart nodded his head, a smile creeping across his face. "I thought so."

After Bart left the Bizkaia House, he checked on Paulina, then started home. When he passed Peter Sonna's hardware store, he had an idea.

"Dr. Bart, what can I do for you?" Sonna asked.

"I want to buy a present—a present for a lady."

"I don't know as how too many of your lady friends would like a present from the likes of my wares, but if I've got what you're lookin' for, I'll sure sell it to you."

"Let me look around and see what you've got."

"All right. You just do that."

It took Bart at least a half hour to go through all the merchandise Sonna had, but at last he found what he was looking for, and when he took his gift to the counter, Sonna was surprised.

"You say this is for a lady friend of yours?"

"It is, and I guess I'll need a pole and about a yard of flannel, too."

Sonna shook his head. "If I gave that present to my wife, I think I'd be sleeping out back with the dogs for a while."

"If I know my girl, she's going to appreciate this," Bart said. "Could you put some brown paper around it?"

"Sure enough."

Leaving the hardware store with his purchase, Bart thought about what he had said. *If I know my girl, she's going to appreciate this.*

Three things were wrong with that statement.

First of all, he didn't know Pia. Second, she wasn't his girl. And third, who was he to think she'd appreciate his gift?

It was time to find out if he had misjudged her.

When Bart stepped into the boardinghouse, he saw several of the men gathered around the dining table. He did not see Pia, however.

"Bart, come join us," Dabi called.

"Thanks," Bart said, and slipped onto the bench across from Dabi. He slid his packages under the table, hoping no one had noticed.

"What brings you here two nights in a row?" Dabi asked.

"Would you believe me if I said the food?"

"Sure, and tonight you're in for a treat. Nikola got a mess of doves today, and *Ama* smothered them in poblano chilies and olive oil. Oh, and then the garlic, of course," Dabi said. "You'll like it."

"Does that mean I'm invited to stay?"

Just then Floria entered the room carrying a big platter, which she set on a sideboard.

"Come and get it," she said in heavily accented English.

She was followed by the Carranzas, each carrying more food, and when it was in place, the others rose quickly and moved toward the sideboard.

Bart hung back, waiting to see Pia's reaction to his being there yet again. He was not disappointed.

When she saw him, she smiled and led her mother to him.

"*Ama*, this is Dr. Wilson. He wrote *Aita*'s letters to us."

Bart didn't understand all the words, but when he heard his own name and the word *aita*, which he knew meant "father," he could assume what she was saying.

The mother responded, and Pia nodded, then turned back toward Bart.

"This is my mother, Zuriñe Carranza."

Bart acknowledged Zuriñe, noticing how much Pia looked like her mother—the flawless golden skin, the same dark eyes, and the hair coloring, except that Zuriñe's was beginning to gray.

"*Ama* wants to know if you actually know my father, or did you just write letters for him?"

"Yes, I do know him. He's much respected, not only by his fellow Basques, but by the outsiders as well."

Another exchange between Pia and her mother.

"And is he doing well?"

"Yes, the last time I saw your father he was strong and healthy."

Pia translated, and Zuriñe nodded in appreciation.

When everyone was back at the table, the four women joined them, and words in Euskera began flying back and forth so fast, and with such intensity, that it was impossible for Bart to follow any of the conversation. That being the case, he didn't even try. He just concentrated on eating the meal and enjoying his frequent glances across the table at Pia. She was animated in her conversation, smiled often, and once or twice pushed back an errant strand of dark hair that fell in a momentary circle around an arched eyebrow. She seemed totally unaware of what a pretty woman she was, and even less aware of the effect she was having on him.

"I am told that all the Bizkaia people have much love and respect for you, because of what you do for them."

The dulcet tones of Pia's voice slipped through staccato phrases of Euskera, and for just a moment Bart could almost believe that he had imagined the comment.

"They're being kind," Bart said. "I'm just a doctor, doing my job."

"You don't look like a doctor," Pia said.

"I don't? Well, what do you think a doctor looks like?"

"They are old men with balding heads and fat stomachs, and they have big noses and their eyes are narrow like this." Pia squinted her eyes in demonstration.

Bart laughed. "Well, I certainly hope I don't look like that."

"Oh, no, you are very beautiful."

Bart had just started to take a swallow of wine, but he coughed and would have spit it out if he had not caught it with his napkin.

"Is something wrong?" Pia asked.

"Did you just say that I am very beautiful?"

"Yes, should I not say such a thing?"

Having heard the exchange, Dabi, Marko, and Julen all laughed.

"What is it?" Pia asked, surprised by the unexpected reaction to her compliment.

"Pia," Marko said, speaking in English, "in our language *eder* can describe a man or a woman. But in English, you don't say a man is beautiful."

"But why not?"

"A man is not beautiful, Pia. A man is handsome."

"Ah," Pia said, putting her hand to her mouth. "I'm sorry, Dr. Wilson. Father Ignacio taught me English, but I didn't learn the difference—beautiful—handsome." She shrugged her shoulders.

"It's all right, Pia. However you say the word, I'm flattered."

"Tell me, Elixabete," Dabi said, returning to their native language, "does Francisco Villota still believe he is the best at pelota?"

Because the previous exchange had been in English, Elixabete had not followed it. Pia was sure that Dabi had asked the question just to change the subject and ease Pia's embarrassment. And for that, she was thankful to him.

"He's very good. They say he wants to play in the Paris Olympiad," Elixabete said. "Right now, there's no one in Guernica who can beat him, maybe in all of the Basque country."

"I know someone who can beat him," Julen Alonzo said.

"Ha! You think there's someone from Muxika who can beat him?" Nikola asked. "I remember once when players from your hometown came to challenge Villota, but there were none who could beat him."

"No, I'm not speaking of players from Muxika, or from anywhere else in Bizkaia," Julen said. "I'm speaking of Dr. Wilson."

When Bart heard his name mentioned, he looked up, but because he had not been concentrating on the conversation, he just smiled and nodded.

"I think Bart could beat Villota," Marko agreed.

"You're talking about this Dr. Wilson?" Pia asked as she gestured toward Bart. "You're saying an American can beat an *euskaldun*? I don't believe that's possible."

"On most days he can beat any of us," Dabi said.

Pia looked with renewed interest at Dr. Wilson. She had to admit he looked athletic, with strong arms and shoulders. Many times she had watched the boys and men of Guernica play pelota, the ball whizzing back and forth as it hit the *frontis* with such speeds that it was only a blur.

"Dr. Wilson, may I see your hand?" Pia asked in English.

Bart held out his hand, not knowing what to expect.

Pia took it in hers and turned it over, rubbing her thumb over his palm. "It's just as I thought. He has no calluses. How can you tell me he is that good?"

"Because in America, we use the *xistera* most of the time," Dabi said. "The basket makes the ball go even faster than a man's hand, even the hand of Francisco Villota. Wait until you see the doctor play. Then you'll know how good he is."

"Bart, we aren't being fair to you," Marko said, speaking in English. "Here we all are talking about you, but it's nothing bad, I assure you. We're talking about your skill as a pelota player."

"Well, I'm not skilled enough," Bart said. "It hasn't been that long ago that I was beaten by a gentleman from Winnemucca."

"He wasn't that much of a gentleman," Dabi added with a laugh. "I lost five dollars betting on you. If he had been a gentleman, he wouldn't have taken the money."

Those who understood English all laughed, and at that moment Pia realized she was still holding Bart's hand. She quickly dropped it and looked around to see if anyone had noticed.

Elixabete had noticed and was glaring at Pia.

∽∞∾

When the meal was over, Dabi extended an invitation to Bart. "Won't you join us in the bar? Cristobol tells us he tried to teach you to play *escoba*, but you didn't do so well."

"Mr. Egana is being kind. I didn't pick it up at all," Bart said. "I'd love to stay, but I've played hooky long enough today. I need to see if anybody needs me back at the office."

Bart watched as Floria, Zuriñe, and Elixabete cleared the food from the sideboard and returned to the kitchen, while Pia gathered the plates from the table. That left Bart and Pia alone in the dining room. This was the opportunity Bart was looking for.

"Pia?"

When she heard his voice, she looked up. "You're not joining the men in the bar?"

"No, I have something for you." He reached under the table and brought out his package.

"Oh, Dr. Wilson, I can't accept something from you," Pia said, thinking of what Elixabete would say to her if she accepted a gift from a man she hardly knew, and especially this man—a man who wasn't Basque.

"You haven't seen my present." Bart handed the bulky package to Pia.

She took it, trying to feel what was inside.

"Go ahead. Open it."

Pia set the object on the table and began tearing the paper away. She saw a metal clamp with a lever attached to it. "I'm afraid I don't know what this is."

Bart reached under the table and withdrew the pole and the yard of flannel. Tearing the flannel into three pieces, he attached one of the pieces to the clamp, then inserted the pole.

"It's a mop." He began pushing it back and forth. "When you want to wring the water out, use this lever, and it does it for you. You'll never have to scrub on your hands and knees again. What do you think?"

"It may be the nicest present anyone has ever given me." Without thinking, Pia stepped forward and kissed Bart on the cheek, a light kiss that was intended as a way of saying thank you.

But Bart caught her in his arms and looked into her eyes. She returned the gaze, her eyes both inviting and vulnerable.

Before Bart realized what he was doing, he returned the kiss, barely making contact with the soft and pliant lips beneath his. He felt her gasp, stiffen, then surrender to him, and though every ounce of his being wanted to deepen this kiss, to take it to its limits, reason prevailed, and quickly he backed away. She continued to stare at him, saying nothing with words, though by expression questioning why he'd withdrawn, as if asking if she had upset him in some way.

"I, uh, had better get back to the office," he said, turning away from those big, brown, wounded eyes.

Later that night, as Elixabete's slow, rhythmic breathing spoke of sleep, Pia lay in the bed, staring at the window. There was no moon tonight, but she could see the dark velvet sky spread with stars. What was it about Dr. Wilson that so attracted her? Not that it mattered. Any relationship with a man who wasn't Basque was forbidden in her culture. She must put him out of her mind.

Pia wasn't the only sleepless one that night. At that very moment Bart was sitting in the living room of his apartment with only a single lightbulb for illumination. He was drinking whiskey and listening to "The Blue Danube" on his Symphonion Disc music box.

Bart took a sip, feeling the burn of the alcohol as it went down his throat. Dozens of pretty, young, unmarried women in town had let him know in every way possible that they were available to him. Even a few married women had hinted that they were approachable. But the last thing he needed was to get involved with a married woman.

"Or a Basque woman," he said aloud, the spoken words contrasting starkly with the bells and chimes of his music box.

SIX

People continued to pour into town for the Intermountain Fair, coming from Idaho, Utah, Oregon, Washington, and Montana, and Bart was sure he had never seen as much activity in Boise as there was now. The Short Line had cut the fares and doubled the number of trains coming into town, "Uncle" John Hailey had put on extra stagecoaches, and every hotel was filled to capacity.

Technically it was the third day of the fair, but since the queen had arrived from Lewiston late on the first day, and it had rained the second day, the queen's parade had been rescheduled for today. All the establishments along Main Street, especially the saloons, hotels, and restaurants, were doing a brisk business as an estimated five thousand people were on hand.

"Dr. Vilson!" a woman called, and Bart recognized her voice—and its accent—immediately.

Smiling, he turned to see Helena Alexander, the attractive wife of Boise's Bavarian mayor, and touched the brim of his hat. "Mrs. Alexander, Moses must be very proud of the success of the fair. Who would have thought so many people would come?"

"It is the races. My husband—he says there are one hundred horses at the stable, and thirty more to come today."

"I think you're right. Monday night the grandstand was almost full, and the fair wasn't even officially opened."

Mrs. Alexander cocked her head to the side and smiled. "Is that why I did not see you at Judge Beatty's reception Monday evening when the queen arrived?"

Bart cleared his throat and dipped his chin. "Would you believe me if I said I forgot?"

"No, I do not believe you, but everybody knows Dr. Wilson. He likes the ladies and the ponies, and Monday, the ponies pull you more than the ladies."

"I'm sure I missed an entertaining evening."

"*Ja*, you did, but most of all you missed meeting Miss Vollmer. *Ach*, so beautiful is that young lady! I know that all will be watching her in the queen's parade today. Wait until you see her. Will you be walking with the doctors in the parade?"

Bart smiled. "Now, Mrs. Alexander, if I walk in the parade, how would I be able to see the beautiful Miss Vollmer? But I believe my father will be walking in the doctors' line, so the practice of Wilson and Wilson will be well represented."

"This is good, *ja*?"

"It is indeed. I think the mayor should be very proud of what he has brought to Boise, and this éclat will be remembered for many years to come."

"*Danke.* I will pass your kind words on to Moses."

"You're welcome. And I promise I will try to meet Miss Vollmer."

Leaving the mayor's wife and picking his way through the ever-growing crowd, Bart hurried on to the Bizkaia House. As soon as he entered, he heard a burst of women's laughter, and looking into the parlor, he saw Mr. Egana sitting with Floria, Zuriñe, Elixabete, and Pia.

"Dr. Wilson," Floria said. "Won't you join us?"

"I'm happy to see the four of you enjoying yourselves. Speaking as a doctor, I will tell you that it's not good to have all work and no play."

Pia translated what he had said, and Mrs. Carranza commented, which brought a laugh from everyone.

"*Ama* says it's because we have a mop that lets us get our work done more quickly, and she says to tell you thank you," Pia said as a flush began to creep across her face.

"Did you tell your mother you thanked me quite properly?"

"I did not!" Pia's eyes widened as through clenched teeth she said, "Some people can understand more English than you think."

Bart chuckled and then turned his attention to Mr. Egana. "How are you feeling, my friend?" Bart patted Mr. Egana on his knee.

Mr. Egana tried to answer but was unable to put it in English, so Pia translated his answer for Bart.

"He said that sometimes after he eats, his stomach hurts, even if he hasn't eaten too much."

"Tell him to put a spoonful of baking soda into a glass of water and drink that, and maybe he should not eat so many hot peppers for a while."

Again, Pia translated, and she continued to translate for her mother and sister, and sometimes even for Floria, who could, as Pia had intimated, understand much more than she could speak.

Bart had a good visit with the women as they enjoyed a rare moment of relaxation, and Mr. Egana was able to share some stories with Bart that had previously been too much for his English skills.

"When do the men get back from the high country?" Bart asked. He was referring to all the sheepherders who would spend the winter at the boardinghouse, but he was particularly interested in when Sabin Carranza would be expected.

"Nikola says it should be less than a month now," Pia said.

"Are you getting anxious?"

"I am," Pia said, a wistful smile forming. "I was only eight years old when my father left, and I worry that I won't recognize him when I see him."

"You'll know him. I promise you. His face may be more wrinkled and his hair may be gray, but when you see his eyes—then you will know."

"I think you're right," she said as she fixed her stare on Bart's eyes. "Your eyes are the clearest blue I've ever seen. I know I would remember them, even the little crinkles at the corners."

"Do you know what those are called?"

"No."

"Crow's-feet."

Pia furrowed her brow.

Bart laughed. "I guess it's an old medical term."

Just then, from somewhere outside, they heard the bleat of a trumpet.

"What was that?" Pia asked, looking toward the window.

Bart pulled out his watch and looked at the time. "It has to be the start of the parade for the Intermountain Fair. Have you ever seen a parade?"

"Oh, yes, many times in Guernica. We have parades to celebrate the feast days at Santa Maria de la Antigua."

"This is not a church parade. You need to come watch it with me. It will be going down Main Street, and that's only a block away."

A broad smile spread across Pia's face, but it was quickly replaced by a look of caution.

"Of course this invitation is for all of you—you, your mother, and your sister," Bart said hastily.

Pia's smile returned and she extended the invitation to the others.

Bart watched them talking back and forth for a moment, but he was unable to follow the conversation.

Then Pia turned to him. "My mother says she and Floria must stay here, because with so many people in town for this fair, they expect more Basques to be here for supper, but Elixabete and I will come."

"Good," Bart said, "but if we want to find a good place to see the parade, we should leave now."

Pia and Elixabete followed Bart outside as he made his way down to Main Street. When they found a place to stand, they watched as Mayor Alexander presented bread and salt to Bessie Vollmer, the queen of the fair.

"Why is he doing that?" Pia asked Bart.

"It's symbolic. The bread stands for hospitality and the salt stands for loyalty."

"I don't understand. I thought in America, no one wanted a queen, but yet this woman gets all of this," Pia said, indicating the crowd of people. "In the Basque country, King Alfonso took away our freedoms, and even now our people try to get out from under the rule of the government of his son."

"It's not the same. This queen has no purpose other than to look pretty and raise money, and when the fair's over, she'll go back to being the same person she was before."

"Raise money?"

"Yes—it cost a penny a vote and she got the most votes, so she's the queen."

Just then the queen climbed into an open carriage pulled by four white horses. Following behind were two maids of honor and twelve ladies-in-waiting, all in their own carriages.

"Did they lose because they don't have any money?" Pia asked.

Bart laughed. "That's probably true."

"Then I shall never be a queen."

"Believe me, you don't want to be this kind of queen," Bart said, taking her hand in his. "Let's move on down the street a little farther because the bands won't start to play until they've marched awhile."

Bart did not drop Pia's hand as he maneuvered her and Elixabete through the crowd until they reached the Overland Hotel. There they stood under the overhang as the parade passed in front of them.

A company of infantry from Fort Boise led off the parade, followed by the queen's carriage and her entourage. Behind the queen came the governor, the mayor, and the state militia. The volunteer-fire-department band was next, and then over eight hundred schoolchildren marched in time to the music. Next were the local artisans' organizations and a great number of local businessmen. Bart saw the doctors, but he did not call Pia's attention to his father.

The last marchers were the women of the Columbian Club, the majority of whom made up the National American Woman Suffrage Association.

True to Marjane's prediction, those who were watching the parade began their haranguing calls.

"Why aren't you women home cooking supper?"

"Ain't you women got a man that can rein you in?"

"Look at 'em! Who'd want one of them women?"

"If you're goin' to act like a man, at least put on some pants!"

"Hey, Governor! Mayor! Look behind you!" someone shouted. "You want those women to be votin' you outta office?"

"I don't know about the governor," Mayor Alexander shouted back. "But I'll take a vote anywhere I can get one."

Those who heard the mayor's response laughed.

"Don't listen to any of these catcalls, Marjane!" Bart called. "I'm proud of you!"

Marjane looked over toward Bart, but she didn't

acknowledge him. Instead she just held her sign up higher.

"Women, exercise your right to vote!" she shouted, then the other women, all of whom were carrying signs and all of whom were just as stern looking as Marjane, repeated her call.

"Women, exercise your right to vote!"

When the final unit of the parade passed them by, the crowd began to break up.

"All right, ladies," Bart said. "Our next stop is the fairgrounds."

Pia relayed the invitation to Elixabete.

"No, I don't think we should go with him," Elixabete said.

"Why not? We live in Boise, now, and everyone is going to the fair. I think we should go, just so we know something about our new hometown."

"He is not *euskaldun.*"

"He isn't asking to marry us, Elixabete. He just wants to escort us to the fair."

Elixabete shook her head. "I don't think it's right. Tell him no, and let's go back." She started pulling on Pia's arm.

"I'm going," Pia insisted as she pulled her arm free.

Elixabete turned and began walking up Eighth Street, headed for the Bizkaia House.

Bart hadn't been able to follow the conversation, though he could tell by Elixabete's reaction that it had been a confrontation of some sort. Finally Pia turned to him.

"My sister thinks she should go back to the boardinghouse. But if you don't mind escorting me, I would love to go to the fair."

"It would be my pleasure, ma'am," Bart said with a happy smile.

Hundreds, perhaps thousands, of people were converging on the fairgrounds, and Pia felt excited as she took in the sights, sounds, and smells—some familiar, others strange and exotic. She was also acutely aware of Bart's proximity, and she realized that if she were alone in this hubbub, she would be frightened. But she felt no anxiety at all, so confident was she in Bart's ability to protect her from any mishap.

"Popcorn! Get your popcorn here! Roasted peanuts, hot popcorn!"

They walked by a glass-sided wagon just before they reached the turnstile. Pia could hear a popping sound coming from the cart, and she saw small, white-bead-looking things spilling from under the lid of a big pot.

"What? What are Cretors?" Pia asked.

"Cretors Popcorn wagon," Bart said. "Would you like some?"

"Some what?"

"Popcorn." Bart stepped over to the wagon. "It's exactly what it sounds like—corn that is popped. I'll bet you've never tasted it."

Bart bought two sacks of popcorn and handed one to Pia. She watched him take a handful, put some in his mouth, then make a face of pure joy. Hesitantly she took a taste, chewed, then broke into a big smile.

"Basques should have this!"

Bart laughed. "I knew you'd like it. But this is just the beginning. Come on."

Just after they passed through the turnstile, a man and woman approached them.

"What are you supposed to represent, my dear?" the woman asked.

"I beg your pardon?" Pia replied.

"Which tent? Where will you be?"

"What makes you think she'll be in a tent?" Bart asked. "She's here to enjoy the fair just like you are."

"Oh, but her costume. Surely she's some kind of performer."

"She's not a performer," Bart said harshly. "The young lady is wearing her national dress. Now, if you'll excuse us?"

When they had moved away from the couple, Pia stopped. "Bart, am I improperly dressed?"

"Absolutely not, your dress is beautiful," Bart said, lifting her chin with his finger, "and so are you. And I am using the right word."

Pia was surprised at the things she saw at the fair. There were ordinary animals such as horses, pigs, cattle, and sheep on display, and locally grown apples, pears, plums, and apricots.

"Why do so many people come to see things that they could see in their own backyards if they wanted to? I thought there would be exotic animals or plants from faraway places," Pia said.

"They want to see the best," Bart explained. "Look, here is a pig with a blue ribbon. That means it won a prize."

"You mean it's like the queen. If you pay enough money, you get to be the best?"

Bart laughed. "I guess it's sort of like that, except

in this case, the winners get money. They don't have to pay."

"I think money is very important in America."

"To some people it is."

"But not to you?"

"I wouldn't say that exactly."

For some reason, Pia was saddened by Bart's answer. She felt comfortable when she was with him, but in that simple exchange, the difference in their cultures was magnified.

The Basque man came to America to work hard, save enough money, and return to Spain so that he could buy a *baserri* for himself. He didn't expect his farmstead to be large, maybe only a few acres, but it would be enough to make him happy.

In America, everything seemed to be about who the winner was.

Leaving the agricultural exhibits, they walked along the line of booths until Bart stopped in front of one with a huge sign above it that read:

THE COLUMBIAN CLUB
IDAHO CHAPTER, THE NATIONAL AMERICAN WOMAN
SUFFRAGE ASSOCIATION

The three women inside the booth were calling out to people who were walking by, apparently trying to convince them to accept some sort of ribbon, but the women weren't getting many takers.

The writing on the ribbon read A WOMAN VOTER.

"Madam, surely you won't turn your back on the hard-won right for women to vote, will you?" one of the young women called out to a female who walked by without even acknowledging her.

"Doesn't look like you're having much luck, Marjane," Bart said as he moved toward the booth.

"Every one we reach is a victory, no matter how small," Marjane replied. "And who is this?"

"This is Miss Pia Carranza," Bart said.

"Basque, I assume?"

"Yes, how did you guess?" Bart asked sarcastically.

"There's no need to waste a ribbon on her, then, is there? If she doesn't understand English, and she's not a citizen, then she can't be a voter."

"Pia, this woman with such refined manners is Marjane Wilson."

Pia gasped. "Your wife?"

Bart laughed. "No, thank goodness. She's my sister."

Pia smiled. "I'm pleased to meet you."

"Yes," Marjane said, ignoring Pia's greeting. "Madam, won't you take a ribbon? Step up and meet Abigail Scott Duniway," Marjane called to a woman who was passing the booth at that moment.

"What is this?" the woman asked, stepping closer.

"It's about women voting, ma'am. And Mrs. Duniway was the push behind getting the right to vote in Idaho. Would you like to meet her?" Marjane turned to an older lady who was sitting in a chair behind a table.

"Come on, Pia, we don't want to stand in the way of a woman with a cause. Let's move on." Bart thought Marjane's behavior toward Pia had been offensive. If the purpose of the suffrage movement was to improve the dignity of women, he thought that respect should be applied to all women.

"She is the one you called out to during the parade, isn't she?" Pia asked.

"Yes."

"I don't think your sister likes me."

Bart tried to find the right words. "It's not that she doesn't like you, because she doesn't even know you, but she is so focused on her cause that sometimes she doesn't realize she's being rude."

"Hey, Doc!" someone called.

Recognizing Don Walton's voice, Bart turned toward him. As usual, Tim O'Leary was right behind him.

"Howdy," Bart said. "Are you boys enjoying the fair?"

"You bet. We just got the inside scoop on Jack Doland. He's the best steer-roper in Montana and he's here," Walton said. "Do you want us to put some money down for ya?"

"I thought Willie Benton was your man," Bart said.

"Willie's good, but I don't think he can beat this here Doland," O'Leary said. "How about it? How much ya willin' to put down?"

Bart reached in his pocket and pulled out a silver dollar. "That's all I'm going to bet. Miss Carranza and I might need every cent I have."

"Don't listen to him, miss," Walton said, turning to Pia. "You have him buy you anything you want 'cause he's going to be rich."

"You think my dollar bet is going to make that much?"

"That's right, 'cause nobody knows about Doland 'cept us," O'Leary said. "He's a real ringer."

"I'm sure he is." Bart shook his head. "Come on, Pia. Let's let these gentlemen find another mark."

"You'll wish you'da given me more, come the steer-roping contest. You just wait," Walton said as the two hurried away.

"They are your friends?" Pia asked.

"Yes. They aren't what you would call high society. But you'll meet a lot like them around here. The salt of the earth."

"Bart," Pia said, a quizzical look on her face. "I thought I knew English, but in this conversation, I don't understand *howdy* or *steer-roping* or *ringer* or *mark* or even *salt of the earth.*"

Bart laughed. "I can tell I'm going to have to spend a lot of time with you, Miss Carranza. It's for your education, you understand." Taking her hand, he led her toward the industrial display.

Bart and Pia were both fascinated as they walked among the new inventions. Pia stood in front of an electric fan, letting the breeze blow her hair, while Bart watched the reaction of people when they put their hands under a screen for a fluoroscope. Invariably they would gasp in surprise and fear as they looked at their own skeletal bones. Some of the women were so disturbed by the vision that they nearly fainted and had to be taken out.

Bart had read about this, but this was the first time he had ever seen such a device. He was immediately struck with how valuable such a thing would be for a doctor, and he wondered if any medical use was currently being made of the machine.

When they moved to the display of gems found in

Idaho, Pia was amazed. "People can just go out and pick these up off the ground?" she asked as she held a cherry-red stone.

"Yes, if you know what you're looking for. What you're holding is an opal. Most of the time they're a pale blue or white, but in Idaho you can find a red one like you're holding or a salmon-pink one like this." He pointed to another stone.

"I don't think I've ever seen so many different kinds of gems."

"We have rubies, garnets, diamonds, sapphires—you name it; but most people who come here are looking for silver or gold. Do you want to see how they recover gold?"

"I'd like that."

They walked on until they reached an area where a gold-stamping machine was being demonstrated. Steam was escaping from the engine, and the building was filled with the thunder of crushing rock. At the bottom of the portable stamping mill, a water sluice and shaker separated the crushed rock so that the tiny bits of gold would be freed.

As this was a new version of the stamping process, miners from all over the Boise Basin were gathered to watch the demonstration. Bart and Pia observed for a moment or two, but the sound was too great for them to stay long.

As they were walking away, someone called out, "Bart, my boy, is that you?"

"I can't believe it," Bart said quietly, before he turned around.

Pia was surprised by Bart's reaction and turned with him to see an old man and woman coming toward them, both grinning broadly. The man was wearing ill-fitting, faded clothes, and the woman was wearing a black-and-white-checked gingham dress and a starched bonnet.

"I didn't expect to run into you today. Did Frank let you off your leash?" the old man asked.

"He doesn't know I'm here," Bart said with a large and genuine smile. "What are you doing here?"

"Why, I came to see the elephant, boy," the old man replied, his smile as broad as Bart's. The two men hugged, then Bart hugged the woman.

"Pia," Bart said after the hugs, "this is my grandfather Eli Wilson, and my aunt Suzie Yarborough."

"Hello, darlin'," Eli said, extending his hand.

"My, Bart, what a lovely young lady!" Suzie said, and she, too, extended her hand.

"I'm pleased to meet you, Mr. Wilson, Mrs. Yarborough," Pia said as she dipped her head.

"What *are* you doing in Boise?" Bart asked.

"I came to see this new stamping machine I heard about," Eli said. "And I want to visit with a few of the old-timers who came into town for this shindig Moses Alexander thought up."

"Is there an elephant here?" Pia asked.

"An elephant? No, I don't think so," Bart replied.

"But your grandfather said . . ."

"Oh, my, don't listen to that old coot," Suzie said with a laugh. "That's just an expression he uses when he wants to see something new."

"Oh." Pia took a deep breath. There was so much she had to learn.

"Have you had your supper?" Eli asked. "Suzie and I were about to go get something to eat."

"My!" Pia said. "Is it time for supper?"

"It's a little early, but I'm as hungry as an ox," Eli said.

Pia felt guilty and apprehensive. She had no idea how much time had passed. She knew she should be at the Bizkaia House helping to prepare the evening meal.

"Bart, I really should go back to the boardinghouse."

"The boardinghouse?" Eli asked. "You can't get a decent meal at one of those places. Too much garlic."

"Grandpa, Pia owns one of the boardinghouses, and I love all the garlic."

"You always were a strange boy," Eli said. "If you own the place, honey, let somebody else do the work. Come on. I hear Johnny Lemp's introduced a new beer and he's serving it with fresh kraut and German bratwurst. You don't want to miss that, now do you?"

A part of Pia wanted to break and run now, but it was too late. Even if she left this very minute, she knew that all the work would be done. Whatever reprimand she was going to get, it would come whether she was fifteen minutes late or if she was two hours late.

Eli led them to a large tent filled with long tables covered with red-checked oilcloths.

As soon as they sat down, a big pitcher of beer and four pewter mugs were set in front of them.

Eli poured the beer. "Drink up." He lifted a mug and drained it.

"Eli, you old coot, you didn't even ask this young

lady if she wanted any of this. She may be one of Marjane's temperance friends," Suzie said.

"Believe me, she's not," Bart said, "but she may not want to take a drink anyway."

Pia wondered what Bart meant when he said *believe me, she's not* with reference to one of Marjane's friends. She couldn't tell if that was a good thing or a bad thing.

Other women were in the tent, drinking from the mugs. She watched Suzie to see what she did, and soon she, too, was drinking the beer, so Pia decided it must be something women in America did.

She lifted the mug to her lips and took her first sip of beer. When she tasted it, she thought she had never had a more vile-tasting drink in her life, and she screwed up her face in an attempt to swallow it.

Bart leaned over and, in front of everyone, kissed her gently on the lips.

"I'm so sorry, Pia. That was your first drink, wasn't it?"

Pia nodded.

"You don't have to drink it if you don't want it."

"But that wouldn't be very polite, not after the old coot bought it for me."

Suzie had just taken a swallow of her beer, and she laughed so hard that she sprayed beer out on the table. Eli laughed as well.

"What is it?" Pia asked. "Did I say something wrong?"

"No, honey, you didn't say anything wrong," Eli said. "I am an old coot."

"I'm afraid I've been a very corrupting influence on you," Bart said. "I think I'd better get you home."

⤺⤻

Later, as they were leaving the fairground and walking back toward the trolley tracks, Pia asked the question that had been plaguing her.

"What is an old coot?"

Again, Bart laughed. "It means a strange old man."

"Oh! Then I insulted your grandpa!"

"No, you didn't," Bart said. "Generally that's a term that is used with affection. And Grandpa is a strange old man."

"What makes you say that? I liked him."

"You saw the way he was dressed, didn't you?"

"Yes."

"Don't you think it's odd for a millionaire to dress like that?"

"Millionaire?" Pia replied in a weak voice. "Does that mean he has lots of money?"

"Yes," Bart said without further elaboration. "Here's the trolley." With that, the subject of Eli and his money was closed.

"Why did you not come home with your sister?" Zuriñe asked angrily. "Elixabete went to the parade and she knew to come to the boardinghouse when it was over."

"I'm sorry, *Ama*. I didn't realize I would be gone so long. I'll do all the work cleaning up after supper. No one else has to do anything."

"That is not what is bothering me. What concerns me is that you, an unmarried woman, were alone with a man. And not just any man, but an American man."

"*Ama*, Dr. Wilson . . . we were never alone. There were people everywhere."

"That makes it even worse," Zuriñe said. "Everyone could see your indiscretion."

Dabi had just stepped in to the kitchen and caught the end of the discussion between Pia and her mother.

"What will people think if they saw you with Dr. Wilson?" Zuriñe added.

"They won't think anything about it," Dabi said. "Mrs. Carranza, Bart Wilson is a very good friend. He is a good man, and a friend to all *euskaldunak*. He would not do anything to harm Pia."

"It is not right," Zuriñe said with a sigh of surrender. "But if Dabi speaks highly of Dr. Wilson, then this once, I accept his opinion. But I just wish that you would show a little more judgment. When your *aita* comes, it will be time to find a husband for you, and no man wants a despoiled woman."

"I'm sorry, *Ama*," Pia said, and she wasn't just saying the words. She knew what she had done today was wrong. She would have to be more careful about letting her feelings for the handsome doctor overcome her good sense.

SEVEN

Owyhee Mountains

Sabin Carranza awakened before daybreak. Looking at his calendar, he turned the page, marking off the first day of December. Rolling off the three-foot-high box that stretched across the back of the sheep wagon, he opened a drawer beneath the corn-husk mattress and withdrew a clean pair of socks. He dressed quickly and stepped outside to relieve himself.

"Good morning, boys." At the sound of his voice two dogs came out from under the wagon, nuzzling his hands and begging to be rubbed behind the ears. "Did you sleep well? You've got to do your job today, keep the bunch close together, because we've got to get the sheep and the wagon across the creek."

In the way of most sheepherders who spent many months in isolation, Sabin treated his dogs, his horse, and his sheep as if they were people, explaining patiently what was expected of them. The dogs were so well trained that a mere word or a hand signal would send them to the appropriate place.

"Let's give Zaldi his oats, because it's up to him

to move the wagon today. And you boys are going to have to bring the girls down on your own."

Sabin went around to the back of the wagon as the wind whipped against the canvas roof. Withdrawing a measure of oats and filling the wooden box, he took it to where his horse was hobbled.

When he returned to the wagon, he knelt to start the fire that he had laid the night before. Usually, he would cook breakfast on the stove in the front of the wagon, but he had purposefully let it go out because he would be moving the camp today.

When the fire was going, he set his metal grill over the stones he had piled around it and started his coffee. He put some bacon and several pieces of mutton into an iron skillet, and when the meat was cooked, he ate what he could and shared the rest with his dogs, Esti and Bekindi. Having cleaned the pan as best he could, he went back into the wagon and began securing everything in preparation for the move.

"If Dabi doesn't get here soon, we're going to run out of coffee."

He checked each of the tin canisters that sat on a triangular shelf across from the wood-burning iron stove. He had enough flour for maybe one more loaf of bread, a couple of days' worth of cheese, little coffee, and a couple of hard crackers.

"But we won't starve. We'll live on mutton."

By the time Sabin had the wagon ready to move, the sheep were up from their bedding ground. The leader of this band of close to a thousand sheep was Toki, a wise old goat who was always first to awaken in the morning, and always in the lead in finding a trail over the rough, mountainous terrain to more pastureland. Sabin had hung a bell around her neck, and the sound of it would summon the sheep to her, each of them finding its own specific position within the band. Sabin had, long ago, learned that the sheep were as jealous and possessive of their place in the herd as a person would be of land he had staked out for his own.

Here, the sheep, after having come down from the higher elevations, were on good drying grassland that was as good as eating hay. After Toki led the band to drink, they spread out down the mountain, while Esti and Bekindi kept a watchful eye over the flock.

Toki's bleating reminded Sabin that she had not yet been milked. Grabbing the pail and stool, he set out down the slope until he reached the goat.

"Sorry, old girl, I guess I was just too busy this morning to think about you," Sabin said as he sat down on the three-legged stool and started squirting little streams of milk into the pail.

He was heading back to the wagon when a low growl from Esti alerted Sabin to danger.

"What is it, girl? What do you see?"

Sabin heard the bleat of frightened sheep then, and he suspected what it was. Putting the milk in a safe place, he grabbed his rifle and moved quickly to a small hill where he had a view of the band's right flank. That was where he saw the coyote, hunkered down and moving toward an outlying ewe. Jacking a shell into the chamber, he raised the Winchester to his shoulder, aimed, and fired.

The coyote yelped, leaped up, and fell back to the

ground, where it lay still. Sabin hurried out to check and saw that the animal was dead. Picking it up by its back legs, he whirled it around a few times to build up the momentum, then hurled it as far away from the sheep as he could.

Not more than fifteen minutes later he heard the distinctive cry of the *irrintzi*.

"He's here, Esti, Dabi's here." Sabin answered with a call of his own: *"Ruuu-ubru-uu!"* Then he broke out in a run, causing the sheep to scatter. Esti stayed with Sabin, but Bekindi, the older of the two dogs, started bunching the sheep immediately, and soon they were grazing quietly again.

When Dabi rode into camp, he was smiling broadly. "It won't be long now, Sabin Carranza, until you will be with your family."

Sabin was so overcome with emotion that for a moment he could not speak. He turned away from Dabi and bent down, ostensibly to tend to Esti's foot. When he got control of himself, he rose. "Sometimes when the sheep are grazing quietly and all is well, I try to picture what my little ones look like."

Dabi chuckled. "They're not little ones anymore. You have two beautiful daughters. Pia is small, more delicate, with the coloring of her mother, brown flashing eyes, while Elixabete has your blue eyes. She is the best worker, but Pia has the best mind. Did you know she speaks English as well as Marko?"

"Are the other herders beginning to come in from the winter range?"

"Yes, there are some, but the Bizkaia is not full yet."

"Has anyone asked to marry either of my daughters?"

"There are many Basques who would have them, Sabin, but out of respect for you, I don't think anyone has asked for them specifically."

"This is good. An old man has much time to think in these hills. And what of my wife? Is she well?"

"She is. My mother is enjoying her help and her company. It was a wise thing for you to invest in the Bizkaia, and it is running well. My father thanks you."

Sabin nodded. "Shall we get Zaldi hitched to the wagon?"

"Yes. I believe Gorka's band is a day or two ahead of us. When we join the two together, I'll stay with the sheep until I get them to the winter bedding ground. It's time for you and Gorka to go to town."

Sabin smiled broadly, but said nothing.

Boise

Over the last several weeks as the temperature turned sharply colder, the number of illnesses associated with the cold increased. Bart and his father were kept so busy treating the increasing numbers of patients that Bart had not been able to visit the Bizkaia House as frequently as he had in the past.

It was Nikola who came to the office in search of Dr. Bart. He had a note from Pia asking him to come when he could.

"Pia? Is anything wrong?" Bart asked when he arrived.

"It's Mr. Egana," Pia said. "He is ill and he's been

vomiting all night long. We didn't know until he came down about an hour ago."

Egana was in the parlor lying on the couch with his shoes off, but fully dressed. Bart took his temperature and saw that it was 102.

"What are you doing down here?" Bart asked. "Why aren't you in your room?"

"No people. Like tending sheep," Egana said.

"Yes, well, you need to stay in bed, covered up for a while. And you don't need to be down here around other people where you can infect them. You don't want to do that, do you?"

When it was apparent that Egana didn't fully understand what Bart was saying, Pia translated Bart's words.

"He doesn't want to make anyone else sick."

"Good. All right, Mr. Egana, as soon as we get your shoes on, Pia and I are going to help you back to your room."

With Pia on one side and Bart on the other they assisted the man up the stairs and down the hall to his room.

"We have to get you in bed now, my friend," Bart said as the old man sat down, coughing and gasping for breath. "Pia, help me get him undressed, would you?"

"Undressed?"

Bart started removing Mr. Egana's shoes. "Yes, unbutton his shirt."

"All right," Pia said a little hesitantly.

As Bart unlaced and removed Mr. Egana's shoes, Pia unbuttoned his shirt. She let it hang open, but went no further.

Bart took the shirt off. "Now tell him to lie back and we'll take off his trousers."

Pia hesitated for a moment.

"Go ahead."

Pia translated, and Egana looked surprised. "Young girl to take off pants?"

Now it was Bart's time to laugh. "Calm down, Mr. Egana. Miss Carranza is my nurse."

"*Bai*. And I am old. Too old."

Egana lay back and Bart unbuttoned his trousers, then took hold of one leg. "You take the other leg," he said, and nodding, Pia did as Bart instructed. They slid his trousers down, and Pia breathed a sigh of relief when she saw that Egana was wearing long underwear underneath.

Bart pulled the cover down, and he and a less nervous Pia helped Egana get into bed.

"Now you stay here. Your nurse here," Bart said, patting Pia on the back, "will bring your food to you and she'll check on you to make sure you have everything you need."

After they left Egana's room, Bart spoke quietly to Pia.

"I hope I didn't embarrass you in there."

"You didn't. It's just that I've never undressed a man before."

"Really?" Bart asked, raising his eyebrows as a smile crossed his lips.

Pia flushed at Bart's reaction.

"I'm sorry, Pia. I'm so used to teasing my sister that my comment just came out. But what we just did, nurses do all the time."

Downstairs, Bart took a small bottle of clear liquid from his bag and showed it to Pia.

"This is oil of eucalyptus. Lay a towel across his mouth, just under his nose, then put no more than four or five drops on the towel so he can breathe in the fumes. That will keep his nose clear and should help reduce the coughing. And if we can get the coughing down, it might also help with the vomiting.

"I want you to keep a close eye on him. Keep him warm, and make certain he has a lot to drink," Bart said. "Oh, and when you go into his room, tie a handkerchief around your face. That way if he has something that may be contagious, it won't be spread around the boardinghouse."

"I'll take good care of him," Pia said.

Through the open door of the bar, they heard a sudden burst of laughter.

By now nearly all of the sheepherder residents of the Bizkaia House were back from the mountains. As a result, the bar, which was quiet most of the time, was crowded with men who were enjoying not only drink, but company, for the first time in ten months.

"And when I shot that coyote, he was five hundred yards away, I tell you. Five hundred yards!"

"You mean when you shot *at* him, Bittor. I think maybe you didn't hit him," another voice said. This was Salazar, the bartender who worked for Bizkaia House.

"Yes, I did. I hit him right between the eyes!" Bittor said loudly.

"I think Bittor shoots best when no one is there to

see," Salazar said, and again there was a loud burst of laughter from the others in the bar.

"If alcohol kills germs, I don't think many of our boarders have a chance of getting sick," Pia said as she tilted her head toward the bar.

"I can't say that I blame them. If I'd just spent ten months out on a mountaintop with no one to talk to, just listening to sheep bleat all day long, I'd be ready for a good stiff drink myself," Bart said. "I admire them, Pia."

"You may be the only one. Except Basques, of course. Dabi says that cattlemen hate sheepherders. They call us tramp sheepmen."

"They're just jealous."

"How could they be jealous of someone who does what these men do?"

"I think they are jealous of men who can work as hard as the Basques do. Some think your people come to work a short time, save all the money they make, and then go back home."

"Why is that bad?" Pia asked, thinking of her own plan to go back to Guernica.

"Because we want you to like us."

"To hear Dabi and some of the others talk, they think most would just as soon we all go back to where we came from."

"Then let me reword that. I want you to like me."

"All the Basques like you."

"I'm glad they do, but I'm not talking about all the Basques, I'm talking about you. I want you to like me."

"But of course I like you. Why would I be different from all the others?"

"You are different, Pia."

"But I don't want to be."

Bart smiled and lifted her hand and kissed it. "It's a good thing that you are different. Believe me, it's a good thing. Come, walk me to the door."

When they entered the dining room, Pia noticed a man standing just inside the door of the entry hall.

He had a gray beard, gray hair, and blue eyes set deep in a weathered face. He was wearing a red flannel shirt and denim trousers.

Something about him was familiar; a recognition resonated deep within her memory. But, this couldn't be her father, could it? This man was old. And she remembered him as being so much taller. But even as she thought that, she realized that it was a matter of perspective. She had been a young girl when he left, so naturally he seemed taller to her. She looked to Bart with a quizzical expression on her face.

Bart, with a big smile on his face, nodded.

"Aita!" Pia shouted, and she ran to the man, who reached out strong arms to bring her into an embrace.

"My daughter! You have to be Pia. Dabi told me you favored your mother. Where is your mother? Your sister?"

"They're in the kitchen," Pia said.

"Fetch her if you would, Pia, and tell her that her husband has arrived."

Excitedly, Pia hurried toward the kitchen.

"Dr. Wilson," Sabin said, extending his hand to Bart. "Who is so sick that we need the doctor to call?"

"It's Cristobol Egana."

"He's still here, eh? I thought he was ready to die last spring."

"He's not going to die. Not with your daughter around. She takes good care of him."

"*Ama!* **Elixabete!** *Aita* is here!" Pia said as she burst into the kitchen.

Elixabete ran past Pia on her way to the door, but Zuriñe only nodded. She finished slicing the loaf of bread she had before her, and then drying her hands on her apron, she walked into the foyer.

"Hello, Sabin," Zuriñe said, extending her hand. "Floria thought you wouldn't get here until next week."

"Dabi stayed with the band so Gorka and I could come into town," Sabin replied, shaking her hand.

"He's a very thoughtful boy. That was nice of him."

"How have you fared over the years?"

"I have fared well."

"That's good."

"You've met your daughters?"

"Yes, they seem to be fine young women," Sabin said. "Are they helpful to you?"

"Yes, they are helpful."

"That is good."

Another outburst of laughter came from the bar.

"Most of the men have returned?" Sabin asked.

"They have."

"Then you have much to do. I'll join the men in the bar. Pia, will you take my rifle and bedroll to the room where I am to stay?"

"Yes, *Aita*," Pia said as she picked up his belongings.

Bart had been observing this reunion. As the conversation was in Euskera, he did not understand
most of what was said, but he thought he could
read the emotions, and what he had seen were no
emotions at all, at least between Sabin and Zuriñe.
Pia and Elixabete seemed genuinely happy to see
their father, but after thirteen years there was no
outpouring of any kind of affection other than the
embrace Sabin had given his daughter. Perhaps it
was because an "outsider" was present.

"Pia, I'd better get back to my own place, so you
can enjoy getting reacquainted with your *aita*," Bart
said. "Just don't have so much fun you forget about
Mr. Egana."

"I'll take care of him, but you will check on him
again, won't you?"

"I'll be back," Bart said as he waved to the others.

A big cauldron of *cocido madrileño* had been sim-
mering on the stove all day, hardly bubbling. The
combination of boiling salt pork, fresh lamb, and
chicken filled the air with its aroma and the promise of full and rich flavor. Floria tasted the broth
and then added garbanzo beans, onions, leeks, and
lots of garlic. Zuriñe and Elixabete had baked close
to three dozen loaves of bread, some mixed with
chopped black olives, others with dried tomatoes,
but all were drizzled with olive oil. This would be
the first meal Sabin and many of the herders had
eaten since coming in from the range. Both Floria
and Zuriñe were determined to make it as much

like a meal that might have been served in the old country as they could.

Pia and Elixabete set the three long tables, making the places as close as possible to accommodate all those in residence. At present the herders were either in the bar or the parlor, each one trying to outdo the other with his experiences in the mountains. The bears, the coyotes, the rattlesnakes—when one started a story, another had an even more daring tale to tell. Because they were all talking at once, and because the wine had been flowing, the boardinghouse literally vibrated with the loud and totally unintelligible conversation.

"Elixabete," Pia said, "were you surprised by the way *Ama* and *Aita* greeted each other?"

"What do you mean? Why should I be surprised?" Elixabete replied.

"It's been thirteen years since they've seen one another. Don't you think they would have wanted to kiss, or at least hug?"

"Pia, it is you who surprises me! A man and a woman do not express feelings for one another in public, at least not a Basque, and they certainly wouldn't be hugging or kissing." Then Elixabete added, "Or holding hands with a man who is not even an Amerikanuak."

"What do you mean?"

"I saw you with Dr. Wilson. You were holding his hand when you were checking his calluses for the pelota. And then at the parade. He didn't take my hand to guide us through the crowd."

Pia started to respond, but then she thought better of it. What would Elixabete think if she knew Bart had kissed her?

Just then Floria brought the steaming stew and placed it on the sideboard. "Girls, go help your mother bring in the bread."

Elixabete, Pia, and Zuriñe carried in the baskets of hot bread and set them on the tables. Floria was already seated beside Lander, and Sabin was sitting across from them. A place was beside Sabin.

"One of you go sit beside your *aita*," Zuriñe said. "I believe there is room."

Elixabete moved toward the place, but Pia pulled her back. "That place is for you, *Ama*."

"But where will you sit?"

"We'll sit with Marko and Nikola, and if I were to guess, that's Gorka and Luken sitting beside them," Pia said.

Zuriñe's face lit up. "It is. I saw them this afternoon when they came into the kitchen to see Floria. Yes, it is better that you sit with them."

At thirty-one, Gorka was the oldest of the Segura brothers. Next in line was Dabi, then Marko, then Luken, and finally Nikola, who, at nineteen, was the youngest. Within moments the four Segura brothers and the two Carranza sisters were talking, laughing, and remembering the years past.

When the meal was over and the kitchen cleaned, Elixabete and Pia moved their belongings to the cellar, where they would be sleeping. The room, if one could call it that, was lined with rocks and had no window. Two half beds were against the walls, and Pia chose the inside wall, thinking it would be warmer. She closed her eyes, fighting back tears, as she pictured her own room back in Guernica— the blue-and-white quilt that her grandmother had made for her, the curtains billowing in the breeze as the scent of wisteria wafted through the open window—all of that she had given up, to come to this place to scrub floors and wash sheets and make bread.

"Steerage, will I never get out of steerage?"

Elixabete had stepped out into the storeroom where the bins of potatoes, carrots, parsnips, turnips, and onions were kept. There was a table where Floria sat when she washed and candled eggs before setting a hen. Elixabete sat down and turned on the bulb in the candle box. Carefully, she held each egg up to the light, checking to see if the egg was fertilized.

Before long, Pia heard three Segura boys come down the steps. They joined Elixabete at the table, and soon Pia heard the four of them enjoying a lively conversation.

Elixabete preached propriety to Pia all the time, and she knew she should go out and join them. If it was not right for Pia to hold Bart's hand, it was certainly not right for Elixabete to talk to three men alone.

But Pia didn't care.

She turned over to face the rock wall and tried to go to sleep, but it wouldn't come.

Why were her people so enamored with America? The life of a Basque man or a Basque woman was hard. Would it be so wrong to marry someone who was not a Basque?

The next morning, Bart went by the Bizkaia House before going to the office. He told himself that it was to check on Mr. Egana, but he knew that wasn't the only reason. He was coming to see Pia. It was foolish of him, he knew, but he enjoyed her company.

He and Pia, having been with Mr. Egana, were coming down the stairs when a woman came in through the front door, highly agitated and speaking in rapid Euskera. The only word Bart could understand was *doctor*, so he knew she was here for him. He looked over at Pia.

Without being asked, Pia said, "Her mother, Mrs. Garatea, is sick."

"Do you speak English?" Bart asked the woman.

"Ez dut ingelesez hitz egiten."

"She doesn't—"

"—speak English. I do know that phrase. If she doesn't speak English, I'm sure her mother doesn't either. That makes it hard."

"Would you like me to come with you?" Pia offered.

"Yes!" Bart replied enthusiastically. "Yes, that would be wonderful!"

After Pia had offered to go, she began having second thoughts. Her mother had been upset when she was with Bart at the fair, when thousands of people were around them. What would she think if she went with him now?

"I'll ask my mother."

"You go," Floria said, speaking in English so Bart could understand as well. "I'll tell your *ama*. It is good. You help Dr. Wilson."

"Thank you, Mrs. Segura," Bart said.

Grabbing his case, Bart left with Pia, following the woman to her house. There, Bart found the woman suffering from a bad case of bronchitis. Using Pia as his translator, he gave her some tincture of bryonia to alleviate the chest pressure. He also left instructions to use oil of eucalyptus, to stay warm, and to stay hydrated.

"Tell her to drink as much hot sassafras tea as she can," Bart said. "That should make her chest less congested."

When they left the Garatea house, Bart walked as far as Eighth Street with Pia. "Do you know how much of a help you are to me? Have you ever considered becoming a nurse?"

"You're being kind, Bart, but I don't think I could do that."

"Don't say no yet. I want you to consider it."

When they reached the corner of Main and Eighth, Bart turned toward Grove and Pia went toward Idaho.

As she walked, she thought about what Bart had said. A nurse? No, she couldn't do that. Not because she didn't think she would be good at it, but because she couldn't trust herself to spend that much time with Bart Wilson. He had said that he wanted her to like him, but then he had said, *It's a good thing you are different.*

What did that mean? He was a man; she was a woman. No matter how much time they might spend together, would he ever see her as anything but a Basque woman? And why did it matter?

She was a Basque woman and she was proud of

it. If Bart Wilson couldn't accept that, then so be it.

As she saw the big sign saying BIZKAIA HOUSE, BASQUES WELCOME, she turned up the walkway with her head held high. Then she had a devastating thought. Bart had asked her to think about being his nurse. Why had she jumped to the conclusion that he was asking for anything more?

"I want to hire a nurse," Bart told his father later that same day.

"A nurse? Why in heaven's name do you think we need a nurse? And where would you find one? Has Clara Barton moved to Boise?"

"I have the person in mind, and she's especially suited for the job. I want to hire Pia Carranza, a Basque woman. She's fluent in English, and she would be perfect as a translator."

"Carranza? Is she related to that sheepherder who got bitten by a rattlesnake a few years ago?"

"That would be Sabin Carranza. She's his daughter."

"I didn't know he had family in Boise."

"He sent for his wife and daughters after he became Lander Segura's partner in the Bizkaia House, and now they help Floria run the place." Bart chuckled. "He was still out with the sheep when they arrived, and I think he was quite surprised when he met them. In his mind, his daughters were still little girls, like they were when he left them thirteen years ago. They have both become very competent young women."

"You seem to know a lot about this particular family."

"I've taken an interest in them," Bart said. "I wrote a couple of letters for Sabin."

"I don't know, Bart." Frank rubbed his chin as he spoke. "I've never really seen the need for a nurse, and if we did have one, don't you think it should be Marjane?"

"Ha. You'll never get Marjane to stay home long enough to work for us. Is she back from Oregon yet?"

"I think your mother got a letter telling us she'll be home for Christmas at least. It seems Abigail Duniway is publishing a newspaper, and she has Marjane helping her."

"That answers your question, then. Do you think for one minute Marjane would be interested in working with us, when she's working with one of the most ardent suffragists in the Northwest?"

"I suppose you're right."

"And besides, the advantage that Pia has is that she speaks English as well as I do, and she also speaks Euskera. The biggest problem I face when I'm with the Basques is that most of my time is spent trying to make them understand what I'm doing or what I want them to do. If I had Pia, that problem would be solved."

Frank was quiet as he thought about Bart's suggestion. "It could work, I suppose, but you know how peculiar the Bascos are, especially when it comes to their women. They work them to death, and if Sabin brought his family over here to work in the boardinghouse, what makes you think he'd let her work for you?"

Bart smiled at his father. "If I know one thing

about the Basques, it's that they're frugal. If I pay her, I'll bet Sabin will be more than happy to let her work for me."

"You say *if* you pay her. Bart, if you were practicing medicine on your own, you'd starve to death." Frank picked up the receipt book and began to read: "Nathan Smith, will pay when he can; Hank Rouse, out of work; Mrs. Leutgert, two chickens; Chester Nason, no charge; Mrs. Wadleigh, a loaf of bread. Should I go on?" Frank turned two or three pages in the book.

"I have the money to pay her," Bart said, silently thanking his grandfather for the recent infusion of cash. "Pop, did you notice, not one of those names you read is a Basque name? The Basques always pay."

Frank drummed his fingers on his desktop. "I'll tell you what. If you can get her to work here, you hire her, and you pay her from your own pocket for a month. If it works out all right, and if there's no trouble with . . . those people . . . I'll consider having her salary come out of the office expenses."

Bart noticed how his father had set the phrase *those people* apart, as if they were somehow second-class citizens. On the other hand, he had gotten Frank's tacit approval and didn't want to say or do anything that would seem confrontational.

"All right," Bart agreed. "I'm willing to accept that."

The next morning, Bart was excited as he walked the two blocks to the Bizkaia House. Even though Pia had told him she didn't think she could be a nurse, he knew he could convince her—that is, if he could convince Sabin to let her do it.

When he entered the dining room, the families and many of the boarders were seated around one of the tables.

"Doc, how is it you always know when we're eating?" Marko asked good-naturedly. "Come have some of my mom's Gypsy eggs."

"You know I want to, but that's not why I'm here."

"Then why are you here? It looks like you've cured Mr. Egana."

Bart looked toward the old man, who sat next to Pia. "It wasn't just me. Pia did her part in taking care of him. Isn't that right?"

Mr. Egana nodded his head and grinned. He caught enough to know he was the subject of the conversation.

"Well, at least have a cup of coffee with us," Marko invited.

"I can do that."

Pia rose to get a cup of coffee for Bart, and when she set it in front of him, she placed her hand on his shoulder. It was the most innocent thing she could have done, something any woman would have done, yet she felt guilty and moved her hand quickly.

Bart sensed her reaction and looked up at her, holding eye contact just long enough for it to be obvious to them, if not to anyone else in the room.

"Pia, have you had time to consider my offer to hire you as a nurse?" Bart spoke the question in a louder voice than he would normally have used.

Sabin jerked his head up. "A nurse? Pia?"

"No, *Aita*, I am not a nurse."

"But she could be, Sabin. She has helped me with Cristobol, and last week she went with me to see Mrs. Garatea, and I don't know what I would have done without her. I would use her to help me with the Basques, but I would also use her with my other patients as well. She has a kind and . . ." Bart was ready to say *loving*, but he chose not to go on with his thought.

Pia was still behind Bart, and he heard her taking the coffeepot back to the kitchen. He wished she had stayed; he believed he could tell by the expressions on her face whether she genuinely did not want to work for him, or if she had just said no out of respect for her elders.

Without Pia present, a flurry of Euskera was going between Sabin, Zuriñe, Floria, Marko, Julen, and even Mr. Egana. Bart noticed that the only one definitely staying out of the conversation was Elixabete, and she was glaring at him. He tried to smile at her, but she looked away.

After several minutes, Marko spoke. "Sabin has decided that he thinks it would be a good thing. With so many Americans equating us with the Spaniards, and with all the talk of the Cuba Libre movement, he thinks more of us should find ways to work with outsiders, and since you are almost an insider, he thinks working for you would be good."

"Thank you, Sabin. I appreciate that, but Pia wasn't here for the discussion. She should have a say in this, too."

"Why?" Sabin asked.

"Because if I bring her into my house, and she doesn't really want to do this . . ."

"Let me guess," Marko said. "With Marjane's crusade for women, she would, no doubt, think you are taking advantage of Pia."

Bart chuckled. "You know Marjane better than I thought you did."

Marko then explained the situation and everyone else laughed as well, while Julen went to the kitchen to get Pia.

When Pia entered, she sat at the end of the table.

"You will be working for Dr. Wilson, Pia, and you will do whatever he tells you to do," Sabin said.

"But what about the work here?" Pia asked.

Floria smiled and held up her finger as if telling her to wait while she asked a question. "Dr. Wilson, will you pay Pia?"

Bart laughed out loud. "Of course I will."

Floria spoke to Zuriñe, and Zuriñe nodded.

Bart saw a smile on Pia's face then. He had been holding his breath without even being aware of it and let out a big sigh. The smile had to mean she was accepting his offer.

It isn't fair, Elixabete complained that night as she lay in her bed in the dark.

"What isn't fair?"

"It's going to be just like it was in Guernica. There, you were teaching children for Father Ignacio, while I worked hard in the bakery. Here, you will be helping Dr. Wilson, while I work cleaning and cooking."

"It isn't the same," Pia said. "In Guernica, I was not getting paid for teaching the children. Here, I will be paid. I have been thinking, and I have decided you should get half the money I make."

"You will give me half the money?" Elixabete perked up at the suggestion.

"Yes, because while I'm gone, you'll have to work harder. But I'll work here, too, when I get back from Bart's office."

"All right. That seems fair."

"Thank you. If you were going to be upset with me, I wouldn't do this, but, Elixabete . . ." Pia turned over, repositioning her knees so they didn't hit the rocks of the wall.

"'But, Elixabete,' what?"

"Nothing. I'm just glad we got it worked out."

Pia was about to tell Elixabete how much she was looking forward to this, but Elixabete wouldn't understand. Even Pia didn't understand the giddiness she was feeling.

The next morning, Pia was up early, having slept little.

She dressed in the traditional clothing worn by Basque women: a black, gathered skirt with a floral band, with a red flounce below the band, and a wide-sleeved waist. She had the apron on, but then she removed it. She pulled her hair back in a severe bun, much as she had seen Bart's sister wear at the fair.

For the first time since coming to America, she wished that she had different clothes. It wasn't that she was embarrassed, but she remembered when Bart had defended her when a woman had thought she was a performer. Would his patients accept her as a nurse if she was dressed this way? She didn't think so, but she couldn't help it. This was all she had.

She climbed the stairs to the kitchen, and when she entered, Floria was there putting on a pot of beans that had been soaking overnight.

"Don't you look pretty," Floria said when she saw her.

"Thank you," Pia said unenthusiastically.

"You don't sound very excited, Pia. Do you not want to do this?"

"I want very much to do it. It's just . . . it's just that I didn't sleep very well last night." She could not bring herself to tell Floria that her clothes were bothering her.

Floria walked over and clasped Pia's face in her hands. "My dear, all of us are so proud of you. Even Marko. Oh, I almost forgot." She went to a shelf and pulled down a package wrapped in brown paper. "Marko said to give this to you."

Pia took the bulky package, wondering what it could be.

"Go ahead, open it."

When Pia opened it, she found a stylish gray wool skirt and a cream silk blouse. There was a card written in English: *To do our best, we have to look our best. Good luck in the world of the outsiders. Marko*

"Marko. Only Marko would understand."

"What is it?"

"It's a skirt and blouse."

"Why would he buy that? Just a waste of money." Floria picked up the skirt and examined it. "Look how ugly it is—no trim—nothing. You don't think he thinks you should wear this plain old thing, do you?"

"I'll bet he thought I might ruin my good clothes working as a nurse, and maybe this is like a uniform," Pia said, trying hard not to say anything that would indicate to Floria that she might be ashamed of her dress. "I'd better wear it today, just to make sure."

"I don't know. You really look pretty."

"Let me go down and change before *Ama* comes." Pia hurried down the steps, knowing full well that her mother would insist she wear the traditional dress.

Bart was anxious for Pia to arrive. He had come into the office early and was actually seeing a patient when he saw her coming up the walkway. She was wearing a hooded cloak, and she had it pulled tight against her body, but he would recognize her anywhere. Her petite frame, her coloring, her walk. What was it about her that so captivated him?

Maybe it was because never once had she tried to seduce him. *Seduce*. That was a strange choice of words. Usually, the word was applied to men trying to win forbidden women, but in this town, it was just the opposite. He knew he had a reputation—even his own father believed the things said about him—and in fairness, many of the things said were true. But never once had he been the pursuer. He was always the pursued.

But in 1897 America, in Marjane's world of the

poor disenfranchised woman, the much mistreated female, no one would believe him. If a man and a woman slept together, it had to be because the man was the aggressor. But in his world that wasn't always the case.

"Doc, are you woolgatherin'? I ain't got all day," the patient said.

"I'm sorry, Toby, where was I?"

"You was lookin' at my throat. Did you have another rough night?"

"I guess I did. Now open your mouth and say *ah*."

Frank Wilson saw an attractive young woman coming up the walkway. He knew many of the ten thousand people in Ada County, and, he thought, most of the people in Boise, but he did not recognize this woman. Straightening his tie, and smoothing his jacket, he stepped out into the waiting room.

"Good morning, ma'am, what can I do for you?"

"I'm looking for Dr. Wilson," Pia said.

"Well, that would be me. Would you like to step into my office?"

"I thought I would see Dr. Bart Wilson."

"Oh," Frank said, somewhat taken aback. "He's with a patient right now, but if you care to wait, you may."

"Thank you." Pia took a seat on one of the wooden benches that lined the walls of the waiting room. She dropped the hood to her cloak, but did not remove it.

Frank observed the woman carefully. She was striking, with a classic beauty. He would guess that she was French, but her accent was definitely British.

"Are you a new resident to our fair city?" Frank asked, hoping to find out more about her.

"Relatively speaking. I arrived in the fall."

Relatively speaking. Not exactly the vocabulary used by the cloying social climbers who usually pursued Bart, or at the other end of Bart's acquaintances—the bar girls, the streetwalkers, the sodbusters, or the Bascos.

"I'm sorry my son is making you wait so long. Are you sure I can't help you?"

"I'll wait."

"All right. He shouldn't be too much longer." Frank walked back into his office, but he left the door ajar. Obviously this woman knew Bart personally. Would it be too much to hope that she was more than just a patient? No, a woman who was obviously that cultured wouldn't have much in common with Bart.

Frank didn't have long to wait.

When Bart's patient left, he hurried out to greet Pia. "There you are!" She stood and he took her hands in his. "Your hands are cold." He drew them up to his chest. "Have you met my father?"

"We spoke, but I haven't officially met him."

"Then come. It's into the lion's den."

"I heard that," Frank said, coming out of his office. "Young lady, don't believe everything this man says. I'm Frank Wilson and I'm pleased to meet you." He extended his hand.

"Pop, meet our newest employee, Pia Carranza."

Frank's mouth slackened as his eyes widened, then his brow furrowed.

"But . . . but, you said . . ."

"She was Basque," Bart said, finishing the sentence. "And she is, and she's very proud of it!" He squeezed her hand and Pia flashed an electrifying smile.

For the next week, Bart and Pia and Frank worked side by side. She greeted the patients, took their money or whatever they had to barter, and served as a helper in the examining rooms for both doctors. Bart was glad she was there, not only because he was enjoying her company, but also because Frank was much less critical of him when she was around.

When the week was over, Frank called both Bart and Pia into his office.

"I want to tell you I was wrong," Frank said.

A grin crossed Bart's face. "Pia, quick. Get a pencil and write that down."

Pia was confused and looked from one man to the other.

"I want you to know, I'm very impressed with you, Pia. I think Bart can attest that this week has been the smoothest this office has ever run, and it's all thanks to you."

Pia beamed under the praise.

"Now tell me, what had you planned to pay this girl?"

"Six dollars a week," Bart said, drawing out his money clip.

"I don't think so." Frank opened the drawer of his desk and withdrew a cashbox. "I think she's worth nine dollars a week."

"Oh, Dr. Wilson, I can't take that," Pia said.

"And why not?"

"Because a sheepherder gets only thirty-five dollars a month. If a woman gets more money than a man, won't that be bad?"

It was Bart's turn to laugh. "Don't ever let my sister hear you say that! Of course you can make more money than a man if you do your job well, and believe me, that you have done. I think we should celebrate."

Bart took Pia's arm in his as they walked down Eighth Street toward the Bizkaia House. When they got to Main, instead of walking the additional block, Bart crossed the street to the Overland Hotel.

"Bart, where are we going? I have to get back to the boardinghouse."

"Tonight, you're going to be late. Have you had one meal that you didn't eat at the boardinghouse or at the office?"

"I thought I was going to have a meal, but you wouldn't let me finish it after I insulted your grandfather."

"At the fair?

"Yes, in the tent."

"Sometimes I do forget my manners. But not tonight. This will be our first real date." He opened the door to the Overland Hotel, and after removing their wraps, he ushered her to the dining room.

When they stepped in, the room was crowded, but there was a hush about the place. A harpist, sitting on a raised platform in the corner, played soothing music for the diners as they sat at tables covered with crisp white cloths.

When the waiter seated Pia, he turned up the wick on the clear-crystal lamp that illuminated the table and handed each of them a menu.

"I hope you enjoy your evening, Dr. Wilson . . . ma'am."

For a few moments, Pia just sat there. There were so many people, and yet the loudest sound she heard was the clinking of silverware against the china plates. If this was Bart's world, she wondered how he could ever enjoy the raucous meals at the boardinghouse.

When she picked up her menu, she noticed that Bart had been watching her.

"You are a beautiful woman, Pia." He reached over and took her hand in his.

"I shouldn't be here." Pia looked down at her free hand and saw the hands of a washwoman and a scrub lady. "I should be home helping Elixabete." When she said this, a knot began forming in her throat, because at this very moment the boarding-house was the last place she wanted to be.

In her mind, she and Bart were like any of the other diners in this place, enjoying a quiet Friday evening, away from their cares and troubles.

"What do you have to do tonight? You don't have to wash sheets and you don't have to mop floors and the meal is already served. You know right now, everyone is sitting around the table, and soon the men will get up and go to the bar and the women will clean up the dishes. Pia, you've put in long hours this week, and I say you deserve to be away. And anyway, I remember your father saying you were supposed to do anything I said. Well, tonight I'm saying you should be with me." He squeezed her hand before he released it. "Now what would you like to eat—or shall I choose for you?"

"You may choose."

❧

When the waiter brought the first course and set it before them, Pia's eyes lit up.

"Bocarte!" Pia exclaimed. "Do you know these are tinned in Cantabria and I love them?"

"I'm glad I chose well. I don't know where these sardines came from and I don't know where Cantabria is, but they may well have come from there."

"It's a province in Spain right next to Bizkaia." She picked up the toast tips and savored the briny tidbits. "This makes me think of home."

For the rest of the meal, Pia talked animatedly about Guernica, about her work with Father Ignacio and the children, about the trip over on the *Lucania*, and about her experience at Ellis Island.

Bart asked enough questions to keep the conversation going, but never once did he talk about himself. When the last bite of the graham pudding dessert was taken, Bart pulled out his watch.

"Do you know it's almost ten o'clock?"

"It can't be! We just got here."

"This has been one of the most pleasant evenings I've had in a long, long time. Thank you."

When they stood to leave, Bart noticed several of the town luminaries eyeing them—Mayor Alexander and his wife were at one table, Senator Shoup and his wife at another, Calvin Cobb and several men from the *Idaho Statesmen* at still another. Normally, Bart would have stopped to speak to each of them, but not tonight. He was with the one person whose company he truly enjoyed.

EIGHT

Didn't Dr. Wilson tell you whether or not you would be going to work today?" Elixabete asked when Pia awakened. "It's Christmas Eve and we need you to help get ready for the celebration this evening."

"He didn't say. I suppose he thinks people get sick if it's Christmas or not, and he should be there if someone needs him."

"Well, maybe he will let you come home early. Mrs. Segura says we have people coming into town from the entire Boise Basin for mass tonight. She says we'll be bedding people down on pallets all over the house, and you should be here to help get ready."

"I'll go on to the office, and if I can, I'll come home early."

Pia dressed quickly, thankful that she had used some of her money to buy a heavier coat and some wool dresses. The winter had so far been mild, seldom falling below freezing, but Mrs. Segura had insisted that it could get much colder.

When Pia opened the door to leave the boarding-house, she was surprised to find the first snowfall of the winter. Nature had added its own enhancement to the Christmas garlands that were being twined around light poles, while wreaths with red bows were being hung on doors.

As Pia got closer to the office, she saw Bart out clearing the walkway. When he saw her, he grabbed a handful of the soft, fluffy snow and, making it into a ball, tossed it at her. When she ducked, he laughed out loud.

"Miss Carranza, you're in for it now." He came running toward her with a handful of snow, intending to rub it on her face, but when he reached her, he stopped short. An errant snowflake had fallen on her cheek, and removing his glove, he brushed it away. He stood motionless, his eyes shining as his gaze began to soften. "I love . . ." he started, then hastily added, "snow. Have you seen it before?"

"It doesn't snow in Guernica, at least not like this, but you can see snow up in the mountains."

"How would you like to go to the mountains?"

"What do you mean? Is the office not open today?"

"It is, but Pop can handle it. Go in and stay warm for a bit, and I'll be right back."

"Where are you going?"

"You'll find out. I promise you're going to like it."

Pia went inside, and not knowing exactly when Bart would return, she took off her coat and began sweeping the office, trying to contain the snow she had tracked in.

"I suppose you're the Basque woman I've been

hearing so much about. I'm Marjane Wilson, Bart's sister." She held out her hand to meet Pia.

"Hello." Clearly Marjane had no memory of their earlier meeting at the fair.

"I thought you were the nurse. I didn't know they hired you as the janitor."

"If something needs to be done, I think it should be done," Pia said, neither confirming nor correcting Marjane's assumption.

"It's too bad that's not what all Spaniards think."

"I'm sorry?" Pia said, not understanding what Marjane meant.

Just then Frank Wilson came down the stairs from the living quarters.

"Merry Christmas Eve, ladies, I trust you two have met?"

"Not really. I didn't get your name."

"Pia Carranza."

"Pia. That's a pretty name, even if it is Spanish."

"Marjane, where are your manners? Of course it's Spanish."

"Well, I'm just saying. She might want to change it to Pearl or Pauline or something like that. Pop, I'm here because President Cleveland's secretary of state won't do anything to help the starving people of Cuba, but President McKinley's new secretary is asking for donations to be sent to the consul general. He's specifically asking for quinine, and since I'm sure you don't get much call for it out here, could we send some?"

"Marjane, I've lived through your suffragette campaign, and I tolerate your temperance foolishness, but why are you getting involved with the Cuban War for Independence?"

"To quote Miss Carranza, 'If something needs to be done, I think it should be done.' When two hundred and forty thousand Spaniards—Miss Carranza's people—have invaded one tiny island, I think something should be done."

"Well, Miss Wilson, you're not getting my quinine, and that's that."

Just then the door opened, and Bart came in, stamping his feet as he did. "*Miss Wilson*—that doesn't sound good." Bart walked over to Marjane and kissed her on the forehead. "Are you trying to take away his whiskey again?"

"No," Frank said. "She's trying to take away my medicine. I'm going to go lock up my supplies before she goes after that, too."

"It never stops with you two," Bart said, shaking his head. "You remember Pia, don't you?" He casually draped his arm around Pia's shoulder.

"Have we met before?"

"At the fair," Pia said.

"Well, why didn't you say something?" Marjane turned and started for the stairway. "Oh, Bart, will you be my escort tonight? The Sonnas are having a reception just before we all leave for church."

"I'm not going," Bart said.

"Why not?"

"Because I've been invited to the Bizkaia House. Isn't that right, Pia?"

"Yes," Pia said nodding, even though if he had been invited, she didn't know it.

"You can't tell me you really enjoy being with—oh, never mind. I would think you would want to be with your own family on Christmas Eve." Marjane stormed up the stairs, leaving Bart and Pia alone.

"I'm sorry I said that, but I don't want to go to a party at Peter Sonna's house."

"You know you're more than welcome at the boardinghouse. *Ama* says there are going to be so many people in town tonight, one more won't make any difference."

"Now you're hurting my feelings."

"Oh," Pia said, "I didn't mean to. What did I say?"

"I want it to make a difference—a difference to you." He touched her nose lightly. "Now get your coat on. Come see the surprise I have for you."

Once outside, Bart stopped, then made a sweeping motion with his hand. "Voilà, m' lady's chariot waits. Only this time it's a sleigh, thanks to Julen Alonzo."

In front of the doctor's office, a horse stood sedately in harness before a bright red sleigh.

"Have you ever taken a sleigh ride?"

"I don't think so."

"Well, you're in for a treat. We're going to play Santa Claus up by Bogus Basin." Bart pulled out two red nightcaps from the big bag that was on the back of the sleigh. "Here, put this on, Mrs. Claus."

"I hope Mrs. Claus is benevolent."

"Of course she is. Doesn't Santa Claus come to your house?"

"I don't think he ever has, but Olentzero came."

"Did he give presents to all the good little boys and girls?"

Pia laughed. "I guess he did. As the story goes, he was a giant who was a charcoal burner. He carved wooden toys and brought them down from the mountains in his charcoal bag."

"Well, we'll just pretend this is a charcoal bag then, and we won't care if it's Santa or Olentzero that delivers the presents."

Bart helped Pia into the sleigh, then went around to the other side and climbed in. Positioning the buffalo robe and blankets that Julen had provided, he reached an arm toward Pia.

"Snuggle up beside me," Bart said as he shivered a little. "We'll stay warmer if we sit close together."

Pia felt him press against her, so close that she felt the contact from her legs, to her hips, all the way to her shoulders. Bart was right, she did feel warmer, but its cause was from more than just the body heat of their proximity.

The sleigh skimmed over the snow, moving so quickly and smoothly that it was almost as if they were flying. Their movement was accompanied by the rhythmic thud of the horse's hooves, the swish of the runners, and the musical jangle of the bells attached to the horse's harness. Pia was enjoying the ride and thought nothing of it until she realized they were heading out of town.

"Where are we going?"

"To Bogus Basin. It's a couple of hours away, but I thought you'd enjoy the ride. Some miners live up there in some run-down shacks, and they've got squaw wives and a whole passel of kids who seldom see anybody. I try to make a run out there every two or three months, just to make sure everybody's healthy. A few years back, I got the idea of bringing Christmas presents to them, and they seem to enjoy it." He hesitated. "And so do I."

When they finally arrived at the settlement, Pia watched in absolute delight as the children raced out to welcome Bart as Santa, and she joined in happily to play Mrs. Claus. They visited one remote house after another while Bart bestowed toys and fruit on the boys and girls. In every case the children were joyful, and the parents were appreciative. It was late afternoon before the last gift was delivered.

Bart pulled out his watch. "We have plenty of time to get you home to help get everything ready for Christmas Eve."

"I know you were teasing about coming to the Bizkaia tonight, but I really want you to come. You've shared your tradition, and I would like to share mine. Will you do it?"

Bart was quiet for a long moment as he watched the emotions cross Pia's face.

"I'll come, just for you." He pulled her closer to him, making sure the buffalo robe was tucked snugly around them.

They rode without speaking for several miles, the jingling bells the only intrusion into the silence. A light dusting of snow began to fall. Bart had never felt this much contentment with any other woman in his life. At a break in the trees, Bart pulled the sleigh off to the side of the trail.

"Is something wrong?" Pia asked.

"The horse has worked pretty hard today. I thought I might give him a breather. And I thought you might enjoy the scenery."

The valley Bart pointed to was, indeed, beautiful. The streetlights of Boise were beginning to come on, and they contrasted with the dark ribbons of the river and the canal. The sun sank low in the west, setting the snow afire with a brilliant golden-red band that competed with the deep-purple notches of the crags and draws now in late-afternoon shadow. The color spilled down from the mountains to lay its brilliant hues all across the snow-covered valley. It was one of the most beautiful sights Pia had ever seen.

Or was the beauty heightened by the situation? Here she was, alone in a sleigh, miles from the nearest habitation, with the most handsome, kind, generous, and, above all, most *interesting* man she had ever known.

Bart's arm reached around Pia's shoulder, and it seemed like the most natural thing in the world when he pulled her even closer to him. She turned to look at him and knew that he was going to kiss her.

"Pia." Bart's voice was low, almost a moan. He did not advance toward her, but his gaze held hers, as if he was asking—no, pleading—for permission. This would not be their first kiss . . .

But this kiss would be different.

Hesitantly, tentatively, she moved toward him, her face upturned, her eyes never breaking contact with his. When their lips touched, it was like the brush of a feather, so light, so gentle.

Bart's discipline crumbling, he put his hand behind her head and pulled her to him, meeting her lips with his own, demanding more.

Almost as if by some primeval instinct, Pia's response was eager and willing. She wound her own arms around his neck, pulling him to her, and when she felt his mouth open on hers, she opened hers as well, trusting Bart completely.

Bart's invading tongue was foreign, frightening, but pleasurable beyond any previous experience of hers, and she followed his tongue with her own, exploring his mouth as he had hers, first darting in and out and then lingering as he tickled her palate. Then he unfastened her coat as his hand moved to cup her breast. And even though her breast was covered by the cloth of her dress, it was on fire . . . sending that fire throughout her body as he began the gentle kneading of the breast against his hand. Oddly, the movement caused the most curious and strangely pleasurable sensation to pulse between her legs.

She instinctively knew that this was what it was like to love and be loved by a man. But she was filled with anxiety. She knew that she shouldn't be doing this, that she should tell him to stop. But she was powerless to stop herself. She wanted, more than anything else, for him to continue to go on until . . . until what? She didn't know, she just knew that there was more—and she wanted it.

Abruptly, Bart removed his hand from her breast and pulled her tight against his body, holding her as he molded her to him. He laid his head against her shoulder as he fought to control his breathing, and when he felt his heartbeat return to normal, he raised his head to peer down at her. What he saw were two sensual brown eyes staring up at him, radiating a childlike trust.

"Oh, Pia." He laid his forehead upon her head. "I cannot tell you how much I want you, but it can't happen here. You're much too special to have something taken from you unless it's something you want to do, too."

Pia moved and took his face in her hands. "Bart, I do want what you want."

"I know you do, angel, but it's not going to happen in the middle of a snowstorm. Put your head on my shoulder and let's get you home."

An hour later, Bart pulled up in front of the boardinghouse, where the sounds of an accordion were already filling the air. He climbed down and then clasped Pia's waist to lift her from the sleigh. When her feet touched the ground, he did not release her and was rewarded when she lifted her head for a kiss.

"Merry Christmas, Mrs. Claus." He moved the tassel away from her cheek and kissed her, allowing his lips to linger on hers.

"You're not coming in?"

"I don't think so."

"But you said . . . please come, Bart."

Bart let out a big sigh. "Let me take the sleigh back."

Pia kissed him soundly, a broad smile on her face, then turned and ran toward the door. "You won't be sorry," she called just before she disappeared inside.

Bart slapped the reins, and the horse, knowing the way to the livery stable, set out at a brisk trot. Without Pia beside him, Bart felt melancholy. This was Christmas Eve, the time when the whole country was enjoying family, but he felt all alone.

He had told Pia he would join her, but no matter how hard he tried to fit in, he was still an outsider—not to her, because she could communicate. But if he went back tonight, he knew that much of the conversation would of necessity be carried out in Euskera. She would try to translate for him, but that wasn't the same as understanding the words as they were spoken.

For the first time, he truly empathized with the Basques. Not only was there a language problem, there were always those who looked down on them, called them dirty Bascos because they took jobs that no one else was willing to do and excelled at them.

Now with the Cuban problem, newspapers across the country were constantly beating the drum about the atrocities the Spanish were inflicting on the revolutionaries. No one would listen when the Basques tried to explain that they were not the Spaniards, even though, technically, they all came from the same country. Sabin, Lander, Marko, Julen—all of them who spoke English—had explained countless times that the Euskadi, the autonomous community of the Basque Provinces, did not ask to be, and did not want to be, a part of Spain.

By the time Bart reached the livery stable, he had decided. He would go to their Christmas celebration. Helping people understand the Basque culture would become his personal mission, and he vowed he would exert as much energy toward his cause as Marjane did toward hers.

He smiled when he stepped out of the sleigh. Wouldn't Frank Wilson be proud of his children now?

Even though Pia was busy putting up makeshift tables, finding more benches, and making sure there were enough eating utensils, she managed to keep an eye on the door. She was rewarded when Julen and Bart arrived, and she watched as Bart anxiously scanned the crowd. When he found her, he flashed a smile and waved at her, then followed Julen into the bar. Pia was so excited she dropped a handful of spoons, causing a racket that brought the conversation to a halt for only a second as she scrambled to pick them up.

"Pia, watch where you're going," Elixabete said. "If you had been here, we would've had all this done. You knew we were going to have all these people, but, no, you were gone all day. And don't tell me you were at the doctor's office, because Dabi went down there to get Mr. Egana something to stop his cough and nobody was there."

"I'm sorry. I went with Bart to deliver Christmas presents."

"Humph! I suppose you'll find something to do every day until the Feast of the Kings."

"How many guests do you think we have?"

"I'm guessing, but I would say close to fifty people including the Seguras and us."

"Are there any other women besides the four of us?"

"Francisco Yribar brought his wife, Teresa, and Estebe and Gabina Aguirre are here, but that's all I've seen. It's your duty—your obligation—to spend time with your countrymen, not Dr. Wilson."

"Do you not like the money I'm giving you?"

"That's a stupid question! Of course I do, but these men spend so little time in town, we have to be extra-nice to them. And who knows? Maybe we'll find someone who wants to marry one of us."

Pia didn't answer. She thought back to the afternoon she had spent with Bart and the feelings he had awakened in her. Looking around the room, she saw dozens of men, most of them near her own age, but none of them aroused her the way Bart did.

Just then Lander Segura stepped up on a bench.

"Ruuu-ubru-uu!" Lander called, and an answering *irrintzi* came from every sheepherder in the house.

"Welcome to my house and to my table. I ask that you partake of my hospitality this Christmas Eve, enjoying my food and drink. You are my guests, so eat and rejoice, drink and be merry, as we celebrate the birth of our Lord this night. But I am reminded by Floria and Zuriñe that on the twenty-sixth, should your stay be longer, you become paying guests. At seventy-five cents a day." Lander's comment was met with laughter. "To tempt you to part with your money, the liquor will be free until the bar closes, the music will be loud, the dancing will be quick, and if my sons will clear off the court, the pelota will be fast." This last comment was met with a loud burst of applause, with much handshaking and backslapping.

"And now, women, get to the kitchen and bring on the food."

For Pia, the traditional Christmas dinner could have been any one of many such dinners she had enjoyed, going back as far into her childhood as she could remember. The aromas were like those of Guernica, and as she and the other women made countless trips back and forth from the kitchen, she found herself a little nostalgic for her homeland. Those aromas were emanating from a rich fish stew that was made from many kinds of fish, mixed with herbs, and cooked until it all blended together.

Zuriñe and Elixabete had made over six dozen rounds of black bread, each crusty loaf uniform in size and shape. Pia made several trips to the cellar to bring up a half dozen five-pound *tommes*. The nutty cheese, made from sheep's milk, had been aging since last spring, and the gray-brown rind looked near perfect. The desserts were spice cakes and a pastry cream baked inside a light, sourdough crust. All of this was served with a never-ending flow of sweet wine made from honey.

Unlike Pia, for whom the meal had stirred so many memories, Bart just loved the food. If he had no other reason for celebrating Christmas Eve with the Basques rather than at the Sonna residence, the food was enough. In spite of the language barrier, Bart was enjoying the evening. He only wished that he could sit with Pia, but she and the other women were busy replenishing the food and drink for the men.

The two additional women were both close to

Pia's age, and one appeared to be several months pregnant. Bart would have to suggest to Pia that the woman come by the office just to get acquainted, should she have need of a doctor before the baby was born. If he had his way, she would stay at the boardinghouse until the baby was born, but most of the Basque women preferred to stay with their husbands, even if it meant their child had to be born in primitive conditions.

After a meal that lasted at least two hours, with the talk getting louder and louder and the "discussions" more and more pointed, Lander stood again.

"Gentlemen, gentlemen," he said to try to get everyone's attention. "I think we have proved tonight that what the outsiders say about us is true. When three Basques get together, no two will agree."

There was much clapping and foot stomping when Lander sat down. Julen Alonzo was next to rise and began speaking in English.

"As all of you know, one of our traditions is the poetry duel. I have discussed it with several of you, and we have all agreed that this year, the poetry duel be conducted in English."

"Why would we do it in English?" Bittor asked.

Dabi rose to join his friend. "We will do it in English because it will help us with learning the language," Dabi said, though he certainly had no problem with English. "And it will also enable our friend Dr. Wilson to enjoy the contest."

"Not just enjoy it, participate in it," Julen suggested.

"I don't know," Bart said, holding up his hands. "I'm not much of a poet."

"Surely, Doctor, you won't be afraid to face me, will you?" Pia asked.

"Oh, you have been challenged now, Doctor," Salazar said. "Would you run from a woman?"

"All right, all right, I'll do it," Bart said. "But if I make a fool of myself, don't say you weren't warned."

The rules of the game were simple. Two contestants would face each other, and one would begin by giving a rhyming couplet. The second would have to respond, keeping to the subject at hand. And they could not use the same rhyming word twice.

Bart asked if he could listen to a few of the contests before he was expected to participate, and Dabi agreed that would only be fair.

Three spirited bouts, admittedly made more difficult because they were being conducted in English, were enthusiastically followed by the onlookers, with much cheering and encouragement.

"All right, Bart, you've heard three battles. Do you think you are ready?"

"As ready as I'm going to be, I suppose." Bart held his hand out toward Pia. "Ladies first."

Pia nodded and began her first two lines.

If a fish and a bird were to meet
Could something between them be sweet?

Surely this wasn't mere coincidence, was it? Bart asked himself. Was Pia trying to tell him something? Bart responded:

*Such different things these creatures be
Almost like the difference between you
   and me.*

Pia waited a moment. The rules gave her a whole minute to respond.

*But would the Lord put love in their heart
If he meant for them to be apart?*

Most of the residents were watching the duel with curiosity, but Bart saw no indication that anyone was seeing through the carefully constructed words to the double entendre each line presented. He took his turn.

*Is it by culture or by nature's law
That the creatures cannot be together at
   all?*

"Pia, you have one more line," Dabi said, holding up his finger, then he pointed to Bart. "And you will have one line to finish. Then we will judge."

*We have come to the end, will our hearts be
   broken?*

Pia studied Bart's face after she delivered her last line. He looked at her with such intensity that it was as if they were completely alone in the room. Then Bart delivered his last line.

No, we will find a way. On this I have spoken.

"Very good!" Marko said, applauding. The others joined him in applause. "Under the circumstances, I would say it was exceptionally good."

The judges met to make their decision; then, after a few minutes of discussion, Marko announced, "We have declared the contest between Pia and Bart to be a tie."

Again there were cheers and applause.

NINE

Julen stood then and held out his hands, asking for quiet. "Mr. Segura, Mr. Carranza, with your permission I would like to speak," he said in English.

"Go ahead, Julen, what do you have to say?" Lander replied.

"I want to say a few words about Bart Wilson. Some of you have met him for the first time here, today, and you may wonder how it is that an outsider has been invited to celebrate Christmas with us. But I don't consider him an outsider, for he is a true friend of the Basques. He is a doctor who will come when we call him and he treats us with dignity."

Bart was a little uncomfortable listening to Julen's accolades and lowered his gaze to study the dessert plate in front of him.

"I can attest to what Julen is saying," Pia said as all eyes turned to her. "Dr. Bart Wilson is the most compassionate man I have ever known."

When Bart heard Pia's voice, he looked up and

found her staring at him with a look that he could only call adoration. In that moment, in a room filled with rowdy people, Bart admitted to himself that his feelings for Pia Carranza were something more than casual respect. He knew that he was in love with her.

"Well, let's hope Dr. Wilson shows compassion tomorrow," Julen said, "but if he does not, I am holding the bets. Who says the doc comes out the pelota champion?"

"No way, Julen," one of the men shouted. "Regeti will be here, remember? Surely Regeti will be the champion."

"There won't even be a game if the playing court at church isn't cleared," Luken said.

"You can count on me," Nikola said. "I'll have the snow cleared.

"What do you mean we can count on you, little brother?" Gorka asked. "Didn't I hear *Aita* ask you to get the tables moved so we could start the dance? But are the tables moved?"

Several of the others laughed.

"I am but one man," Nikola said. "I can't move them all by myself."

"Ha. You are still a boy, or you would know that he meant organize others to help."

"Come, Nikola," Julen said. "I'll help you."

"As will I," Luken said.

Bart said nothing, but when he saw what they were doing, he grabbed one end of a table, while Dabi grabbed the other. Within a few moments the tables were moved up against the walls so that the center of the room was ready for dancing. Pia and

Elixabete began sweeping the floor, getting it ready while the guitarist tuned his instrument.

To the music of the guitar and castanets, they danced the fandango, and because Pia coaxed Bart out onto the floor, he was soon dancing as well, although not nearly as gracefully as some of the other men who had been dancing since they were children. Bart and Pia danced the first of the three-part *trikitixa*, but when the vocals were added, Bart took his seat and Luken took his place. Because there were so many more men than women, Bart didn't dance again as the six women present danced every dance. As a doctor, Bart wanted to tell Gabina Aguirre she should sit down, but perhaps her due date was farther out than he guessed.

Sabin and Lander were standing to one side, keeping time with the music by clapping their hands. Sometimes they sang along with vocalizations when they knew the song, but always they passed the bota bag as the wine flowed freely.

"Look at our children," Lander said. "How well they get along."

"I think my daughters have always admired and respected your sons," Sabin said.

"That is good that they feel that way."

"Why do you say that?"

"In Guernica we were first neighbors." *First neighbor* was the Euskera term for the one who lived nearest to you. "And in Idaho you have been a loyal and trusted friend. Now we have put our money together to form this business, and if tonight is any indication, it will be successful."

"You are wise, Lander, and you have made a

prosperous man out of me. Not many men have been able to bring their families to America."

"Look around at how few women there are in this place." Lander took another squirt of wine. "We need to form one more partnership, my friend."

"And what would that be?"

"Our families. We need to join our families. I have sons—you have daughters. Where else will my sons find Basque women to be their wives? Your daughters could have their pick of any man here tonight, but there aren't enough women to go around. Let my sons speak for them this very night, and while everyone is here, we will hold the wedding on the Feast of the Kings."

"In twelve days?"

"Yes, why should we wait? Look at Estebe. He is happy because his Gabina is about to give birth. We are growing old, Sabin. By next Christmas, your daughters will stop calling you *Aita*, and they will call us both *Aitona*. Don't you think Zuriñe would like to cuddle a little one once again?"

Sabin smiled broadly. "The bota bag, please. Let us drink to our grandchildren. But we have a problem. You have five sons—I have two daughters. Which sons will my daughters marry?"

"Whichever one she chooses."

"But that will not be fair. My daughters respect all your sons, and if they choose one, won't that cause strife between the families?"

"You are a wise one, my friend. It is written in the Good Book, 'The lot causeth contentions to cease, and parteth between the mighty.' We will cast lots tonight and it will be settled. Do you agree?"

"I do."

Lander left the room and returned a few minutes later, carrying a clear-glass bowl in which Sabin could see five folded pieces of paper.

Lander rapped a spoon against the bowl, causing it to ring out, getting everyone's attention. "Ladies and gentlemen," he said as he looked around the room, seeming to focus on each person individually. "You all know my good friend and partner, Sabin Carranza. We have an announcement to make. Salazar, go to the cellar and bring up more wine."

"Yahoo!" someone shouted, and the others joined in the shout.

"And now, I'm going to ask Sabin's daughters to come up here and help us out."

Pia had no idea what this was about, but for some reason she suddenly felt nervous. She looked over at Elixabete, and though Pia didn't see the same sense of anxiousness that she felt, Elixabete was obviously just as confused by what was about to happen.

"Come, Elixabete, Pia," Sabin said, motioning for them to come to the spot where the musicians had been playing.

Pia looked over at her mother to see if she could read anything in her mother's face, but her mother, too, was just as confused.

Nervously, Pia joined her sister as they moved to the side of the room. When they got there, Lander held out the bowl.

"Elixabete, you are the oldest, so you are first. Pull out one of the pieces of paper I have in this bowl, but don't look at it until I tell you to."

Elixabete reached into the bowl and pulled out a small folded paper.

"Pia," Sabin said, nodding toward the bowl.

Pia then drew.

"Now, Elixabete, open the paper and read what is written there."

Elixabete did as she was directed. "Gorka."

The five Segura brothers were standing together, and they all looked at each other, silently asking if anyone knew what this was about. Gorka motioned that he had no idea.

"Now, Pia, it's your turn," Lander said.

Pia was so anxious it nearly overwhelmed her. What could all this possibly be? Whatever it was, she wasn't sure she was going to like it.

When she hesitated, her father prodded her. "Go ahead, Daughter. You're going to be very happy."

Pia unfolded the paper. "Marko," she said barely above a whisper.

"Gorka, Marko, come forward," Lander said. "Will the musicians start the music while we watch a special dance?"

Pia let out a big sigh as Marko approached her. "I wasn't sure what that was all about," Pia said.

"Nor was I," Marko replied as they started the intricate steps of the dance.

Everyone clapped wildly as the two couples danced, and when they were finished, the four bowed to the crowd. They started to move out of the center of the floor, but Lander stopped them.

"Ladies and gentleman, you see how well our children dance together? They have known one another since they were children, and now—Sabin, come stand beside me—the Segura family and the Carranza family are going to be one. Sabin and I have decided that these four young people will be joined in holy matrimony after the service for the Feast of the Kings, January sixth, 1898. That is twelve days from Christmas, and you and every Basque within traveling distance is invited to the wedding. We intend to make this the biggest Basque wedding Boise has ever seen."

"What?" Pia gasped out loud, but Zuriñe, who was standing close by, reached out to put her hand on her daughter's arm and, by so doing, to stifle any further outburst.

"Huzzah!" one of the sheepherders shouted, and the other responded.

Pia looked over at Elixabete, expecting to see her as horrified as Pia was. But, to her great surprise, Elixabete was smiling as broadly as was her father, while Gorka was embracing her.

"It would appear that our fathers have put together a merger," Marko said.

Bart was stunned and made breathless by what he had just heard. But, he asked himself, why should he have been stunned? If he was truthful with himself, really truthful, wasn't this what he'd expected all along?

Everyone in the room rushed to the center of the floor, surrounding the Segura and Carranza families, leaving Bart alone and unobserved standing over by the tables. While all the shouting, huzzahing, laughing, and congratulatory conversation was going on, Bart moved quietly and unobtrusively toward the door. With one last glance toward the throng of people surrounding Pia, he stepped outside.

Pia was anything but happy. Never before had she felt such heartbreak, and she glanced toward Bart, wanting to catch his attention, but he wasn't looking at her. Pia was certain he was intentionally avoiding her because she knew that the expression on his face mirrored her own. She glanced quickly toward Marko, but he was surrounded by well-wishers and was so distracted at the moment that Pia might as well not have been present. And with all her heart she wished that she were not present.

Looking back toward Bart, she saw that he was heading for the door. She saw, too, that he was leaving without his coat. Stepping out of the crowd, unnoticed because of the jubilation, she hurried to get his coat and take it to him.

"Bart?" she called out to him as she stepped down from the front porch. "Bart, wait!"

Bart had nearly reached the street when he stopped and turned back toward her.

"Shouldn't you be standing beside your future husband?"

"You forgot your coat."

He accepted the coat, but said nothing.

"Bart, you have to know this wasn't my doing."

Bart shrugged his shoulders. "It doesn't make any difference. I should have expected something like this. I know better than anyone that Basques always marry another Basque. Marko is a very lucky man."

"I . . . I didn't choose this. You saw what happened."

"Can a Basque defy her father?"

Bart stared directly at Pia, and never had she been able to see so deeply into anyone's eyes. She felt as if she could see all the way to the scars on his soul, and as she stood there, mesmerized by what she was seeing, disturbed by what she was feeling, she felt herself drawn to him. She licked her lips, then opened them slightly as he moved toward her. He kissed her. It wasn't unexpected, but what did surprise her was her reaction to it. Here she was, standing under the lamplight, kissing one man while, inside, another man was receiving congratulations over his upcoming marriage to her.

She was so confused. Bart was right. She would not defy her father, especially when his pronouncement had been made before such a large gathering. To say no would cause both Lander Segura and Sabin Carranza to lose face, to say nothing of Marko. On January 6, she would be a married woman— married to a man she didn't love.

The realization of what her fate was to be made her shudder as she hugged Bart tighter to her.

"You shouldn't have come out here without a coat," Bart said without emotion.

His tone caused Pia to be even more upset. In her mind she knew he was accepting what had just happened and was preparing to walk out of her life.

"No, Bart, no. I don't want this. I want you." She lifted her head and she became the aggressor. She kissed him with an intensity she didn't know she possessed. Remembering the pleasure his kiss had given her this very afternoon, she opened her mouth and began teasing his lips with her tongue until he opened his own mouth and allowed her entry.

Dropping his coat, he drew her to him, forcing her body to make contact, pushing his swelling member against her. More than anything else he wanted this woman—not just in a sexual way as he had taken countless women before, but in a protective way. Pia did not deserve to be forced to marry someone she didn't love, and he was sure she didn't love Marko.

When he thought of Marko, his ardor slackened, and he was brought back to reality. He found the strength to break off the kiss and stepped back from Pia.

When they parted, Pia's heart was beating so hard she was sure he could hear it. Pia reached up to touch her mouth, and feeling the heat still lingering on her lips, she held her fingers there for a long moment.

"I'm sorry," Bart said.

"I'm sorry, too." She leaned into him once more, lifting her head toward his. He bent to her, deepening the kiss, and Pia knew it would be their last.

Unable to control her emotions, she grew limp in his embrace, losing herself in it, surrendering to him, totally pliant in his hands, subservient to his will, feeling herself spinning into a bottomless vortex.

Bart tightened his fingers in the silky spill of chestnut hair, then did what Pia could not do. He found the strength to gently tug her head back to break the kiss. She stared up at him with eyes that were filled with wonder, innocence, and raw desire.

"Pia, I . . . you'd better get back inside."

"Bart, please." But please what? Please don't go? Please forgive her? Please understand? How could he, when she didn't understand herself?

"Good-bye, Pia." Bart turned and started back toward his own house.

"Good-bye." She stood in the cold watching until she couldn't see him anymore. She felt as if a part of her had slipped away.

"Pia, where have you been?" Elixabete asked when Pia went back into the house. "Were you outside?"

"Yes, I went after Bart."

"You did what?" Elixabete asked, challenge in her voice.

"I went after Bart. He forgot his coat."

"I'm glad he was here tonight."

"Why do you say that?"

"Because I feel that he . . . and maybe even you . . . were forgetting who and what you are. What *we* are. We are Basques. And being here to witness what has happened—to know firsthand that you are to be married to a Basque—will put a stop to this foolish idea that he . . . or maybe even you . . . might have had."

"You're right, Elixabete," Pia answered, her voice dispassionate. She headed for the kitchen, and when she stepped through the door, she saw that it was overflowing with dirty dishes. Putting on an apron, she filled a dishpan with hot water, then tackled the hard task before her as tears streamed down her cheeks.

"To hell with the Bascos and their damn ways!" Bart said as he kicked the door open to the stairway that led up to his apartment. Going to the dry sink that he used for a bar, he poured himself a drink. "Merry Christmas." He held the glass up as a salute and sat down before the fireplace inset, the coals long since burned out. He should have started a fire, but that would have made his apartment seem cozy, and he wasn't feeling cozy.

He felt as if he'd been punched in the gut. When Lander Segura made his grand announcement, it made Bart physically sick. He wanted to get away from that place as quickly as possible, and then Pia followed him, which made it even worse. If he could accept that she would be happy, he could deal with it better, but even though Marko could provide for her, he knew she didn't love him. And he was powerless to help her. Her father had spoken. He threw the glass at the cast-iron inset, shattering it to pieces. He rose and, putting on his coat, left the house. He needed to clear his head.

"Bart, you made it!" Peter Sonna greeted him when Lee Gow showed Bart into the parlor. "Marjane said you weren't coming, but I knew you couldn't stay away. All the young ladies have been absolutely bereft by your absence."

"Bart! Where have you been?" Lily Newman said. "Get over here, you handsome thing. We've got mistletoe."

"Do you now?" Bart said, going over to the door where several of the celebrants were gathered to take advantage of the little parasitic plant.

By the end of the evening Bart had tasted enough lips—and consumed enough alcohol—that the kisses he'd shared with Pia should have been a distant memory.

But they weren't.

Elixabete was still bubbling over with excitement when the two sisters found their way to the cellar and their beds.

"This has been the happiest Christmas of my life," Elixabete said. "You should have been out there dancing with Marko."

"Someone had to clean up the kitchen."

"Well, it shouldn't have been you."

"And just who should have done it? *Ama?* Floria? Or maybe the pregnant Gabina?"

"One thing is for sure, you won't have to do it next year. Gorka says we'll get our own house. Maybe it will be at the home ranch. But you . . . you will have a big house, I'll bet. I think Marko makes lots of money working for Mr. Moore."

"We'll still be right here, Elixabete. Washing sheets, cleaning floors, and baking bread."

"Why do you say that? You don't know."

"*Aita* brought us here to work in a boardinghouse. Do you think being married will change that?"

"You are not trying to accept this. Marko will be a wonderful husband for you, and if we are living here, you will see your husband every day. Gorka will go back to the sheep, and I will be like all the other women who marry shepherds. You are the lucky one."

"Yes," Pia replied quietly. "I am the lucky one."

Pia lay quietly, thinking about what had happened tonight. She had to admit that it had not come as that much of a surprise to her. She had known all along that her father would select her husband. She had even known that in all likelihood it would be one of Lander Segura's sons. And if it had to be, Marko was probably the best suited for her. But she'd had no way of knowing that when the time came for her to be married, she would be in love with someone else.

In love with someone else? Was that true?

She touched her lips where, still, she could imagine the heat of his kiss.

Bart didn't wake up until past noon. He wasn't sure how he had gotten home last night, but he was glad he was alone. He took a bath, shaved, and had just gotten dressed when he heard a knock on his door. For a moment he felt elated, thinking it might be Pia! Hurrying to the door, he jerked it open with a huge smile on his face.

"Oh, it's you."

"Merry Christmas to you, too," Marjane said.

"I'm sorry, Sis, I didn't mean it like that. Come in."

"I don't have time to come in, and neither do you."

"What do you mean, neither do I?"

"Bart, are you still drunk this morning? You aren't making a bit of sense. This is Christmas, remember?

You're spending the day with your family, or did you forget?"

"I didn't forget," Bart said, although he was lying.

"Mr. Chee's ham is out of the oven, and Pop doesn't think he can wait until two o'clock. He sent me out here to tell you to come now."

"All right." Bart reached for his coat, but as he put his hand on it, he thought of Pia, bringing it to him last night. He decided not to take it. "Let's go."

"Aren't you going to wear your coat?"

"I'm not going to freeze going across the backyard."

"Actually you're right, it's not that cold. Even the snow is beginning to melt."

Marjane and Bart trudged through the kitchen, where Chee was putting the finishing touches on dinner, the aroma causing Bart a hint of nausea.

"Good afternoon, Chee. Everything looks good."

"Very good. You will like."

"Yes, I will like it," Bart said.

"Well, I see you managed to sober up in time for dinner," Frank said when Bart came in. "If it hadn't been for your sister, I don't know where you would have spent the night."

"Frank, please, it's Christmas Day," Anna said.

"You're right. I'm glad you're with us."

Somehow Bart managed to get through the dinner and was even able to laugh at a few of the stories of Christmases past. After dinner they went into the parlor, where Anna played the piano and they all sang Christmas carols. Bart had almost forgotten what a beautiful singing voice Marjane had. She usually kept her talent subjugated to her passionate political commitments.

Finally the long day was over, and Bart went back to his apartment, pleased that for his mother's sake no one had said anything that caused any disagreement.

TEN

The next day was a Sunday, and Bart had just made himself a ham sandwich when he heard a commotion in the alley. When he looked out, he saw Julen Alonzo pulling up in a four-in-hand carriage.

"Julen, what are you doing here?" Bart yelled down from the window.

"The pelota tournament. I've been bringing everyone to the church. They're ready to start, and you're not there."

"What pelota tournament?"

"What tournament? Have you forgotten? We're having a pelota tournament today. Basques from all over the valley are gathered at the *frontis* behind the church. And you're playing."

Bart shook his head. "I don't think so, not today. This is a special day for Basques, and I don't think you need an outsider."

Julen's expression was crestfallen. "Bart, you have to play. I've got money bet on you to advance through all the brackets until the final. So do a lot of the others who have seen you play. There's more than a hundred dollars bet, just on you."

"There's snow on the ground. How are we going to play pelota with snow on the ground?"

Julen smiled. "There's no snow on the court. Luken and Nikola worked all day yesterday, and today it is dry."

"All right, I'm coming down."

Sundays were always special days for the Basques, not just on the day after Christmas. They gathered together to celebrate their own culture by dancing, playing cards, playing pelota, or just visiting.

Today was especially significant because all the best pelota players in the basin had come to participate. This included Edurne Retegi, who was from one of the other Basque boardinghouses in Boise.

"Dr. Wilson," Retegi said, and then continued in Euskera. "I've heard that the American thinks he is a *pelotista*. Is he good enough to be in this tournament?"

"He is good enough," Dabi said.

"I am told he is in my bracket. I hope that we meet, so that I can trounce him," Retegi said, hitting his hand against his fist.

"You may be sorry what you wished for," Dabi said. Then to Bart in English he said, "Mr. Retegi is ready to play against you."

Bart smiled and extended his hand. "Thank you, Mr. Retegi. I, too, am looking forward to our game."

Bart saw that Marko was also playing in the tournament, and though the two had played against each other many times, splitting victories between them almost evenly, Bart very much wanted to beat him today. He tried to tell himself that it was his natural competiveness coming out, but he knew it was more than that. He wanted to beat Marko to prove that he could hold his own against any Basque *pelotista*. And—this was more personal and, he confessed to himself, vindictive—he wanted to prove to Pia that he was the better man.

As he looked over the brackets, though, he saw that while he was in one bracket, Marko was in another. The only way the two could meet was if each won every game in his individual bracket until they reached the finals. That meant that Bart would have to defeat Retegi, whom everyone seemed to acknowledge was the best pelota player here.

Bart easily won his first two games and was now sitting on the sidelines watching Marko play against José Archabal, his third match of the day. Archabal was good, but Marko got the better of him and advanced to the final match.

Now it was up to Bart. If he defeated Retegi, he would face Marko. When Bart took the court, he could feel his leg muscles begin to tighten. Crossing his legs, he bent low to stretch. When he stood, he was surprised to find Pia standing behind him.

"Pia, why are you on the court? This match is about to begin."

"I have something for you." She withdrew a piece of red cloth.

"What would I want with this?"

"Look at Retegi. He is wearing the green sash representing his home district. You need a sash, too."

"But I don't represent anything."

"You are wrong, Bart. You represent . . . here, let me put it on for you." Pia interrupted her thought. She wanted to say that he represented her, but she couldn't. If he won, he would be facing the man she was to marry.

Pia hesitated just for a second, then she placed the sash around Bart, aware of her closeness to him. She could feel the tight muscles of his body, and as she was tying the sash, she had a fleeting remembrance of having these arms wrapped around her. She wanted to embrace him now, but this was certainly not the time, and when she looked into his eyes, she saw a determined look.

In that moment, she was sorry she had done this. What if she had broken his concentration and Retegi won the game? Would Bart think she had come out to distract him, so that Marko would play Retegi and not him? Bart put his hand down to make a slight adjustment to the sash, and he took her hand. Pia felt a sudden heat from the touch, much more than mere body heat.

"Thank you. I will wear your sash with honor," Bart said.

"What is this?" Retegi asked. "Is he afraid to face me?"

"Are you ready, Bart?" Dabi asked.

"I'm ready."

"Then the game will begin."

Bart quickly jumped to a quick three-point lead, but Retegi's skill had not been oversold. He came back and went ahead. During the game Bart was aware that Pia was cheering for him, as were many of the other occupants of the Bizkaia House. As one of them explained, if Bart won this game, then he would play Marko, and that would guarantee a Bizkaia House victory.

Bart played better than he had ever before played in his life, and when he scored the game point, he was roundly cheered by everyone, Marko among the loudest.

Now, after a few minutes' rest, Bart and Marko were to meet.

Bart won the flip of the coin and served first. Bouncing the ball on the court, he brought his arm around, caught the ball in the *xistera*, the long, wicker basket he was wearing on his hand, then slammed it against the *frontis*. It came whistling back at over one hundred miles per hour. Marko caught it in his own *xistera* and whipped it back against the wall.

Pia had watched Bart play all afternoon, and she realized that Julen had been correct in his assessment of Bart Wilson's skill. He had certainly triumphed over Regeti, and now he was playing Marko, matching him shot for shot. Over several years she had seen many skilled players, including the great Francisco Villota, who many regarded as the best in the game. She wouldn't go so far as to say that Bart could beat Villota, but she was certain he could play on a par with nearly any of the young Basque men she had seen play the game. She enjoyed watching him catch the pelota, then slam it back against the wall, his tall, handsome, and beautifully proportioned body moving quickly and gracefully around the court. But hadn't she promised herself that she would try to be impartial in her support for the players in this game? Marko had played brilliantly throughout the day, and she had cheered him on lustily. And right now, the two men were showing skills that were equal to each other's.

The two men raced about the court, catching the ball when it would career off the front wall, even if at an odd angle, then hurling it back. Gradually the score began to climb, fifteen to thirteen in favor of Bart, twenty-one to nineteen in favor of Marko, twenty-six to twenty-five with Bart in the lead. As the ball whizzed back and forth, and the two men ran about, first toward the *frontis*, then away from it, first to the left side of the court then to the right, the crowd cheered them on.

Was Marko playing better than he ever had before? Bart certainly thought so, and he wondered now if Marko had merely carried him in all the many games they had played against each other. No, he knew that wasn't so. He could only assume Marko's intensity in this game stemmed from the same source as his. Marko wanted to be Pia's champion. And why not? Didn't he have every right to be her champion? Wasn't he, after all, her intended?

Maybe Bart didn't have the right to call himself Pia's champion, but he had every intention of proving to her that he was the better man.

At least in this game.

The game reached a tie at twenty-nine points. The first one to make it to thirty would win. Then, after a strike from Marko, the ball met the wall at a strange angle and came back toward Bart as if it were going to be an easy return. But instead of dropping where Bart thought it would, it fell short and . . . he missed it.

Game point went to Marko. After a few cheers and several groans over this outcome, everyone cheered that the match had been well played and all had been entertained.

Bart stood on the court for just a moment with his head down in disappointment. He had failed. He went over to Marko and extended his hand. "Marko, you've never played a better game."

"Nor have you." Marko held Bart's hand for a moment longer. "Thanks for coming today, Bart. I know it was hard for you. I admire your courage, and your grace."

Bart nodded. "Thanks. I'd better get back to my place."

Bart left without so much as a word to Pia. He wondered about the strange comment Marko had made. It had to mean that he knew, that he understood, that Bart was in love with Pia. Marko was a good man who had long been Bart's friend. He made up his mind at that moment that he would do nothing to jeopardize that friendship.

"Bart came very near to beating me," Marko said as he and Pia walked back to the Bizkaia after the pelota game. "It was probably your red sash that did it." Marko laughed, but Pia didn't join him.

"You played very well. You won, and isn't that what counts?"

"Pia, do you want me to win?"

Pia understood that Marko was not talking about

the pelota game. "I don't think we have much choice. Our fathers have spoken, and neither one of us can do much about it. It's not that I don't care for you, Marko, it's just that I don't . . ."

"Love me?"

"Yes, that's it exactly. My mother and father were separated for thirteen years, and when they first saw one another after so long, they shook hands. Is that how a marriage is supposed to be?"

"I don't have an answer. You and I are different, Pia. I work among people who I think have accepted me as their equal. We both understand the language of the outsider, and because of that, we don't see every person as someone who sees us as second-class citizens or else is trying to cheat us out of whatever we've worked hard for. That's why Basques think they have to marry other Basques."

"There's more to it than that. Our language, our culture, it is unique, and I don't want to lose it."

"I agree. But if we are going to marry each other, I want us to be sure that is what we want. On the other hand, if we come up with some reason why we shouldn't get married on the sixth, will you be disappointed?"

Pia threw her arms around him for the first time in her life. "I will be forever grateful if you can come up with something."

"You have that wrong. If *we* can come up with something. But in exchange, I have a favor to ask of you."

"And what would that be?"

"The bank is sponsoring a citywide New Year's Eve party at the Natatorium. Will you go with me?"

"Oh, dear, what would I wear to something like that?"

"Don't worry, I'll take care of it."

New Year's Eve

The ballroom of the Natatorium was festooned with bunting of purple and gold. A huge banner spread all the way across the back wall.

HAPPY NEW YEAR—1898!
WELCOME
THE FIRST NATIONAL BANK OF IDAHO

Christopher Moore, the president of the bank, was pleased with the turnout as he looked over the gathering crowd of people. The governor was there, as were the mayor and every other person of importance in Boise. But Moore had chosen to have this gala event at the fifteen-thousand-square foot Natatorium, rather than at the opera house or the hotel, because he wanted to include all the layers of society.

Frank and Anna Wilson, along with Marjane, were just arriving.

"I don't know why Bart couldn't have come with us," Anna said.

"Because something's put a burr under his saddle," Marjane said. "He's been an absolute grump every time I've tried to talk to him."

"We go back to work Monday, so let's hope he's got whatever is bothering him out of his system," Frank said. "Excuse me, ladies, I'd like to speak to the mayor. We need a new streetlight down our way."

"Oh, Frank, don't bother Moses with things like that. This is a party," Anna said.

"Well, what are you supposed to talk about at a thing like this? You know Chris Moore has just put this thing on to drum up business for the bank," Frank said as he looked around. "Do you know even a quarter of the people here?"

"I do know one more. Look who just came in."

Frank looked toward the door where Bart had just made his entrance.

"Good. I'm glad he got here."

Bart saw Don Walton and Tim O'Leary standing near the bar, so he headed toward them.

"I didn't expect to run into you two here," Bart said as he picked up a cup, then ladled in some punch.

"When Mr. Moore issued the invitation, he said ever'body come, so me 'n' Tim, why, we come any place where there's free food, free drinks, and a lot of pretty women hangin' around," Don said.

Bart chuckled. "Is that a fact?" He lifted the cup to his lips.

"Oh, maybe I'd better tell you. I seen Toby Calhoun dump a whole bottle of whiskey in the punch a while ago," O'Leary said.

Bart took a taste of the punch and screwed up his face. "I see what you mean. That's strong." He then emptied the cup with one drink. "Maybe I'd better get a refill."

"That's our Doc," O'Leary said, refilling Bart's cup.

Then a nearby conversation caught Bart's attention.

"The hell they ain't! They're from Spain, ain't they? What with ever'thing that's goin' on down in Cuba, that makes 'em all our enemies, and I'm sayin' we need to keep a watch on 'em."

The man with the loud voice was Milt Garrison, and he was holding court with half a dozen young cowboys.

"I know some of them Bascos, Garrison, and as far as I know, they just come here to work hard and go back. Seems like they don't never get into no trouble."

"That's just it. They take our money and our jobs, and what do they do with it? Send it right back to Spain. Now that ain't right. We're goin' to wind up havin' to kick them Spanish bastards out of Cuba as sure as a gun is iron. And once that happens, you'd better watch your back around these here Bascos, that's all I got to say. Just watch your back, boys, 'cause they'll turn on us quicker 'n a duck will gobble up a june bug."

"Garrison, you're just sore 'cause Mr. Moore let you go and hired Julen Alonzo," one of the cowboys said.

"Yeah, 'cause that damn Basco will work for just about nothin' and he never quits. Julen do this, Julen do that—whatever the boss wants. He don't never ask a question. That's not normal."

"But they don't call theirselves Spanish. They're Basco."

"Same thing," Garrison insisted.

"No, it ain't. Not if you've ever talked to any of

'em. They hate Spain. Hell, that's why most of 'em has come over here. I heared 'em talk. They say the king took away their rights."

"How long has Garrison been going on like that?" Bart asked with a nod toward the obnoxious young man.

"About ten minutes or so." Walton chuckled. "Truth is, he can't find anybody that'll listen to his hogwallerin' more'n a couple of minutes."

True to Walton's comment, the cowboys who had been gathered around Garrison drifted off, and he moved on to another group.

"Here you are," Julen said as he pulled the carriage up in front of the Natatorium. "Just in time for the dancing."

Marko stepped out and helped Pia down. "Are you ready?"

"I feel so out of place," Pia said. "Why did I agree to this?"

"Don't feel like that. We belong here just as much as anyone else does."

Pia took a deep breath as she looked up at the building, every window gleaming brightly. "Look at those towers—and the arches."

"I know what you're thinking. They're Moorish."

"Why would anyone want to put up a building that would honor the Saracens? I don't understand."

"Because these people don't dwell on things that happened in AD 700. Do you think one person at this party knows the Moors tried to kill all the Basques back then?" Marko asked.

"Probably not."

"For certain they don't, and especially out here. Everyone wants to make money, and that's why we're here. Mr. Moore wants us to mingle with the crowd and show everyone that we 'Bascos' are just like everyone else."

Pia hesitated. "Marko, wait."

"What is it?"

"I'm afraid I've made a mistake. I . . . I don't belong here."

"Pia, if you don't want to go inside, we'll go back. But that will be because you don't want to go, not because you don't belong here. We belong here as much as any other person at this dance."

Pia curled up her fingers, then took a deep breath. "All right." She nodded. "All right, let's go."

Bart was laughing at something Don Walton had just said when he glanced toward the entrance and saw Marko and Pia arriving. Like Bart, and many of the other gentlemen of Boise's society, Marko was wearing evening dress, a black tailcoat, with a gold waistcoat underneath. But it was Pia who caught Bart's attention.

He had never seen Pia in anything but the clothes she wore to work, or the native dress of the Basque. Tonight she was wearing a green velvet gown with metallic embroidered insets of brown moiré. The neckline was low enough to show a hint of cleavage. Her attire was the equal of that of any woman present, including the wives of the wealthiest men. Her beauty far surpassed anyone else's, and to see her coming in on Marko's arm sent a dagger to Bart's heart.

"Wow!" O'Leary said. "Look over there! Who is that with Segura?"

"I'm not sure," Bart lied. He stepped out of the ballroom and went into the indoor-pool area, allowing the fumes from the warm water piped from the hot springs to clear his thinking. Walking up to the upper balcony, he planned to go to the billiard room, but all the various social rooms were closed for the evening.

He was certain Pia had not seen him exit the ballroom and decided it would be best if he left. He was on his way to the cloakroom when Marjane came looking for him.

"And just where do you think you're going? The dancing is about to begin, and I need a partner, and you're the only man who will dance with me."

"And whose fault is that?"

"Just dance with me." Marjane took her brother's hand and pulled him back into the ballroom.

"Choose your partners for the Virginia reel!" someone shouted through a megaphone.

Bart followed Marjane out onto the floor, where they joined five other couples who had formed two parallel lines facing each other, ladies on one side and gentlemen on the other. Bart and Marjane were standing at the head of the lines, which made them the top couple. When he looked over the other people in this set, he saw that Marko and Pia were at the other end of the line. He attempted to turn away, but then thought to do that would cause a scene, and it would embarrass Marjane.

The music began, and Bart and Marjane bowed and curtsied to each other, then Marjane advanced

down the middle to meet Marko, the "bottom gentleman," who had stepped out at the same time.
They bowed and curtsied to each other, then
returned to their places. Next, Bart and Pia did the
same thing.

Pia smiled at Bart, but he didn't return the smile,
and she felt rejected. As the dance continued, Bart
and Marjane went through all the routines until
Bart took his place next to Marko, and Marjane next
to Pia. Pia noticed that Bart avoided meeting her
eyes.

Once the set was over and they were again
standing at opposite ends of the line as everyone
applauded politely, Pia caught him looking at her,
but when she tried to return his gaze, he glanced
quickly away.

After the dance, Bart walked Marjane back to
where their mother was standing.

"Wasn't that the Carranza girl in your set?" Anna
asked.

"I believe it was."

"Who are you talking about?" Marjane asked.

"Pia—the Basque girl who works in the office,"
Anna answered.

Marjane turned to look over the crowd. "Which
one is she?"

"The one in the green dress," Bart said, not even
looking for Pia.

"Bart, I was standing right beside her and you
didn't even say anything to her."

"I didn't, did I?" Bart walked away and headed
toward the bar.

"Hmmm," Marjane said. "I have a feeling I know what's bothering the doctor."

"Whatever it is, Marjane, you stay out of it." Anna took her daughter's arm and they walked over to join a group of women who were standing near the refreshment table.

"There you are, Bart Wilson. I saw you dancing with your sister when you could have been dancing with me," Lily Newman said as she intercepted Bart on his way to the bar. "But that's all right as long as you dance the next dance with me."

Lily was attractive, her milky-white skin contrasting with her titian hair. Tonight she was wearing a sapphire-blue dress that was so low cut, the tops of her breasts were exposed. Bart had known Lily for several years. She was the only child of one of the more prominent families in Boise, and she had let it be known that she intended to marry Bart. Until meeting Pia, he had assumed that he would probably marry her eventually. He knew he had not been her first lover, but she was not his first either, so in his mind they would have come to the marriage as equals.

The next dance was a waltz and Bart led Lily onto the dance floor. He took his position, extending his arm for her right hand as he placed his left hand upon her waist. When the music started, Lily stepped closer to him, and he pulled her to him, not caring what the dance's decorum demanded. He thought holding Lily close would blot out the image of the dark-eyed woman in the green velvet dress who was in the arms of another man. But as he whirled her around, Bart was always aware of Pia, no matter where she was.

"I say there, Bart, when are we going to be invited to a wedding?" Columbus Anderson said as they stood at the bar. "It looks to me like Miss Newman will get what she wants."

"Miss Newman always gets what she wants, but I don't think that includes me," Bart said. "What about you, Crawford? Aren't you one of Lily's friends, too?"

Crawford Moore laughed. "I've known Lily as long as you have, but I'm on my way to Colorado."

"Colorado? What's so special about Colorado?" Bart asked.

"My dad thinks anyone who's going to be a good banker needs to know what it's like to work hard, so I'm into cattle ranching there."

"I agree with your dad, but why didn't you stay in Idaho?" Columbus asked.

"Colorado was my idea. If I'm going to make it, I want to do it on my own. Not because my dad owns the bank and the waterworks and every other business he has his hand in."

"Well, if you're going to be off by yourself like that, you really do need Lily to go with you," Columbus said. "Bart can get him somebody else. Isn't that right?"

"It is, and I see someone I'm going to dance with right now," Bart said, nodding toward another woman.

For the rest of the evening, Bart danced every

dance, determined to show Pia her upcoming marriage didn't affect him.

Pia watched Bart as one woman after another danced with him, noticing that the women seemed to be gathering around him, as if they were inviting him to ask them. And why not? If she could, if it wouldn't be a terrible breach of etiquette, she would go up to him and ask him to dance with her.

She remembered that they had danced together Christmas Eve—he had not known the steps to the fandango, but he had picked them up quickly, and they had very much enjoyed themselves. So why, when he was dancing with every other available woman, would he not dance with her now?

What a foolish question. He wouldn't dance with her now because he was present when he learned . . . when she learned . . . that she was to be married.

Pia fought back tears. It had been a mistake for her to come here tonight.

She had been standing off to the side while Marko talked to several of the men. She inched her way toward him, and when she caught his eye, he smiled and asked her to join the group.

"Mr. Moore, I don't think you've met my fiancée, Pia Carranza."

"You are a lucky young woman, Miss Carranza. Marko is a fine gentleman and a trusted employee," Mr. Moore said, extending his hand. "I'm sure you're going to have a wonderful life here in Boise."

"Thank you," Pia said.

"And when are you planning to be married?"

Pia looked anxiously toward Marko for an answer, praying that he would not say in six days.

"We've not decided on the exact date, yet," Marko said.

"Good, because I may need you to make a trip for me this spring, and I wouldn't want to take you away from a new bride."

"I'll do whatever you ask, Mr. Moore."

"You are a good man, son. If only Crawford was as mature as you are. I believe we're almost ready to count down the New Year, so I'd best find my bride, because I wouldn't hear the end of it if I missed the kiss."

"I'm hurt," Lily said, pouting as she approached Bart. "Why have you been avoiding me?"

"Because every time I looked your way, you were dancing with another man. But I've saved the last one for you."

"Five minutes!" someone shouted. "Five minutes to the New Year! Time for one more slow waltz!"

Lily held her arms out and Bart stepped into them as several of the chandeliers were dimmed and the slow waltz began.

When the dance was concluded, someone called out loudly, "Hold your partners for the New Year!"

Bart was about to kiss the New Year in with Lily Newman. She was, in any way she might be described, an attractive woman. He had kissed her many times before and enjoyed it. But tonight her lips would be a poor substitute for those he wanted to kiss. He searched the ballroom for Pia, but in the darkened room he could not find her. It was just as well.

"Happy New Year! Welcome 1898!" someone shouted, and bells were ringing and horns blowing as all the dancers celebrated. Lily moved her mouth up to Bart's.

"Did I tell you," she asked quietly, "that my parents are gone? They are in San Francisco for the holiday. I'm in that big old house all by myself."

Before Bart could answer, she covered his lips with hers.

As was the custom at that hour, Marko kissed Pia. But he could have been her brother, so chaste was the kiss. It was absolutely nothing like the kisses she had shared with Bart. Or like the kiss she saw Bart sharing, right now, with one of the pretty women who had been hovering around him all night.

ELEVEN

Bart awakened in the dark of predawn on New Year's Day. Getting out of bed, he padded barefoot over to the window and drew the curtain to one side. It had snowed during the night, and from the front of the house all the way across the street to the other side was a mantle of white, with only the track of a single horse-drawn vehicle marring the scene.

The waxing moon didn't provide much light, but the snow reflected the electric streetlamps enough to illuminate the room dimly. Looking back toward the bed he had just left, Bart saw a bare shoulder and an arm gleaming in the light.

Bart groaned and put his hand to his forehead. Because he was in Lily Newman's bedroom, it was obvious what had happened. His headache told him *how* it happened. This wasn't the first time he had spent the night with Lily, but it was the first time he'd regretted it so deeply.

As quietly as possible, Bart dressed and, while Lily was still sleeping, let himself out. It was cold, and he pulled his coat around him as he trudged through the snow. His breath made iridescent clouds in front of him. When he reached the street, he began the mile and a half to his rooms, walking in the tracks left by the recent vehicle. He felt guilty. If he could rightly remember, he had not wanted to bed Lily, but he had obviously succumbed to the temptation. No matter how much she enticed him, he should never have gone to her house. He was never going to marry her, and he was wrong not to tell her that.

A man didn't marry someone he didn't love, and neither should a woman marry a man just because someone told her she was going to, even if that someone was her father. All his remorse came back to one thing: his relationship with Pia. But he didn't really have a relationship with her. Why hadn't he said the words when he had kissed her in the sleigh? Three little words: *I love you.* Would that have been enough to give her the courage to resist her father? Maybe in his culture, but not in hers.

In five days, she would be Mrs. Marko Segura, and no matter how lax his morals might be, he had never slept with a married woman. And he would damn sure not start with Pia Carranza.

When he walked past his parents' home, he saw that the light was on in the kitchen. Going up on the porch, he rapped on the glass window before he entered.

"Oh, Mr. Bart, you scare me," Mr. Chee said. "I didn't expect you up so early."

"Is the coffee ready?"

"Yes, sir." Chee retrieved a mug. "You want hair of dog?"

Bart chuckled as he took the cup of coffee. "Not this morning. I want sleep."

"Very good. I see you this afternoon. Mr. Frank— he want black-eyed peas today. He say they bring good luck. You need to eat black-eyed peas, too, don't you think?"

"Chee, my luck has run out. Black-eyed peas aren't going to help."

"You don't know. Maybe little black-eyed girl come back."

"You see too much," Bart said as he started out the door.

Chee laughed. "I hear plenty, too, Mr. Bart. You have good happy New Year."

"You, too."

On Monday morning, the senior Dr. Wilson was looking at a young girl while her mother stood by anxiously. Mrs. Coleman had once made it clear to Bart that anytime she or any of her family came to the doctor's office, it was to see his father, not him. For the moment Bart was sitting behind a desk in the reception room, and he could not only see into his father's examining room, he could also hear the conversation.

"Right now I think it's just a common cold," Frank said to Mrs. Coleman. "But we need to keep an eye on her lest it develop into the influenza. Keep her home from school for a few days. If it's something else, there's no sense exposing the whole classroom."

"Yes, Doctor."

"Mama, I can't miss school. Miss Margrabe depends on me to help teach the other kids how to read."

Frank chuckled. "It's always that way—the boys will stay home from school if they have a hangnail, and the girls will go if they're at death's door. You do what I say, Katie. Stay home and keep warm, and Mrs. Coleman, brew up plenty of hot sassafras tea. If she drinks that, I think she'll be fine in a few days."

"Thank you, Doctor," Mrs. Coleman said as she helped her daughter put on her coat. "Wrap your scarf around your face, Katie. We don't need you to get any sicker."

"Do you need for me to call down to the livery and summon a carriage?" Frank asked.

"No, no. It's just a short distance, and if she's wrapped up good, I think we can make it without any problem."

The office had been closed for the entire week between Christmas and New Year's, so when Pia arrived just as Katie and her mother were leaving, it was the first time she and Bart had spoken to one another since the pelota game.

Frank had walked the Colemans to the door, and when Pia entered, he was effusive in his greeting.

"Pia, my dear, we have missed you! I saw you at the New Year's celebration but I didn't get a chance to speak to you. I believe you were escorted by the Segura boy, were you not?"

"Yes, sir. I was with Marko Segura."

"He's a good boy. I see him down at the bank all the time. C.W. says he's a good worker, just like you are. Bart, do you need Pia this morning?"

Bart was seething as he listened to his father prattle on about how wonderful Marko Segura was. He had intended to meet Pia at the door and tell her she was fired, but Frank had made that plan impossible.

"I won't be needing Miss Carranza," Bart said curtly as he went into his own examining room and closed the door.

Frank turned to Pia and, with a questioning look, shook his head. "Did I say something that I shouldn't have?"

"I don't know, Dr. Wilson. What is it you want me to do?"

"It's Marjane. She's been haranguing me to send supplies to our consul general in Havana, and I'm going to do it just to shut her up. If you'll pack it, I'll show you what I want to go."

"All right," Pia said as she followed Frank into the supply room.

For most of the morning, Bart only came out of his room when he heard a patient enter. He didn't know if Pia was still there or not, but she was definitely out of sight, and that was how he wanted it.

He had never had any experience tear at him the way Pia's impending marriage was. He kept telling himself she wouldn't go through with it, but then he replayed the scene on Christmas Eve when the two fathers had decreed their will. Except for Pia, everyone accepted the news with happiness and joy. Floria, Zuriñe, Elixabete, Gorka, even Marko—they all had been jubilant.

No, Pia would not go against tradition.

Bart had just ushered his last patient of the morning to the door. When he turned around, Pia was standing in his examining room, waiting for him.

"Miss Carranza, have you been in hiding this morning?"

"I've been doing some work for your father."

"You were hired to be my nurse—not my father's handyman. I'm afraid under the circumstances, I won't be needing you anymore."

"What circumstances?"

Bart gave her an incredulous look. "I don't believe that question deserves an answer." He reached for the cashbox and began withdrawing money. "I believe your salary is a dollar seventy-five a day. Here's two dollars for your trouble."

He laid the money on the desk, but Pia stared with unwavering brown eyes. She turned and, grabbing her coat, stormed out the door, leaving the money behind.

"What was that all about?" Frank asked when he heard the slam of the door.

"I believe Miss Carranza has chosen not to work for us."

Pia ran most of the way down the street, choking back the sob in her throat but not the tears in her eyes. When she got to the boardinghouse, she started to go in, but what explanation would she give why she was home in the middle of the day and why she was crying? Instead, she walked without knowing where she was going.

When she arrived at St. John's, she went around back to the pelota court, cleared snow from a bench, and sat down and wept. She felt such conflicting emotions. Bart had dismissed her, ostensibly because she had not helped him this morning, but she knew in her heart that wasn't the reason.

He had said "under the circumstances," and she knew very well the circumstances that he was referencing. He was jealous. He was jealous of Marko, just as she had been when she had watched Bart dance with all the women at the New Year's ball.

If one was jealous, didn't that mean one cared?

In her own case, she knew the answer.

Pia had never been inside the Idaho First, as Marko called the bank where he worked, and when she entered, she was impressed. In the open space, several people were talking to various people behind metal bars mounted on wooden counters. Separating the sets of bars were the thickest sheets of glass she had ever seen. She walked down the enclosures, looking for Marko, but he was not standing at any of the windows marked TELLER.

"May I help you, miss?" a gentleman asked from behind one set of bars.

"I'm looking for Marko Segura. Does he not work here?"

"Oh, yes, but he's back in the counting room. Who may I say is calling?"

"Pia Carranza."

A broad smile crossed the man's face. "We've heard of you, Miss Carranza, but Marko didn't tell us how pretty you are. Wait right here and I'll get him."

When Marko came toward the window, he looked anxious. "Pia, is something wrong? I thought you were at the doctor's office today."

"I'm sorry. I shouldn't have come here, but I thought perhaps there was someplace we could talk. Privately."

Marko looked back at the big clock that hung on the wall. "I've been so busy today, I've not eaten my lunch. Let me get my coat and I'll join you outside."

Pia stepped outside and waited for Marko, who soon came from the back of the building.

"I didn't ask. Have you eaten?"

"No, but I'm not hungry."

"Wait until we get to Lee Toy Chung's place," Marko said. "Then you can decide."

Marko and Pia entered a small wooden building that was facing the alley behind Front Street. It had few tables and only two or three people, all of whom were Chinese.

As soon as they sat down, one of the men jumped up from the table and approached them. "Marko, you bring pretty lady today."

"Lee Toy, this is the lady I'm going to marry."

A big smile crossed Lee Toy's face as he placed his palms together and bowed toward Pia. "You will be very happy. What will you eat today?"

"What did you cook?" Marko asked.

"Hop ho gai din."

"Then that's what we'll have. Now tell me what it is in English," Marko said.

"Fried chicken with walnuts. And rice."

Even though Pia did not think she was hungry, when the food arrived, it was delicious.

"Have you ever eaten Chinese cooking before?"

"I've eaten food that has been cooked by a Chinese man—Dr. Wilson's cook—but I've never eaten food like this. I like it."

"Speaking of Dr. Wilson, why aren't you working there today?"

"I think I was . . ." Pia stopped as her throat began to constrict and her eyes began to tear.

"Fired?"

"Yes." Tears began to roll down her face, and she did not try to hold them back.

"What did you do?"

Pia could not answer.

"It's Bart, isn't it?"

She nodded yes.

Marko reached out to take her hand in his. "He's not pleased that we're getting married."

"He didn't say that."

"But that's what you think. And let me guess—you don't want to get married either."

Pia lowered her head, and in a voice so quiet that Marko barely heard her, she said, "But we have to."

"Why? Because two old men said we have to? Pia, did you come to America because you wanted to? Did I come because I wanted to? Our fathers brought us here. Well, we're here now, and we have the chance to become Americans, not Basques who live in America just waiting until we earn enough money to go back to Euskadi. And in America, no one tells their children who they are going to marry." Marko withdrew his hand from Pia's and hit the table. "We'll just tell them we're not going to do what they say."

"Marko, that's what I want to do more than anything, but I can't. If I did, both of my parents would be heartbroken, and so would yours. We have to think of a way, some logical way, to make them agree that now is not the time for us to do this."

"All right, we'll both try to come up with some reason, and we'll tell them tonight."

Pia was waiting for Marko when he came home from the bank that evening. "Do you have an idea?"

Marko smiled broadly. "I do, but I have to talk to my brothers before I say anything. If I can get them to agree, we're home free."

"'Home free'?"

Marko laughed. "It comes from the game of baseball, and it means—well, it means we get what we want."

"Then I hope your brothers know baseball."

Once again all of the guests were crowded around the table finishing up the meal, and Pia and Elixabete were filling cups and clearing dishes, when Marko stood. Everyone stopped talking and he began to speak. He looked toward Pia and smiled, and she knew they were "home free."

"I want to say that the Segura family and the Carranza family have enjoyed having you as our guests for this Christmas season. I know that many of you are staying until the twelfth day when we celebrate the day of the Feast of the Kings. And this year, you are expecting to have an added celebration with an upcoming wedding. But my brothers and I have discussed this, and we think that is asking you to celebrate too much. We want to put off our wedding until we can honor our patron saint, Saint Ignatius of Loyola, on July thirty-first."

Elixabete, with a loud clatter, dropped a tray full of dishes, and leftover food splattered everywhere.

"I'm sorry," she said as she ran from the room.

Pia began picking up the pieces of broken china as Marko continued, "To go on. We brothers think it would be better if we all got married on the same day, and we would like to invite any of you here to bring your brides over from home."

This was met with loud cheers.

"Marko, that sounds like a fine idea, but I don't have a woman. How am I going to get one to marry me?" one of the men asked.

"You can do what we're going to do," Dabi said as he rose to stand beside Marko. "That is, if our father agrees." Dabi turned to Lander.

"Let's hear your plan," Lander said.

"We want to send our money to Father Ignacio," Dabi suggested. "We can ask him to find women who would come to Boise to marry us. We trust the priest's judgment to find a wife for each of us, and we can trust him with the money. If anyone else wants to join us, we will have a huge wedding next summer. Luken even suggested that we bring Father Ignacio over to perform the ceremony so that we will all be married in Euskera. *Aita*, what do you think?"

"It is not my decision alone. Sabin, do you agree with my sons' suggestions?"

"I am thinking the Bizkaia House can use more helpers. Yes, I can speak for my daughters—they will wait until the feast day of Saint Ignatius."

"I don't want to wait," Elixabete said, returning from the kitchen with Bart's mop and a bucket of water. She turned to Pia. "This is all your fault! You don't want to marry Marko, and you did this, I know you did! I hear you sniffling in your bed—you want to marry Bart Wilson, and now because of you, I can't marry Gorka."

"Elixabete, that is not true," Marko said. "Pia had not heard of our proposal until just now."

Sabin rose from the table. "Elixabete, go to the kitchen. You will do as I say, and I say you wait until July to marry—that is, if Gorka will still have you when he sees what a disobedient wife you can be."

After Elixabete left, the dining hall became subdued as the talk turned to other things. Pia cleaned up the mess, and no one, not even Marko, spoke of Elixabete's accusation.

When the work was finished and Pia went down the steps to the cellar, Elixabete was already in bed, her back turned to the room. Neither woman spoke, but long into the night, it was Elixabete who was crying herself to sleep.

Oh, God, what have I done? Pia prayed.

Silver City, Idaho

For travel in the winter snows, wagons, surreys, buggies, and even stagecoaches had their wheels removed to be replaced by sled-runners. It had taken two days for one of "Uncle" John Hailey's converted stagecoaches to travel from Boise to Silver City. Two of the five passengers who made the trip were Bart and Marjane.

They were going in response to a letter Bart had received from Suzie Yarborough, and he took it out and handed it to Marjane.

*Your grandpa has taken some sick and
has been coughing and wheezing something
awful. I tried to get him to see a doctor here
in Silver City, but he says the doc is a quack,
and he won't go. He wants you to come here,
and he wants you to bring Marjane if she's
not off on some nonsense.*

"You don't think he's dying—that that's why he
wants us to come?" Marjane asked as she handed
the letter back to Bart.

"Don't be worrying just to be worrying. Grandpa
is getting older, but he's a tough old bird. This coughing and wheezing could be several different things,
from tuberculosis or pneumonia or the influenza or,
knowing him, maybe nothing but a common cold,
and this is his way to get us here."

"When did you see him last?"

"He and Aunt Suzie came in for the fair, but you
were too busy with Mrs. Duniway to even come see
him."

Marjane turned away and looked out at the snow-
covered mountains as the horses labored to get to
Silver City. "Do you think I'm wrong?"

"No, I don't think you're wrong, Sis. It's just that I
hate to see you so all engrossed in your causes that
you don't take time for yourself."

"Do you think I'm going to be an old maid?"

One of the other passengers in the stage, who
had been leaning up against the door with his coat
collar pulled up around his ears, suddenly sat up.
"Honey, you don't ever have to bother your pretty
little head with that—not around Silver. I'd say for

ever one like you, they's fifteen like me just jumpin' at the bit to marry ya, and I'll be the first to ask ya right now."

"That's your answer," Bart said, barely containing his laughter.

Marjane hit Bart on the arm and rolled her eyes at him.

When they arrived in Silver City, the stage stopped in front of Caldwell's General Merchandise. Bart and Marjane were just at the door when they saw a horse and sleigh coming down the street, at a pace that made Bart wonder if it was a runaway. As he started to try to stop the horse, it whizzed by the store.

"I'll be back in a minute," the driver yelled as the vehicle passed.

"Was that Aunt Suzie?" Marjane asked.

"I think it was."

True to her word, within a short time the sleigh stopped in front of the store. Suzie jumped out and hugged both Marjane and Bart.

"I couldn't get old Prince to stop with this thing, so we just went down the hill and around the block. Come on. If you're not afraid to ride with me, we'll go see your grandpa."

Bart and Marjane climbed in, and before they were situated, Suzie snapped the reins and the horse was off again. Marjane literally hung on to Bart, afraid she was going to be thrown from the sleigh.

When they arrived at the house, Bart helped his sister down and offered to help Suzie, but she waved him off. "I've got to put the horse away. You two go on inside."

Bart grabbed his medicine bag and hurried into the house, with Marjane following behind. Eli was sitting in a leather chair that had been pulled close to the potbellied stove that was putting out enough heat to keep the entire room toasty warm.

"How are you doin', Grandpa?" Bart asked.

"I'm not about to die, if that's what you mean. Of course, if you listen to that old woman out there, I'm already on my deathbed."

Bart opened his bag and took out the thermometer. "Let's see what we have here," he said, sticking the thermometer in Eli's mouth.

"First thing you do is stuff this thing in my mouth?" Eli complained, while trying to hold in the thermometer. "We couldn't have a little conversation first?"

"Quit talking." Then with a laugh, Bart added, "And I won't have to ask how you're doing, I'll be telling *you*."

Bart left the thermometer in for a while, then checked the temperature: 103 degrees. "Hmm. That's not good."

"What's not good?"

"Your temperature. It's too high."

"Did you need a gadget to tell me that? Hell, I could have told you that. My skin's tingly."

"That's *allodynia*. How do you feel?"

Eli smiled broadly. "I feel like I got my money's worth with you. How many more five-dollar words do you know?"

"Not enough. Now seriously, how do you feel?"

"I'm just tired all over and I ache everywhere. I've got a headache and a sore throat and sometimes I'm so cold I can't stand it, and the next thing I know I'm sweatin'."

"It sounds to me like you've got a classic case of influenza."

"That's just what I been tellin' him," Suzie said as she came in the door. "He didn't have to get you to come all the way up here just for that."

"Do people die from the flu?" Eli asked.

"Sometimes," Bart said. "But I'll try to keep that from happening to you."

"Whaddaya mean you'll *try*?"

Over the next several days Bart treated Eli and kept him comfortable. In the meantime both Bart and Marjane tried to entertain him, playing cards and checkers with him. Marjane went into great detail about her activities with the women's suffrage league, and the women's temperance league.

When Bart and Marjane had been there for more than a week, sleeping on the floor in the loft and enduring the lack of indoor plumbing, they both were pleased when Eli seemed to be feeling a lot better.

"When are you two goin' back to Boise?"

"I guess when you get tired of us," Marjane said.

"That's gettin' pretty damn close," Eli said. "I put up with Suzie hovering over me all the time, but you two—I don't know about that."

"We love you, too, Grandpa," Marjane said.

"Well, that's good to know, because I need to talk to you about a few things. About your future."

"Our future?" Marjane asked.

"Yes, your future. I want to know, do either one of ya think you'll ever get married? Marjane, what with all your palaverin' and such about women votin' and people drinkin' and all, do you really think you'll find a man who'll put up with all that?"

"Eli, what an awful thing to say to your grand-daughter!" Suzie scolded.

"Don't harp on me, woman. I'm gettin' old, I don't have time for dancin' around the truth. All I can do is talk straight. So tell me, Marjane, do you think you'll ever get married?"

"I don't know, Grandpa," Marjane replied quietly. "If I could find somebody who'd have me, I might get married."

"You can find somebody," Bart said, then laughed. "On the stage coming up to Silver City, she turned down a good-looking man who would have married her this afternoon."

Bart intended his comment to be lighthearted, but Eli didn't take it that way. "It's not that easy, Bart. You've got to find somebody you love." Without hesitation, Suzie came over and patted Eli's shoulder. "Look at me. I'm married to a woman who would just as soon spit at me as look me in the eye." For several moments, the room was quiet, except for the sound of the occasional piece of falling wood in the stove. "I thought when I got rich, that would bring her out, but not money—not moving her son and you two out here—nothing could entice her to come. Bart, that little ole gal you brought to the fair. What's happened to her? I got the impression you sort of liked her."

"I did."

"Did? Does that mean you've lost her?"

"Yes, I think she got married while we've been up here, Grandpa."

"Well, that explains things. I wondered why you've been sittin' up here holding an old man's hand when you've got more than enough to do in Boise. You really love her, don't you?"

"Yes. She was—is—the most genuine woman I've ever known."

Marjane was listening to this exchange, and when Bart looked toward her, her eyes were glistening. "I'm sorry, Bart, I had no idea."

Bart shrugged his shoulders. "It's over. She married a Basque—not because she wanted to, but because she had to."

"Do you think she loves you?" Marjane asked.

"She never said, but I know she doesn't love Marko."

"Marko? Marko Segura?"

"Yes."

"But he's your friend."

"I know. I think I'll go for a little walk."

Within a week after Marjane and Bart returned to Boise, Marjane left for Iowa to join Carrie Chapman Catt in that state's suffrage movement. Bart went to the depot with her to see her off.

"I'll bet Miss Catt has no idea what a hard worker she's getting," Bart said.

"It's Mrs. Catt," Marjane said. "If I could find a husband like George Catt, I'd marry him tomorrow."

"Oh? What's so special about Mr. Catt?"

"Carrie made him sign an agreement before she would marry him that she could be gone four months of the year, just so she could work for the suffrage movement."

"And Mr. Catt agreed to that?"

"He did. He thinks his role is to make a living so Carrie can have the money to go around the country making speeches on behalf of women, and I think it's wonderful."

Bart smiled. "If there's another man like that, I hope you find him."

"I know there will be."

Bart nodded. "I think every person has a soul mate out there someplace."

"Oh, Bart, you had yours and you lost her. Are you going to be all right?"

"Of course I am." As he said it, he looked away from his sister and kicked at a rock that was on the platform.

"It hurts me to see you so hurt."

"Board!" the conductor called just then.

"I guess that's you." Bart picked up Marjane's bag and carried it to the steps of the train. He hugged her, then kissed her on her forehead. "I'll be fine, Marjane. I've decided I'm going to keep my nose to the grindstone, and that'll keep Pia out of sight and out of mind. And who knows? Maybe Pop and I will get along better, so in the end it'll turn out to be a good thing."

Bart watched his sister move through the car, then he waved one last time as the train pulled out for Nampa.

He'd be fine, he had told her. He had also told her he would keep himself busy enough to keep Pia out of his mind.

And that's exactly what he did. For the rest of the month he dedicated himself to work. When he and Frank weren't seeing enough patients to keep both doctors busy, Bart volunteered his time at the Tuberculosis Sanitarium, or, as it was more commonly known, the Pest House. His favorite service was at the Soldiers Home, where retired Civil War veterans lived. In addition, he called on Dr. Collister and Dr. Springer and agreed to see their patients at both Saint Alphonsus and Deaconess Hospitals.

The more he worked with the less fortunate patients, the more he thought about what he had wanted to do when he graduated from medical school at Washington University in St. Louis. His intention had been to go to Chicago to work alongside Jane Addams and Ellen Starr in the immigrant houses. It would be a noble thing for him to do, it would be personally satisfying, and most of all it would get him so far away from Boise that there would be no chance he would ever run into Pia or Marko again.

Setting down at his desk, he took out paper and pen and began writing to Jane Addams at Hull House.

"You shouldn't work so hard, Pia," Floria said. "You've washed all the windows, and in every room you've moved the beds. The Bizkaia has never been so clean."

"It needed to be done."

"I know you miss Marko, but let's hope he doesn't have to be away too long." Floria brushed Pia's hair away from her face. "What does my son know about setting up a cattle ranch?"

"It can't be that much different from raising sheep, and Marko does know that business."

"If Mr. Moore's idea is to teach his son how to work, why does he need to take somebody from Idaho? I'm sure he could have found someone in Colorado who could do the job just as well as Marko."

"Marko told me Crawford specifically asked for him to go, and I think it speaks highly of Marko."

"Oh, yes. When the Americans want to find people who will work hard and do all the dirty work, they turn to the Basco, but then for no reason they turn their backs on us," Floria continued. "Look at you and Dr. Wilson. We accepted him as one of us, and what did he do? For no reason, he fired you, and even more strange, he hasn't darkened our door since Marko beat him at pelota. You would think he would be man enough to accept that Marko beat him fair and square."

"You would think so," Pia said, not at all liking the direction of the conversation. "Perhaps I should air some of the quilts. It looks like it's going to be a clear day."

"That would be good. I'll have Elixabete help you."

Pia and Elixabete were beating quilts hung on a wire line stretched from the house to a poplar tree when a man came around the corner of the house.

"Pia Carranza?"

"I'm Pia Carranza."

"Then this is for you." He handed her a yellow envelope that said *Western Union* across the face of it.

Pia knew this was a telegram, but she had never before received one, and with trepidation she opened it.

"What does it say?" Elixabete asked.

"'Come quick. Gabina dying. Bring Bart. Dabi.'"

"What do you think is happening?"

"I don't know, but Dabi wouldn't have sent this if it wasn't something very bad." Pia hurried toward the back door.

When she got inside, she grabbed a few clean cloths and sheets and began stuffing them into an old flour sack.

"Pia, what are you doing?" Zuriñe asked when she entered the kitchen.

"It's Gabina Aguirre. She must be having trouble with the baby. Dabi sent a telegram, asking me to come, and to bring Bart."

"You can't do that."

"What do you mean I can't do it? Dabi says Gabina is dying."

"Then send Dr. Wilson alone, but you can't go with one man when you are betrothed to another."

"*Ama,*" Pia said, looking directly at her mother, "Marko Segura and I are not married, and even if we were, what could happen if I take a doctor to a dying woman?"

"People will talk."

"What people? The Basques will understand what

I'm doing, and I don't care what the Americans say. I just hope that Bart will go with me, but if he doesn't, I'm going by myself."

"Pia, I don't like it," Zuriñe said.

"I'm sorry." Pia grabbed her coat and, with the flour sack in hand, ran out the door and hurried down the street.

Bart was sitting at his desk when he looked up and saw Pia standing in the doorway. His first reaction was joy, but then he saw the worried expression on her face.

"Pia, has something happened?"

"I got this telegram from Dabi." She handed it to Bart.

"Gabina is dying? Do I know who this is?"

"It's Gabina Aguirre. You met her Christmas Eve."

"The pregnant one?"

"Yes. We wanted her to stay with us until the baby was born, but she insisted on going with Estebe out to the lambing grounds."

"The lambing grounds? Do you think she's out on the range?"

"I don't think so, but I don't know. Most of the time all the herders bring their wagons in and stay at the home ranch until all the lambs are born."

"Let's hope that's true. Have you been out to the ranch?"

"No, but surely someone in Mountain Home can tell us how to get there."

"Let's get Marko to go with us. I'm sure Mr. Moore will let him off in an emergency."

"Marko's not here. He's in Colorado with Mr. Moore's son."

"How could he . . . it doesn't matter." Bart looked at the clock. "The train for Nampa should be leaving about now. Let's pray it's not on time."

Bart wrote a quick note to Frank, telling him he was going to Mountain Home, and then after checking the supplies and equipment in his medical case, he grabbed it. "We don't have time to get a ride. Do you think you can keep up with me?"

"I can."

The train station was only a few blocks away from the doctor's office, and when they turned on Front Street, Bart saw that the train was at the station, the smoke and steam enshrouding the engine.

The conductor was standing on the platform, and the stationmaster was holding some papers.

"Pia, can you do that Basque thing?"

"What . . . do . . . you . . . mean?" Pia asked as she gasped for breath.

"That call—the *irrintzi.*"

Pia stopped and, holding her sides, yelled. *"Ruuu-ubru-uu."*

It got the desired effect. Everyone, including the stationmaster and the conductor, looked down the street. Bart waved his hand wildly.

"It must be an emergency, Doc," the stationmaster said when Bart arrived.

"It is. Two tickets to Mountain Home," Bart said, fumbling for his money clip.

"Don't worry about payin' now. I'll just let old Frank take care of it. This train's got to get out of here if it going to meet the eastbound, and we're already a little behind."

"Today, I'm glad you were, Abe," Bart said as he helped Pia onto the train.

Once they were settled, and their breathing returned to normal, Bart turned to Pia. "That was close. We wouldn't have made it without your *irrintzi*."

"It did come in handy. Bart, thank you for doing this."

Bart reached over and took her hand. "If there had been time to find him, I would have sent my father."

"Why? Do you not want to help us?"

"You know better than that. And you know why it's not good for us to be together." He withdrew his hand from hers and lay back in the seat, closing his eyes.

Pia looked over at Bart. Could he possibly be unaware that her wedding had been postponed? She started to tell him, then held her tongue. Pia sat there by the window, looking out at the snow-covered mountains, the mantle of white interrupted only by the deep green of the pine trees.

They reached Nampa in just over half an hour, where they stepped down from one train and up into another, heading east. Less than four and a half hours from the time Pia had received the telegram, Bart and Pia were in a hired buggy hurrying out to the lambing grounds.

They could hear it before they could see it, the air rent with the bleating of thousands of sheep. Lambing was in full process, with mothers calling for their young, and the baby lambs trying to adapt to the new, cold world into which they had just been thrust.

The sheep were in several bands. Those ewes heavy with lambs were in corrals, while the rest were outside. Patches of snow still remained, but most was gone, either melted by the sun or swept away by the trampling feet of thousands of animals.

In addition to the herders were the lambers, men who specialized in helping the ewes birth their young. Men were riding around on horses, and moving on foot, calling to each other, shouting loudly to be heard over the crying and bleating of the sheep.

All the sheep wagons that were normally out in the field were here for the lambing. Two dozen of them were in four neat rows of six, as carefully laid out as the plat of a town.

Dabi was the first to see the approaching carriage and hurried toward them.

"Bart, I'm so glad you're here," Dabi said as he extended his hand. "Gabina's in bad shape. *Aita*'s seen a lot of births, and he says there's something not right about this one."

"Where is she now?"

"Her wagon is the last one on the third row."

Bart nodded. "Is anyone with her? Elixabete, maybe?"

"Elixabete?" Dabi replied in a questioning voice. "Why did you think she would be here?"

"I thought since Gorka was here, she'd be spending as much time with her husband as she could."

Dabi chuckled. "Didn't Pia tell you? Nobody got married, so, no, Elixabete's not here."

Bart glanced quickly over toward Pia, who, embarrassed because she had not told him, cut her eyes to the ground. He didn't say anything to her but, instead, turned his attention back to Dabi. "I'll need as many clean sheets and bandages as you can find."

"Bart, this is a lambing ground," Dabi said. "Where do you expect me to come up with clean sheets and bandages?"

"I've got a whole bag full," Pia said. "I brought them from home."

"Good girl," Bart said. "I should have thought of it myself."

"No reason you should have. You've never been around when the lambs are being born, but I have. I knew that everyone would be so busy, there's no time for anything else."

Within minutes of their arrival, Estebe came running to meet them.

"Eskerrak zu hemen!"

"What did he say?" Bart asked.

"He's very glad we're here," Pia translated.

Estebe motioned for them to follow him, and Bart, Pia, and Dabi made their way through the bleating sheep until they got to Estebe's wagon.

When Bart stepped into the wagon, he was overcome by the oppressive heat from the stove. The canvas top was supported by ridgepoles, but Bart's six-foot-two-inch height made it impossible to stand upright, and when he got to the rear of the wagon, he saw that the bed on which Gabina was lying was less than four feet wide.

"The first thing we've got to do is get her out of here," Bart told Pia. "Find out if there's somewhere we can take her so I can examine her properly."

As soon as Dabi heard Bart, he ran to get a wagon, not taking the time to hitch up a team. He enlisted the help of several of the herders, and when they had Gabina in the wagon, they pushed and pulled until they stopped in front of a small cabin.

"This is mine," Dabi said, "but I'll be in the lambing shed tonight, so you can use it."

"Pia, get out your sheets and put them on the table, and, Dabi, you and Estebe help me get her up on it."

When she was lying as comfortably as she could, Bart checked her pulse and found it was racing at over a hundred beats per minute. He opened his bag and got his cuff out and took Gabina's blood pressure and found it to be 180/110.

"Ask her if she has a headache, or if she's having trouble seeing."

Pia reported that Gabina had those difficulties and felt nauseated.

"Ask Estebe to step outside with me for a minute. Dabi, you come with me so I can talk to him, and, Pia, keep her as comfortable as possible."

When they were outside, Bart ran his hand through his hair and explained, "I'm sure he knows his wife is a very sick woman. When a ewe can't have a lamb, sometimes you have to help it, and I'm afraid that's what I'm going to have to do with Gabina. But with a person, there are a lot of risks."

Bart waited and watched Estebe's face as Dabi spoke.

"Tell him, if we don't get the baby out of her, she may—" Bart paused in midsentence, then continued, "Just tell him we have to get the baby out. I'm going to take the baby from her. I'm going to cut into her stomach."

When Estebe heard this, he began crying and shaking his head.

"If I don't try, she and the baby are both going to die. I may be able to save one of them or both of them, but if I don't try, there is no chance either of them will survive."

"No, no, no!" Estebe said, the only word he knew in English.

"Bart, I trust you. Do what you have to do, and I'll keep Estebe away," Dabi said.

"Thank you, but what if I fail?"

"You can't." Dabi took Estebe by the arm and guided him away.

When Bart went back into the cabin, Pia was rinsing Gabina's face with cool water. "Look at her eyes, Bart. They're almost swollen shut."

"You're going to have to help me, Pia. There's a good chance Gabina and her baby may die."

Pia gasped and covered her mouth with her hand.

"Have you ever heard of a cesarean section?"

"I think I know what it is. Should I tell Gabina what's going to happen?"

"Just tell her we're going to try to save her baby."

Bart stoked the stove with wood and then put as many pots of water on the stove as he could find.

"Get her dress off her. Then take this carbolic soap and wash her stomach as well as you can. If she has any chance, we have to have her as clean as possible."

Bart saturated a wad of cotton with chloroform, then put it in the bottom of an ordinary drinking glass, packing it in so tightly that it wouldn't fall out. Then he gave the glass to Gabina. "Tell her to hold this over her nose and mouth and breathe deeply."

Gabina did as Bart instructed, and when she had taken enough to make her insensible to pain, it also put her to sleep. Her hand relaxed so that she dropped the glass on the bed beside her.

Pia started to pick it up, but Bart stopped her. "No. Letting her control it is a natural way of regulating it. She drops the glass when she goes to sleep. Otherwise she might get too much. How many sheets did you bring?"

"Several." Pia got her bag and withdrew one.

Bart ripped it in two, then cut a hole in each of the pieces. "Slip this over your head and then put the other one over me, and then let's wash up and start."

Bart took out his scalpel and a surgical needle and threaded it with catgut. "Pia, this is going to be rough. Do you think you can stay with me?"

"I'll do my best."

Bart took a deep breath and picked up the scalpel, then very deliberately made a midline incision down Gabina's distended belly.

When she saw the first drop of blood, Pia became woozy, and she felt light-headed. She stepped back, thinking she was going to faint, but she had promised Bart she would do her best. He needed her and Gabina needed her. Taking a deep breath, she stepped back to her position. At just that moment, Gabina began to move.

"Pia, the glass, put it over her nose and mouth, quickly!"

Nervously, and still not sure what she was doing, but trusting Bart, she picked up the glass and held it over Gabina's nose and mouth.

"Count to five, then pull it away."

Pia counted, then pulled the glass away.

It seemed that in no more than five minutes Bart was holding a baby boy.

"Get some more of your cloths, Pia. You get to give this little fellow his first bath."

Pia took the baby in her arms and he began wiggling and crying. "Oh, Bart, we did it!"

"Not yet. I've got to take care of Gabina."

Pia had never held such a tiny baby, much less given one a bath, but she did the best she could. When she was finished, she wrapped him up and sat down by the stove.

When she looked down at his face, she thought she had never seen anything more precious. She ran her finger over his cheek, and he turned his head toward her finger as his lips moved.

"Oh, baby, I'm sorry. I'm not your mama." She held him to her tightly. Then a horrible thought crossed her mind. What if Gabina died?

Pia looked at Bart, who was still working on Gabina. He was carefully cleansing her and putting sutures in her incision, and he looked exhausted.

When he was finished, he came over to Pia. "Let me look at the little fellow." Bart took the baby and held him, but he began to squirm, so Bart handed him back to Pia. "If you can take care of things for a while, I'd better go find the new daddy."

Bart was exhausted. Gabina had awakened a couple of hours ago, and Wilson had already tried to nurse, so Bart was hopeful all would be well. He couldn't help but chuckle over the name they had chosen. How would Wilson Aguirre ever explain his first name to his Basque friends?

Estebe had helped get his wife into bed and was with her now, and Pia had made a bed for the baby in the drawer of a chest. Bart looked over and saw Pia curled up on the floor, asleep. What would he have done without her?

Opening the door, he stepped outside. Because it had been so warm in the cabin, the cool air felt refreshing. He looked up. The mere quarter moon allowed him to see a vast array of stars. A meteor streaked across the night sky, and he mouthed a quick prayer that it was a promise that infant and mother would be all right.

Looking toward the lambing shed, he saw it lit by several lanterns and watched a couple of lambers working the drop bunch of ewes. He wondered how many lambs would be born tonight, and if they would all make it. He knew that an orphaned lamb was called a bummer.

Please, God, don't let Wilson wind up a bummer.

He felt thankful that Gabina had awakened and that she had nursed the child. That was a good sign, but he knew many things could still go wrong. After all, she had endured major surgery in the most trying conditions. It was imperative that she be kept clean, and he wished that he could stay here and oversee her recovery, but he knew he couldn't be away from Boise that long. Perhaps Pia would stay awhile and take care of Gabina and the baby. He would talk to her in the morning.

In the darkness, Bart had wandered farther than he had thought, and when he was returning, he stumbled into the wagon Dabi had used to bring Gabina to his cabin. Exhaustion was getting the better of him, and he decided to lie down in the back of the wagon and rest for a few minutes. When he crawled in, he was surprised to find the bed of the wagon lined with sheepskin. He lay back on the soft wool, and putting his hands behind his head, he looked up at the sky hoping that sleep would come quickly.

Pia had heard Bart's footsteps as he walked across the floor and then went outside. She lay on the floor waiting for him to return, but when he did not, she thought something might have happened to him. Wrapping the blanket around her, she stepped outside.

With only a sliver of moon, it was dark except for the stars and the few lanterns that were lit in the lambing shed. If Bart was out here, how would she ever find him?

Bart heard someone approaching the wagon, and thinking it might be Dabi to inquire about Gabina, he sat up. Then he saw that the figure was coming from the house.

"Has something happened?"

"Bart, where are you?" Pia called softly.

"I'm in the wagon. Has Gabina gotten worse?"

"Not that I am aware. I can hear Estebe snoring, so I'm thinking Gabina and the baby are fine. It is you I'm concerned about." Going to the sound of Bart's voice, Pia reached the wagon. "Are you going to sleep out here?"

"It's really quite comfortable. More comfortable than the floor you're sleeping on."

Without giving it a thought, Pia climbed into the wagon. "I'll share my blanket with you."

Bart was quiet as he felt the wagon shift with her weight. Within moments, she was lying beside him, putting the blanket over both of them.

"If you want, you can use my shoulder as a pillow," Bart said, moving his arm to accommodate her.

Without question, she moved closer to him. With her head on his shoulder, Pia could feel Bart's slow, steady breathing and the beat of his heart. She raised her hand and placed it on the hard muscles of his abdomen. She swallowed, trying to choke back emotion. In her heart, she knew this was where she belonged, but so many circumstances kept them apart.

Then she felt Bart move, turning toward her. He embraced her, hugging her tightly, and she wound her arms around him.

"Pia, why?"

Pia didn't answer.

"Why didn't you marry Marko?"

"Because I can't. I don't love Marko."

"What does Marko have to say about this?"

"He was the one who suggested we put the wedding off."

"'Put the wedding off'? Does that mean you *are* going to get married—but just not now?"

"I . . . I don't think we'll ever get married. Marko said we would put it off until we figured out a way to get out of it entirely."

"That's good to know." Bart lowered his head to hers and kissed her, a long, tender kiss that was neither aggressive nor passive.

Within minutes he was sleeping peacefully.

Pia lay beside him, encircled in his arms. The February night air should have been cooling, but she was decidedly warm, immediately aware of the heat their bodies were generating.

But there was something else about their body contact. There was heat, yes, but it was a heat that was far beyond mere warmth. It seemed to be generated internally, and at this very moment it was causing strange, tingling sensations all throughout her body. What made it even stranger was that these sensations were extremely pleasurable, pleasurable in a way that she had never before experienced, not even in the previous kisses they had shared.

This was not a sexual encounter, being in his arms as he lay sleeping, but was an expression of the love that she knew she felt for him. She gave him a gentle kiss, not wanting to awaken him, but when she did, he snuggled closer and instinctively tightened his hold on her.

Bart allowed a small smile to play across his face as he felt the fill of her breast in his hand, enjoying the tactile contrast between the soft, smooth skin and the hard, little nipple. He felt her body against his, smooth, supple, and so receptive to his caresses, her lips surrendering to his kisses, the moist warmth of her body as she received him deep into her, the . . .

The early-morning bleating of the sheep awakened him, and Bart lay there for a long moment, withdrawing from the dream, experiencing conflicting emotions about it. He was sorry it had been just a dream, but he was also relieved that he had done nothing to despoil Pia's innocence.

When he opened his eyes, he was startled to find Pia actually nestled against him. Her dark hair was fanned out on the sheepskin beneath them and her eyes were closed. He could see the arch of her brows, the ruffle of her lashes, and the contour of her cheekbones, but it was her lips that were so inviting. Bart knew that if he chose to kiss those lips, he would not be pushed away. He moved to take them, at first gently and then with more pressure. He knew the moment she was awake. She answered his kiss with a kiss that promised a dreamy intimacy.

"Good morning, sleepyhead," Bart said, drawing back with a bemused smile. "We're a fine pair. Leaving our patient while we sleep out under the stars."

"Gabina," Pia said, rising quickly. "What if something has happened?"

Bart pulled her back to him. "If there was anything bad, Estebe would have come out to find us."

Pia's eyes widened. "Bart, Estebe knows."

"What does he know?"

"That we slept together."

"Darlin', what we did is not sleeping together—not the kind that would cause anyone to talk. The first time we sleep together, I'm going to make certain everything is perfect." Bart kissed her on the nose. "But now we really should see what's happening inside."

When Bart and Pia went into the cabin, they found Estebe holding the sleeping baby, his face contented.

"Now that's the picture I like to see," Bart said. "Ask him how Gabina's night went."

Pia reported he said Gabina had had a restless night. Her stomach was painful.

"That's to be expected. Pia, I'll leave some Perry Davis with you, and you can give her some of the painkiller when she needs it."

"You're going to leave it with me? Does that mean you're leaving?"

"I don't have any choice, but I thought if you stayed, you could see after Gabina and little Wilson."

"Bart, I want to go back with you."

"And I want you with me, but Gabina needs a nurse. Find out from Estebe if there's any other woman in camp."

Bart watched, and when Pia began to smile, he knew that there was someone to watch over Gabina.

"Graciana Erquiaga is here."

"Good, as soon as we check on Gabina, we'll go find her."

When they walked over to the bed, Gabina was awake but her face was drawn and pinched.

"Ikusi al duzu Wilson?" Gabina asked.

"Yes, we have seen Wilson. He's a beautiful little

boy who looks just like his mother," Pia replied both in English and Euskera.

"Tell her I need to check her blood pressure." Bart took the blood-pressure cuff from his bag and put it around Gabina's arm. "Ask her if she's still nauseous."

Pia asked the question.

"Ez," the woman replied. *Ez,* "no," was a word Bart understood.

"Headache?"

"Ez."

"Dizzy?"

"Ez."

The blood pressure was 130/85.

Bart put the cuff back in the bag and smiled. "Everything looks fine."

"Gosaria?" Estebe asked.

"He wants to know if he can make us breakfast."

"Tell him thank you, but we want to find Graciana, and besides, I want to eat at the cookshack. You do want to see your father, don't you?"

Pia wrinkled her nose. "Yes, I want to see him."

"Don't worry. Nobody knows what we did except Estebe, and I don't think he'll say a word."

Bart was right to want to eat at the cookshack. When they entered, they saw a man standing over a Majestic cookstove frying bacon and ham, with eggs cooking, and he was flipping hotcakes.

"You must be Sabin's girl," the man said. "And you must be the doc. Let me shake your hand. Harry Miller's the name." He extended his hand and Bart took it.

Bart was curious how an outsider came to be the cook, but he didn't ask. "Estebe was mighty worried last night, but when Dabi went over this morning to see what had happened, he reported the mama and baby are both fine. I gotta hand it to you, Doc. Who would have thought you could do what you did out here away from a hospital and all?"

"You do what you have to do," Bart said. "Do you have enough for a couple of very hungry people?"

"Of course he does," a man said as he entered the cookshack. Sabin came over and sat down opposite Bart and Pia. "How's Marko, Pia?"

Pia looked away, but then trained her gaze directly on her father. "He's in Colorado—working on a cattle ranch, I think."

"A cattle ranch? If he wanted to get out of town, he could be out here helping us, don't you think, Doc?"

"It sounds to me like it's part of his work," Bart said.

"Or maybe he's trying to get out of marrying you," Sabin joked.

Pia laughed nervously.

At just that moment, Dabi pulled up a stool and sat beside them. "Are you going back today?"

"Yes, that is if we can find Graciana Erquiaga. Estebe says she's here with Alfonso, and we thought she could help out with Gabina," Pia said.

"I saw Alfonso working the jugs this morning. He can tell you where his wagon is," Sabin said as he stood to go. "If I don't see you before you leave, tell your *ama* I send my regards." He extended his hand to Bart, but he didn't speak.

"Where do we find these jugs?" Bart asked.

"They're in the main sheep shed," Dabi explained. "When a ewe, especially a young one, won't have anything to do with her lamb, we put her and her lamb in a little jug—I guess you would call it a stall. Sometimes it takes two or three days before the ewe bonds with her lamb."

"It didn't take Gabina long to bond with *her* baby," Pia said. "Wait until you see him."

"I saw him this morning," Dabi said. "Bart, we all appreciate what you did last night. Nobody thought there was a chance Gabina would be alive today, let alone little Wilson, too."

Pia looked up quickly. When was Dabi at the cabin? And what had he seen? At first she was panicked, but then she remembered what Bart had said. *The first time we sleep together, I'm going to make certain everything is perfect.*

No matter what Dabi thought, she knew she had done nothing wrong.

Unless falling in love was wrong.

TWELVE

Pia sat next to the window as the westbound train raced from Mountain Home to Nampa. Only six months ago she and her mother and Elixabete came to Boise for the first time. Then, she had been apprehensive and had vowed to return to Guernica as soon as possible. Now, it was her home.

Father Ignacio had been right. She had committed a passage to memory, from *Gero*, the book he had given her.

When a man leaves his country for the Indies or some distant land, while he is yet within sight of his town or still within its region, he looks back frequently at the mountains of his homeland. But as he goes forth, once he is beyond the view of his town and its surroundings, he adjusts his thoughts to his country of destination, fixing his gaze upon it and his will as well. These words, written by a Basque countryman in the seventeenth century, were valid today. How long had it been since she'd thought of returning to Guernica?

She knew the day she stopped longing for the mountains of her homeland. It was the day she sat on another mountain, fixing her gaze upon Boise, with the man she would fall in love with.

She loved Bart . . . loved him with all her heart and soul . . . and because of that, she was torn. It would be so easy to marry Marko. If only she could love him.

As a Basque woman she understood that she had obligations to fulfill. One of those obligations, perhaps the most important one, was to marry another Basque. The traditions that were the inheritance of a small group of people who lived in an isolated region of the Pyrenees Mountains had been handed down for centuries.

Now with a Basque diaspora in the Americas, these marriages were even more important. The only way to maintain their heritage was to marry within their culture. More often than not, those marriages were arranged, because the survival of the Basque culture took precedence over anything else. She was sure that few if any Basque marriages were the result of love.

Did her mother and father love one another? In their own way, she was sure that they probably did. But she couldn't help but recall the way they had greeted each other after a thirteen-year absence. Until she had come to fetch Bart for Gabina, Pia had not seen him since the Monday after New Year's Day. That was only six weeks ago, and yet she had thought of him every day . . . and she had felt a genuine quickening of her pulse when she did see him again.

And then there was last night. They had slept together—not in a carnal way, but she had never felt more contented in her entire life. This was the man she wanted to marry, the man whose children she wanted to bear. Somehow she must find a way to make it happen.

When they reached Boise, the same young man whom Pia had asked about the Bizkaia House the first day she had arrived was standing on the platform once again selling newspapers, but this time a small crowd was gathered around him clamoring for the news. Something was in the paper that Pia instinctively knew would bode evil.

"Paper, get your paper here! Spain sinks American warship! Get your *Statesman* here!"

"Oh, oh," Bart said. "I don't like this. I don't like this at all."

"Bart, what is it? What's he talking about?"

"I'll buy a paper, and we'll find out."

BATTLESHIP *MAINE*
SUNK IN HAVANA HARBOR
MYSTERIOUS EXPLOSION OCCURRED WHILE
MEN WERE ASLEEP IN THEIR BUNKS
SPAIN WILL PAY

By Associated Press to the Idaho Statesman

Washington, DC, Feb. 17—A report from Havana states that divers have found a percussion hole in the sunken Maine*'s armor plate, which* *leads to the suspicion that a torpedo caused the sinking. Assistant Secretary of the Navy Theodore Roosevelt is authoritatively quoted as saying, "I am convinced that the destruction of the* Maine *was not an accident."*

The loss of life is very high, in excess of 300 men. All the officers were saved except for two, Jennings and Sterritt, both ensigns, who are missing. Captain Sigsbee, who was unhurt, was on the deck when the explosion occurred. A sailor on watch at the bow was unhurt and reports that he saw nothing. It is strongly believed that this dastardly incident presages war with Spain.

"Do you think that's true? Surely Spain wouldn't attack an American ship," Pia asked, concerned.

"We'll just have to wait and see what happens. But now let's get you home so you can tell your family the good news about Gabina."

As they walked the few blocks from the depot to the Bizkaia House, Bart was picking up bits and pieces of conversation that he did not like.

"Who the hell do them damn Spaniards think they are, sinkin' an American ship like that?"

"What gets me is they's so damn many of 'em here in our country, livin' the good life. I mean we got 'em right here in Boise."

"Yeah, well, if they don't look out, they're goin' to find their good life ain't all that good here."

Bart quickened his steps, wanting to get Pia away before she realized that they were talking about Basques. He knew that in her mind Basques and

Spaniards were two completely different entities, but in the minds of these scoundrels, they were one and the same.

By the time they reached the Bizkaia House, the streetlight was already on, and it was casting its light on the front porch.

"Do you have a key to the door?" Bart asked when they stepped up on the porch.

"Why would I need a key? The door's never locked."

"When we left for Mountain Home, how many people were staying here?"

"Just Floria and my family and, of course, Julen and Mr. Egana."

"Do you have a key for this door at all?"

"I don't think so. But, Bart, why are you asking all these questions? We've never had any problem keeping the door unlocked. When you run a boardinghouse, people are in and out all the time."

"There must be some way of keeping this door closed."

"Well, there is the bolt. Sometimes when the wind is blowing hard, we have to throw it to keep the door from blowing open."

"Good. When you step inside, you slide the bolt."

"What if Julen's not home yet?"

"Pia, you're not hearing me. Keep this door locked at all times. If Julen needs to get in, he can bang on the door," Bart said emphatically.

"You're scaring me, Bart. What's going on?"

"Did you hear what those low-life cretins were saying back there at the depot?"

"Yes, I did. They were saying the Spanish had sunk an American ship."

"That's right, and if they get liquored up enough, they may decide to retaliate against anybody they think may have caused it, including Basques."

"Basques? Why? We didn't have anything to do with it."

"I hope I'm just making a mountain out of a mole-hill, but will you promise me you'll lock the door?"

"I will lock the door just to please you, but there's really no need to. Nobody's going to bother four women, an old man, and Julen, who is everybody's friend, and you know it."

Bart put his thumb and forefinger under her chin and tilted her face up toward his. "Thank you. And thank you for being my nurse."

"That was my pleasure. What could be more wonderful than bringing a baby into the world?"

"Bringing your own baby into the world." Bart had not taken away his thumb and forefinger, nor had she turned her head away. They held each other with their eyes for a long moment, then Bart moved his lips down to claim hers.

The kiss was gentle at first, but as she warmed to it, she leaned into him as she wound her arms around his neck and opened her mouth on his. The kiss was long and deep, and then they broke it off.

"You should go inside," Bart said, shaking his head. "And please, as soon as you go inside, lock the door. I'm going to stand right here on the porch until I hear the bolt thrown."

"All right," Pia said, her head still swirling from the kiss. She went inside, closed the door behind her, then slid the bolt into the slot.

"Gabon."

"Gabon," Pia replied. As she walked away from the door, she was pleased that he had used the Basque word for "good-bye." She stepped into the dark of the parlor and looked outside. She saw Bart standing under the streetlamp, looking down the street. Then after a minute he disappeared into the shadows as he started down the street toward his own home.

"I thought you would be back before now," a sleepy Elixabete said when Pia crept into their room in the cellar.

"We got here as soon as we could. Elixabete, you should see Gabina's baby. He's a beautiful little boy."

"Estebe must be proud. What did they name him?"

"Wilson."

"Wilson? Why would a Basque name a child Wilson?"

"I think they did it both in gratitude and in honor of Bart," Pia said.

"Doctors deliver babies all the time, and they don't have babies named after them. That's silly. The child should have been named Estebe."

Pia started to tell Elixabete just what Bart had done to save Gabina and the baby, but she didn't want to go into it. She was too close to the emotions of the past couple of days to discuss them.

"I got to give him his first bath," Pia said, hoping to talk about something uplifting. "I've decided a newborn baby is the most precious thing in the world. Wait until you hold one."

"I intend to. I hope Gorka and I have our own

baby by next spring—that is, if someone doesn't stop us from getting married this summer."

"I'll be so happy for you when you do marry Gorka," Pia said, praying that Elixabete would not say anything about her and Marko.

"I don't think you really mean that, Pia. You could have talked Marko out of putting off the wedding if you had wanted to, but I don't think you really want to marry Marko. Good night, Pia." Pia heard the bed squeak as her sister rolled over.

Pia got undressed and climbed into her own bed. Lying there, under the covers, she couldn't help but compare it to the previous night, when she and Bart had slept out under the stars in a wagon.

Elixabete didn't know how right she was. No, Pia did not want to marry Marko, but how could they gracefully get out of it? She knew that some people became excommunicated from the Church. She wondered if there was a form of excommunication from a culture.

"So you went all the way to Mountain Home just to deliver a baby. I don't suppose you got paid for missing two good days of work?" Frank said when Bart came into the office the next morning.

"Money didn't come up, Pop."

"Son, I hate to harp on you all the time, but no matter how altruistic you want to be, this is still a business, and we have ongoing expenses that have to be met."

"I thought we were in the business of saving lives."

"Of course you're right. But you just go off donat-

ing your time to every cause that comes along—
the Sanitarium, the Soldiers Home, your Basque
friends. I'm sorry, Bart. I'm afraid I don't have your
compassion."

"Well, this wasn't a case of compassion. The
woman would have died without a doctor."

"Oh. What was the trouble?"

"Preeclampsia for certain—may have been
eclampsia."

"You say the woman is alive. Did you have to
abort the baby?"

"No." Bart smiled proudly. "Wilson appears to be
a healthy baby boy."

"Wilson? So she named him after you. How did
you deliver him if she was in eclampsia?"

"I did a cesarean section."

"The hell you did! How could you have done that
without a team helping you?"

"Pia helped me, and we made do with what we
had. When I left, Gabina and Wilson were both alert
and doing well. I hated to leave them, but I knew I
had to get back."

"So Pia helped you," Frank said. "I miss her. Do
you think there's a possibility she could come back
to work for us?"

"She just might," Bart said, thinking back to the
night he had spent with her cuddled in his arms.
"I'll ask her the next time I see her."

"Oh, by the way, did you hear the Spanish blew
up an American battleship off the coast of Cuba?"

"Yes, I saw a paper when we got back last night,
but the article said there was suspicion it might be a

torpedo. Don't you think they'll investigate to make sure that's what it was?"

"I would hope so, but you know it's going to be those bastards that did it. Didn't you listen to Marjane when she was here for Christmas? The Spaniards have been running roughshod over those people for a long time, and they don't want the United States to come down there and help out the Cuba Libre. It just makes sense that they'd blow up one of our ships."

"I hope you're wrong about that."

"In this case, I hope I'm wrong, too. But I'll bet there's going to be hell to pay over this," Frank said. "The whole town—no, the whole country—is up in arms, and that kind of sentiment will lead to a war with Spain sure as God made little green apples."

"You may be right. I just hope that the people here keep a cool head, especially about the Basques."

"What about the Basques?"

"There are a lot of people right here in Boise who think of them as Spaniards."

"Oh," Frank said. "I suppose I can see that. But that's foolish, they're Basques. Anybody should be able to see the difference."

"Believe me, Pop, there's a whole class of people in this town who don't like the Basques at all."

"What did I tell you?" Garrison shouted angrily late that same day. He was in the Lawrence and Smith Saloon, and he was holding up the paper to show the other saloon patrons. "I told you them damn Spaniards was goin' to make war against us. And here they've gone and sunk an American ship!"

"I reckon Spain will rue the day they done that," one of the others said.

"I'd love to get my hands on the sons of bitches that done that."

"Listen to this, boys. It says the Spanish warship *Alfonso XII* was right beside the *Maine*, and our boys heard 'em yell, 'All's well.' Now that was just after the nine o'clock tattoo. Ever' one of our boys was in their hammocks and the lamps was put out. Do ya think that sounds like a coincidence?"

"Nah! That's when they done their dirty work."

"It says here a red-hot bolt from the *Maine* fell on the poop awning of a Spanish warship and set it on fire. Now just guess what the name of that warship was?"

"Hell, Garrison, how are we supposed to know that?"

"It was the—are you listenin' real hard?—the *Vizcaya*. Now where have we heard that word before?"

"Ain't they a boardin'house over on Eighth Street by that name?"

"It's where Julen Alonzo lives, the son of a bitch that got my job over at the livery," Garrison said.

"I don't think they calls it *Vizcaya*. From what I seen, it's the Bizkaia."

"It don't make no damn difference. None of 'em can speak English. What makes you think they can spell?" Garrison asked. "I say we go smoke 'em out. That'll show 'em they can't take somebody's job or blow up our ship. What do you say?"

"I don't know, Garrison. Ain't none of 'em ever done nothin' to me."

"Do ya ever read the Good Book? It says thou

shalt give eye for eye, tooth for tooth, and if you keep readin', it says burnin' for burnin'," Garrison said. "Now don't you think the Lord is a tellin' us to burn somethin' to avenge them three hundred dead Americans?"

"Yeah! Yeah!" the crowd responded.

"Boys, get your torches!"

Because all of the sheepherders were gone to the home ranch, the amount of work required at the Bizkaia House was much less than it had been during the Christmas season. At the moment, only five people were in the house, the four women and Mr. Egana. Because the women didn't have to cook for a lot of people, all five were sitting around the table conversing. Mr. Egana was entertaining the ladies with a story.

"I came to America as an able-bodied seaman on a square-rigged sailing ship. We slept in canvas hammocks slung on the berth deck, and sometimes when the sea was very high, why, those hammocks would start swinging back and forth and it would throw you out like the sling David used when he slew Goliath. Then, in the daytime we would—"

The story was interrupted by a crashing sound coming from the parlor of the house.

"What was that?" Floria asked, and all got up to hurry into the parlor. A big rock was lying on the floor, surrounded by shattered glass. In one of the windowpanes nothing but shards remained.

"Hey! You Spanish bastards!" someone shouted from out front. "Come on out!"

"What is this? What's going on?" Zuriñe asked.

"I think I know," Pia said, thinking that Bart had tried to warn her. "The Spanish sank an American ship near Cuba."

"Isn't that a long way from Boise?" Zuriñe asked.

"Yes, it is, but these people think we are Spanish."

With the sound of breaking glass, another rock came crashing into the parlor.

"We're goin' to burn yer house down!" someone shouted from outside. "Let this be a warnin' to you. If you don't want to get burnt up with it, you'd better come out now!"

"What is he saying?" Zuriñe asked.

"He's saying that they are going to burn the house down," Pia said, frightened.

"They can't do that, this is our home," Egana said, starting toward the front door.

"Mr. Egana, no! Don't go out there!"

Disregarding Pia's warning, Egana opened the door and stepped out onto the front porch.

"You men!" he shouted. "Go away! Just women here! Go away!"

"Are you a woman, old man?" someone shouted, and the crowd, which now numbered almost fifty, laughed and jeered.

"Go away!" Egana said, this time waving his hands as if he were shooing chickens.

"That's it, old man. We'll go just 'cause you say so. Now get back in there and tell them women to git out!" someone in the crowd shouted.

"He don't understand English. This'll git his attention." The man picked up one of the gathered rocks that were lying in a pile. "Make a stone boy out of that," he said, referring to the cairns that the

Basques frequently built on the mountains to provide way markers.

"Why, he'll need more than one. We want a big rock pile," another man shouted, and a whole barrage of rocks was hurled at Egana. Several of them hit him, and he collapsed on the porch.

"Oh!" Pia shouted. "Mr. Egana is hurt!"

Pia opened the door and hurried out to help Egana.

"Pia, get back in here!" Zuriñe called.

"Mr. Egana, can you walk? We have to get you back inside," Pia said as more rocks were being thrown, some hitting her.

"Ain't no need in you takin' him back inside, missy!" someone shouted from the crowd. "You're all goin' to have to come out of there sooner or later. We aim to burn that place down!"

Elixabete came out onto the porch, and as the mob shouted threats, Pia and Elixabete helped Egana get safely inside. As soon as they were back in the house, Pia closed and locked the door, as more rocks were thrown, and more windows were broken.

"Get him back in the kitchen and stay away from any windows," Pia said. "I'm going to go get Bart."

"What do you think he can do to stop this?" Elixabete asked, her voice on the edge of panic.

"I don't know, but we can't just stay here and do nothing."

"Go out the back door and run up the alley," Floria said. "I think you can get all the way to his office without being seen."

❧

Bart looked up in surprise when Pia came bursting in from the kitchen. She was out of breath and her eyes were wide and filled with fear.

"Pia, what is it?" Bart asked, shocked by her appearance.

"Some men," Pia said, panting to get her breath back. "They're in front of the house. Bart, they say they're going to burn it down!"

Without saying a word, he quickly moved to his desk, jerked open the drawer, and pulled out his pistol and holster. He was buckling it around his waist when Frank saw him.

"Bart, what are you doing?"

"Pop, I was afraid of this. There are a bunch of men outside the Bizkaia House and they say they're going to burn it down. Go tell Rube," Bart said. "Come on, Pia, we've got to hurry."

Bart ran back up the alley the two blocks from his office to the Bizkaia House, holding back somewhat because he didn't want to leave Pia behind him. They went in through the back door, where Mr. Egana was stretched out on the table with the three women standing around him. Elixabete had a basin of water and was bathing his head as blood was trickling down his face.

"Is he hurt bad?" Bart asked.

"He says his head hurts," Floria said.

"I don't have time to look after him now, so keep doing what you're doing. Pia, you stay in here with the others. Where's Julen?"

"He had to go to Idaho City for Mr. Moore."

Bart started toward the front door.

"What are you going to do?" Pia asked.

"I'm going to try to stop these idiots."

Bart walked over to the shattered window and looked outside. He saw a gathering of between fifty and seventy-five men, but his attention was drawn to the man who was pouring kerosene on the porch.

"Hey! Bascos!" someone shouted as yet another rock came through the window, missing Bart. "I hope you burn in hell for what ya did to our sailor boys."

The raucous shout was followed by loud laughter as two men pranced by carrying a large banner saying REMEMBER THE *MAINE*.

"Bart, don't go out there, you'll be hurt," Pia said.

"If I don't go, all of us could be hurt. I figure if I can keep them occupied until Pop gets Marshal Robbins here, maybe nothing else will happen. But now I want you to go back in the kitchen and stay there."

Bart gave Pia a hug and then opened the door. He walked out on the porch to the man pouring the kerosene and stood above him, with his arms folded across his chest.

"Good afternoon, boys," Bart said calmly.

"Doc Wilson," Garrison said. "I might'a knowed you'd be here."

"Really? And how did you know that, Garrison?"

"'Cause you're always sniffin' around that little Basco woman. They's some says you got her workin' fer ya."

"Is that a fact?"

"You'd best be gettin' on out of the way, Doc.

We've come here to take care of business, but we've got no beef with you."

"Let's see, you've stoned an eighty-two-year-old man, broken out six or eight windows, and terrified a bunch of women. Is that the business you've come to take care of?"

"We aim to show this bunch they can't blow up an American battleship and get away with it," the man carrying the sign said. "Remember the *Maine*! That's what folks all across the country is a saying."

"I see. You're Harvey Barnes, aren't you?"

"I am."

"I patched you up when you tangled with the barbed wire. Remember?"

"Yeah, I remember. You cut up my pants."

"Tell me, Mr. Barnes, do you really think anyone in this house had anything to do with blowing up the *Maine*?"

"That don't matter," Garrison said. "They're Spaniards, ain't they? And in my mind, right now, all of 'em's just alike."

"Go home, Garrison. All of you, go home."

"Now, that ain't likely to happen," Barnes said. "We asked ya oncest, real nice, to get out of the way. Garrison told ya we got business to take care of, and we aim to do it." Barnes waved his sign. "We aim to 'remember the *Maine*.'"

"If you're going to carry a sign that says 'Remember the *Maine*,' the least you can do is dot the *i*," Bart said.

Bart drew his pistol, fired, and returned it to his holster, doing it so fast that most of the mob didn't even see it.

"What the hell?" someone shouted in surprise. On the hand-lettered sign, a bullet hole was now perfectly placed as a dot over the letter *i*.

"Go home," Bart said. "Marshal Robbins has been called, and I expect he'll be here any minute."

"That old man? Rube don't scare nobody anymore, and right now he ain't here. There's just you, and even a feller who is as smart as you think you are can't stop us all by yourself," Garrison said.

"I don't have to stop all of you," Bart said.

"What do you mean?"

"I only have to stop you, Garrison, and maybe two or three more." Bart drew his pistol again. "I don't really want to kill you, Garrison, so I'll just shoot you somewhere where it hurts a lot. Then I'll charge you to take the bullet out."

Bart pointed his pistol toward Garrison.

"Wait a minute! Wait a minute!" Garrison shouted, holding his hands out toward Bart. "We ain't armed. None of us is!"

"Then I'd say that makes it easier for me."

At that moment they could hear a police whistle being blown, and a moment later a spring wagon came up quickly, pulled by a team of galloping horses.

The wagon stopped and the marshal and four more deputies jumped out quickly.

"Hello, Rube," Bart said easily.

"Doc," Marshal Robbins said. He looked out toward Garrison and the others. "What's going on here?"

"Nothin'," Garrison said. "Just palaverin' with the doc here."

"Really?" Rube walked over to the empty kerosene can. "I suppose you just sort of spilled this kerosene, and it accidentally got on these folks' porch. Is that about how it happened?"

"Like I told you, we ain't doin' nothin'. You may notice there ain't no torches lit. We just want to let these damn Bascos know we don't appreciate them blowin' up an American battleship."

"I don't think any of the folks who live here had anything to do with blowing up the *Maine*," Marshal Robbins said. "Now, you men know we don't have room for all of you down at the jail, so if you decide to go home peaceably, I'll let you go, but if I see any one of you hanging around this house, I'll throw you in jail in a military minute. So it's up to you. Which will it be?"

"What about Wilson? He took a shot at us. What ya gonna do about him?" Garrison asked.

"I'm ashamed of you, Doc. I've seen you win many a shooting contest. How is it that you shot at all these men and didn't hit a one of them?"

"I don't know, I guess I just wasn't shooting as straight as I should have. I could try again, I suppose, and see if I have any better luck this time."

"We're going," Garrison said, "but mark my words, this ain't the last of it."

"Is that a threat?" Robbins asked.

"No, no. I mean we're goin' to war with these Spanish bastards. You can put that down in your little black book. Come on, boys, let's go."

Garrison turned and walked away, the other men following him.

Bart stood beside Rube Robbins, watching as the demonstrators disappeared in the distance.

"I'm glad you made it, Rube."

"Yeah, I'm sorry I was a little late, but there was a big ruckus going on over on Levi's Alley. I think I'll leave a deputy here for a little while just to make certain nobody comes back around and accidentally drops a match on this porch."

"Good," Bart said. "Julen Alonzo had to go up to Idaho City, so I think I'll spend the night here with the women and the old man."

"That's probably a pretty good idea," the marshal said.

THIRTEEN

When Bart came back inside, he saw everyone gathered in the dining room. Egana was now sitting at the table as Pia held a damp cloth to his forehead.

"How are you feeling?" Bart asked.

"What happened?" Egana replied.

"He keeps asking that over and over," Floria said. "And even when we tell him, he can't remember."

"He probably has a concussion," Bart said. "Do you feel dizzy or sleepy?"

Egana just looked at Bart with a vacant stare.

"I'm sure he has a headache and he may soon be sick to his stomach," Bart said. "Let's get him up to his room. He may be confused for a while, and he may not remember much about what happened, but plenty of rest should take care of him."

"What if he gets worse?" Pia asked.

Bart smiled. "I think I'd like to spend the night here, if that's all right? That way, I can keep an eye on Mr. Egana, and I'll be here in case Garrison and his bunch come back."

"Oh! Do you think they will?" Floria asked.

"No, to be honest, I don't think so. But I'd feel better about it if I was here."

Floria translated to Zuriñe and Elixabete.

"Bai, bai," Zuriñe said, nodding.

"Yes, do stay here. I think we would all feel better, especially since Julen is away."

"Good."

Bart helped Pia take Egana up to his room, and after they had made him comfortable, she picked out a room for Bart.

"I want to put you in this room, Bart. This is where Elixabete and I stayed until we were banished to the cellar."

Bart lifted his eyebrows as a slow grin crossed his face. "You know I would never banish you for anything."

"That's not true, Dr. Wilson. Didn't you banish me from working at your office?"

"Well, that's just sort of true. I couldn't have someone work for me that I thought was married. At least not if it was you. By the way, Pop asked me just yesterday if I thought you would come back and work for us. He says he misses you."

"The question is, do you?" Pia said, her voice low and throaty.

As an answer to Pia's question, Bart took her in his arms and kissed her. "Need I say more?"

Just then they heard the tinkling of glass downstairs.

"Oh, no! Do you think they've come back?" Pia asked as she ran toward the stairs.

෨෴෴

When they reached the bottom of the stairs, Elixabete was sweeping up the shards of glass.

"We need to get those windows covered," Bart said. "Do you think Mrs. Segura has any packing crates around? We can use the wood from them. It's light and thin and it would be easy to put in place."

"I think there are some boards in the cellar," Pia said. "I'll get them."

For the next hour, Pia helped Bart cover the windows while Elixabete swept up the glass, and Zuriñe and Floria prepared a meal.

"There," Bart said when he'd driven in the last nail. "That at least stops the wind from blowing in."

Floria had just come in with her arms full of quilts to put over the windows. "One thing about running a boardinghouse, we have plenty of quilts. Put these up and that will make it warmer."

"Oh, Mrs. Segura, I hate to do that," Bart said. "Are you sure you want to make holes in these?"

"Quilts are made from patches in the first place, so if we have to mend them, we will. I think you should put them up."

"Soup's on."

Everyone turned toward the sound of English words, where they saw a smiling Zuriñe. She had just spoken the first English words Pia had ever heard her say.

"I'm proud of you, Mama," Pia said, pointedly saying *mama* instead of *ama*, although she was sure her mother couldn't hear the difference.

∞

The hearty potato soup also had sausage and cabbage and was served with thickly sliced black bread. On a cold night like this, Bart didn't think anything could have been more appropriate, or delicious.

"I'm glad you're here with us," Pia said as they sat around the table. "Do you think those men would have burned our house down?"

"It's hard to say what a mob will do. If they have a ringleader egging them on like Garrison was doing, sometimes you can get men to do things that they wouldn't ordinarily do."

"Humph," Pia said. "Reminds me of sheep. If one or two get frightened and start running, the whole band will run, and if one of them tries to stop, that one will get trampled by the rest."

"That's really a very good analogy. But just remember, all Americans aren't like what you saw tonight. I'm sure these men got their courage from a bottle." Bart smiled at Pia. "You and Elixabete actually showed more courage than any of those men when you went out to get Mr. Egana. Either one of you could have been hurt as badly as he is."

"It was frightening," Pia said, "and I hope nothing comes of it."

Pia rubbed her arm gingerly. With all the excitement, she had not even thought about the rocks that had struck her. She was sure she would have bruises.

"I'd better take Mr. Egana some soup," Pia said, rising from the table.

"Let me go with you," Bart said. "If he's nauseated, let's just hold off on letting him eat. And, ladies, this has been a long evening. I think I'm going to say *gabon*."

"Gabon," Zuriñe said, her own head nodding with fatigue.

As Pia lay in bed, she thought of Bart. She thought of the kisses they had shared, and the promise, only hinted at, of those kisses. The night they had slept out under the stars, with only their body heat keeping them warm, was the night that she knew she loved him.

She wondered if Bart loved her as she loved him. She had seen him the night of the New Year's dance, as one woman after another sought his company. But the most painful thing she had watched was when the buxom, red-haired woman and he had left the dance together, with Bart's arm draped casually around her. Pia could not bear to think where they might have gone or what they might have done.

As all these thoughts swirled around in Pia's mind, she needed an answer. Did she mean anything to Bart or was she just his latest pastime? Sighing, she rolled over in bed and tried to rid herself of these thoughts, but she couldn't.

When she moved, she was aware of aches in her back. She attributed them to helping Bart hold the boards to cover the windows. But maybe they were from the rocks that had hit her? Could she have been injured? She should have asked Bart.

The longer she lay, the more restless she became. Every gust of the wind, every creak in the house, every bark of a dog, caused her to imagine that the mob was returning.

She listened to the slow, even breathing of her sister lying in the other bed.

"Elixabete?" she called quietly. Then, a little louder: "Elixabete?"

Elixabete did not answer.

Pia sat up, then quietly swung her legs over the edge of the bed. Every sense of reason and propriety told her to lie back down, that what she was about to do was unthinkable. Putting on a dressing gown, she opened the door, then stepped out of the room, quietly closing the door behind her.

Pia climbed up the steep, narrow steps from the cellar to the main floor. She knew that her mother and Floria were in rooms just off the kitchen, so she moved as quietly as she could, praying that neither of them was awake. She walked carefully, mindful of all the broken glass that had been scattered all over the floor, hoping that Elixabete had got it all swept up.

She made it across the floor without stepping on any forgotten shards, then, reaching the stairs, she climbed slowly, making certain that her footfalls were silent, and hopeful that the stairs wouldn't squeak. When she reached the second-floor hallway, it was illuminated, though dimly, by one electric lightbulb that hung from the ceiling on a long cord.

She wished the light weren't here. She hoped Mr. Egana was asleep, but if he happened to leave his room for any reason, he would certainly see her. How would she explain her presence?

The answer was, she couldn't explain it. If Mr. Egana saw her on this floor in her nightdress, she would be disgraced.

"Please, Lord," she prayed, saying the words in a whisper, "don't let Mr. Egana see me here."

What was she doing? This was insane!

Taking a deep breath, Pia moved down the hallway, and when she got to Bart's room, she reached for the doorknob.

Bart opened his eyes. Something had awakened him and he lay still. Had Garrison returned and somehow gotten into the house?

The doorknob turned and Bart was up, reaching for his gun, which lay on a table by his bed. He moved as quietly as a cat, stepping to the side of the door, which would hide him as it opened. He pulled the hammer back on his Colt .44, his senses alert, his body alive with readiness.

Bart could hear someone breathing on the other side of the door. A thin shaft of hall light shone underneath, then, as the door opened, a wedge of light spilled into the room.

"Bart?" a woman's voice called, low and husky, with just a hint of rawness to it.

Bart recognized Pia's voice, and he eased the hammer down on the pistol, then pulled the door the rest of the way open.

The sudden and unexpected opening of the door startled Pia and she gasped.

"I'm sorry," Bart said quietly. "I didn't mean to scare you."

Pia stood in the doorway, backlit by the hall light.

"Pia? Is something wrong?"

"I, uh, I shouldn't be here." She turned to leave.

"No, don't go." Bart moved back to let her step inside. He closed the door behind her, then crossed over to turn on his table lamp. A bubble of light illuminated the room.

Bart was dressed in a one-piece garment that covered his arms and legs. It molded to his body, his shoulders straining against the cloth. Now more than ever before, Pia was aware of how powerful he was, with his chest broad and muscular.

"I can't believe I actually came to your room like this," Pia said as her lip quivered. "You must think I am a terrible person."

He smiled at her, and just that—his smile—set her pulse to racing.

"Do you want to know what I think of you? I think you are the most beautiful and the finest woman I have ever known."

A strand of hair had fallen across her forehead, and Bart reached out to push it back. This simple gesture, the lightest touch of his fingers against her skin, sent a jolt all through her body. His fingers slid down the side of her face, tracing her cheek, then under her jawline, resting just for a moment on her neck.

She responded by reaching up to his face, feeling a slight stubble of beard. His jawline felt strong and masculine under her touch. She could feel her heart hammering against her ribs. She had charted a course with only the vaguest idea of where it could go. She knew that by coming here, she had put everything in Bart's hands. She had taken the first step; from here on it would be up to him. She put all her trust in him, not to leave her alone, but to lead her on this quest.

Bart's hand moved up from her neck to take a handful of hair, guiding her head gently, ever so gently, toward him. The first kiss was slow, and deliberate. Then he put his arms around her and pulled her to him for a much deeper kiss, one that set her body aflame. She pressed herself against him, then opened her mouth hungrily to seek out his tongue. That sent new spirals of ecstasy coursing through her, and in that moment she knew why she had come.

His lips seared a path down her neck, then rose to nibble at her earlobe. She was on fire, then she felt Bart's hands tugging at her robe, easing it and the nightgown beneath it up across her legs, then baring her most private part. She felt the air on her naked skin, but instead of cooling her, it fed the flames so that the fire raging within became a conflagration. She lifted her arms to facilitate the removal of her robe and nightgown, and when Bart let them fall to the floor, she was totally naked in front of a man. And not just any man—she was in front of the man whose mere glance could arouse her.

When Bart lifted her into his arms and carried her to the bed, it seemed like the most natural thing in the world. Lying there, she felt the texture of the bedsheet on her bare skin. She watched through lowered lashes as he stripped out of his underwear so that he was as naked as she was. For the first time in her life she saw a man, his penis large and engorged, standing erect from his body. She could not avert her gaze as Bart climbed into bed with her.

He captured her hand in his and she felt his eyes burning into her. She watched his face get closer to hers until their lips were touching. She had thought their previous kisses were sensuous, but in all the previous kisses they had been clothed. Now they lay naked beside one another, and she was discovering completely new emotions.

It was slow, his lips moving over hers, his tongue forcing her lips apart and then darting into her mouth, only to withdraw to enter again and again. She followed his tongue with her own, entering his mouth, then feeling their tongues press against each other. He kissed her hard and passionately, and she pulled her hand free from his, to pull him down upon her body. Then he separated his lips from hers, and she regretted that her action had caused the pleasure to stop.

But that need not have concerned her. His lips trailed down her throat as she tipped her head back to allow him better access. He moved from her neck to her breasts, fondling one globe, and she raised her body to push her nipple into his lips. How did she know to do this? She explored his body by instinct alone. Bart's tongue caressed the nipple until it swelled and throbbed with pleasure.

"Pia," Bart whispered. "I have thought of this, even dreamed about it. Do you have any idea what you do to me?"

When he kissed her again, her hands moved over the smooth skin of his naked body. Then she encountered it—that hard, erect stalk she had seen for the first time but a few minutes ago.

She wrapped her fingers around it, feeling the heat of it, almost believing she could feel it throbbing. Driven by urges she could not explain, she began moving her hand, sliding the velvety skin up and down his shaft.

"No, no," Bart said, pushing her hand away gently.

"Oh, did I hurt you? I'm sorry."

"Oh, believe me, what you were doing does not hurt," Bart said softly, kissing her gently on the nose. "But if you keep doing that, I'm afraid this will all be over before it gets started."

Pia didn't understand exactly what he meant, but she could tell from the tenderness of his words, and his continued ministrations, that he wasn't upset. Bart continued kissing her while his hand moved farther down her body into the soft down at the juncture of her legs, to that place no man had ever touched. Pia could hardly believe what was happening. She spread her legs and thrust up against his hand and busy fingers. She bit her lips to keep from crying out.

"Laguntza! Laguntza!"

It was Egana's voice, and it was loud.

Bart quickly pulled his hand away and sat up, leaving Pia hanging on the raw edge of unfulfilled promise.

"Laguntza! Laguntza!"

"Mr. Egana. What is he saying?" Bart asked.

"He's calling for help," Pia said, so breathless that it was hard for her to speak.

"Non nago?"

"Now he wants to know where he is."

"It's from the concussion." Bart bounded out of bed. He picked up Pia's nightclothes and tossed them to her. "Dress quickly!"

"Why did I come here? Someone will find me for certain," Pia said, anguished.

Bart pulled on his trousers and shirt and moved toward the hallway.

"When you get your robe on, come out in the hall," Bart said. "If anyone sees you, we'll say you heard Mr. Egana and you knew I wouldn't understand what he was saying."

"Non nago? Non nago?"

When Bart stepped out into the hall, he saw Egana heading for the stairs. "Mr. Egana, no!" Bart called. "You don't need to be going downstairs. Let me help you back to bed."

Despite Bart's warning, Egana started down the stairs, going much more quickly than Bart would have expected him to move. Bart had no choice but to follow him.

"Non nago?"

"Where are you? You're in the Bizkaia House. This is where you live. Don't you remember?"

"Nor zara zu?"

"What? I don't understand what you're saying, Mr. Egana."

"Nor zara zu? Nor zara zu?" he asked, more agitatedly than before.

"He wants to know who you are," Pia said, hurrying down the stairs behind Bart.

"You know me, Mr. Egana. I'm Dr. Wilson, and we've been friends for a long time."

From the expression on Egana's face, he clearly had no idea what Bart was saying.

"Tell him what I said," Bart instructed, and Pia repeated it.

Egana began babbling fast, and even more agitatedly.

"Can you speak in English, Mr. Egana?" Bart asked.

Again, Egana spoke a long string of Euskera.

"He has no idea where he is," Pia said. "He thinks he's in Bilbao. And when I asked him to speak in English, he said he doesn't know English."

"He is still disoriented from the blow to his head."

"What's going on in there?" Floria called in Euskera.

"It's Mr. Egana, *Ama!*" Pia answered.

A moment later Floria and Zuriñe came from their rooms by the kitchen. Because they were dressed similarly to Pia, neither of them took notice of her attire, assuming that she, like them, had simply gotten up when she heard the disturbance.

"Mr. Egana is having a spell of disorientation, I'm afraid," Bart said.

"Disorientation?" Floria asked, confused by the word.

"He doesn't know where he is," Pia explained.

"Heavens! You mean he's lost his mind?"

"I don't think so. There are some other things that could be happening to him other than the blow to his head, but he had no difficulty moving around, so I don't think he's had a stroke. If we can get him back to bed and get him calmed down, I think he'll more than likely have a full recovery. Could one of you get him a warm glass of milk?"

Floria understood and moved toward the kitchen, leaving Zuriñe and Pia with Bart and Mr. Egana.

"Pia, I want you to ask Mr. Egana some questions. He doesn't seem to be able to communicate in English at all. Ask him what his name is."

"Zein da zure izena?"

"Christobol Egana."

Bart gave her a series of questions to ask, such as where was he born, could he identify the others in the room, and how old he was. He seemed able to answer all the questions to Bart's satisfaction.

"That's good; he still has his wits about him. He may never remember exactly what happened to him, and that's all right. But the fact that he can respond at all is encouraging."

Just then Floria brought in the warm milk along with a handful of crackers. "I hope the poor old man is going to be all right."

Bart led him to the table and he drank the milk and ate the crackers.

"You have very good ears, Pia. It is good that you heard him and came up from the cellar. If we had to depend on your sister, we would be out of luck," Floria said.

"She is a very sound sleeper," Pia said, hoping that there would be no other comments.

When Mr. Egana finished his snack, Bart helped him to his feet.

"Let's go back to bed."

"Why don't you go up, too, Pia. You might need to explain to him what's happening," Floria said.

Pia and Bart exchanged knowing glances.

When they had Mr. Egana back in bed, they moved into the hall and Bart took Pia in his arms.

"No, no," Pia whispered. "I know *Ama* will be waiting for me."

"That's too bad." Bart flashed a big grin. "Maybe I'd better stay here another night. Of course, you understand it's just to make certain Mr. Egana is all right."

"Of course. Good night, Bart." She stood on tiptoes and kissed him, then ran down the hallway.

As she had expected, her mother was standing at the bottom of the stairs.

"Uhmm, what's going on?" Elixabete asked sleepily. "Did I hear *Ama* and Mrs. Segura talking?"

"Mr. Egana got out of bed and started wandering around the house. We were afraid he would hurt himself, so we all went to see about him. But Dr. Wilson got him back in bed."

"Why would Mr. Egana do that? Was he looking for something?"

"Dr. Wilson said that he's a little confused because of being hit on the head. But he still thinks he'll be fine in a few days."

"I hope so." Elixabete turned over in her bed and grew quiet.

Pia lay in her bed for a long time. She couldn't explain what had just happened between her and Bart, but it had given her the greatest sense of euphoria she had ever felt. Without knowing how she knew, she recognized that what had just happened upstairs was but a presage of what was to come.

She had not heard the words *I love you* from Bart, but surely a man and a woman did not become as intimate with one another as they had just done if there was no love.

❧

Bart undressed and crawled naked into bed. Pia's scent was still on the sheets, and he longed to have her beside him to finish what they had begun. Bart had a history with women, but for all the previous encounters, he had never been through anything quite like what he had just shared with Pia. Even though the act had not been consummated, it was the most intense sexual experience he had ever felt. His blood had boiled, his skin had been on fire, and with every ounce of his being, he had wanted to possess her completely.

But he knew that this wasn't just about the sex. It was her demeanor, her intelligence, and her innocence. That innocence had initially put him off a bit, but now it was one of the things about her that he considered her strongest attraction. Pia had put herself in his hands, and it had been within his power to ravage her or to protect her.

So why was it that he wanted to do both?

At breakfast the next morning Egana seemed to be recovering. When he saw the boarded-up windows, he could remember rocks being thrown, but he didn't remember that he had gone out onto the porch to confront the rioters, and he couldn't remember that he had been struck by several thrown rocks.

"Why did I do that?" he asked. "It was foolish,"

"You were trying to protect us, and it was a very brave thing to do," Pia said.

"It was no braver than you and Elixabete going out to get him back in the house," Floria said.

"Nor any more foolish," Pia said, in both languages so that all enjoyed a laugh.

"What's going to happen to us?" Floria asked. "If those people came once, won't they come again? What would we do if they set the house on fire?"

"Rube Robbins and his men know who to look out for now," Bart said. "I think they'll be keeping an eye on them, and the likelihood of something else happening is practically nil."

Bart was trying to lessen their fears, but even as he spoke the words, he knew that the danger still existed.

"Pia, I was serious when I asked you if you would come back to work for us. Have you given it any thought?"

Pia thought back to their conversation that had been interrupted by the rock-throwing incident. She remembered that he had said he couldn't have someone work for him that he thought was married. At least not her.

She was thinking over her answer when Elixabete chimed in, "What are you waiting for? I know you want to do it, and the money is good. Tell him yes."

"Yes," Zuriñe added. "It is good. What would have happened to Mr. Egana, or to all of us, if Dr. Wilson had not come to help us?"

Bart listened as the words flew back and forth. "What are they saying?"

"When do you want me to come?" Pia asked as a grin started that she could not contain.

"Mr. Egana probably needs a nurse yet today, but how about tomorrow?"

FOURTEEN

When Pia returned to work, Bart enjoyed having her around him, and he made up things for her to do so that she was always in his presence. He knew the relationship was growing beyond the sexual attraction that they felt for one another, and he was pleased. He wanted her to grow to love him as he loved her, and except for a few stolen kisses, there was no repeat of what had happened that night at the Bizkaia House.

Left unspoken, but hanging between them almost as an animated presence, was the question of what was going to happen when Marko returned. Bart knew what he wanted to happen. He wanted to ask Pia to marry him. He knew the problem that would cause with her family, but he was perfectly prepared to make the offer to leave Boise, even to leave medicine if it came to that. They could go somewhere far away from both their families, maybe to St. Louis, or Chicago if he was accepted at Hull House.

He had made up his mind. He was going to ask her as soon as she came in to work today.

No, not today. Not yet. He was going to ask her, but he was going to wait for the right opportunity. He would know when that opportunity presented itself.

"Doc! Doc! Are you here?"

The caller was Tim O'Leary, and he came rushing into the doctor's office.

"You better come quick, Doc. It's Bustamante. He's been hurt."

"Where is he? What happened?"

"He's down at his blacksmith shop, or what's left of it. There was a mob this mornin' that damn near tore the whole shop up. They pushed over his anvil, they broke the billows over his forge, they busted out all his windows, and when he tried to stop them, they took a whip to him."

José Bustamante was a longtime and well-respected businessman in Boise. When Bart got to the blacksmith's shop, he saw Bustamante lying on the boardwalk in front of his shop. Several people were around him, including Don Walton, who was kneeling beside him.

"What I don't understand is why they come after him," Walton said. "Hell, he's Mexican, he ain't Spanish."

"He speaks Spanish," one of those in the crowd said. "Evidently, that's all some of these people need."

During the next week, Bustamante was only the first to come under attack. Amorphous groups seemed to gather spontaneously, just long enough to do damage, then they would break up and a new mob would form with different participants. That made it difficult for Marshal Robbins to get control over the situation.

Crudely made Spanish flags were hung on the door of any business that employed a Basque, and the Basque-owned businesses came under particular condemnation. The other two Basque boardinghouses in town were, like the Bizkaia, attacked by mobs, and though none were burned, windows were broken. Not even Christopher Moore, one of the wealthiest and most influential private citizens in town, was spared, since he employed both Marko and Julen. Bart found that particularly surprising because both Marko and Julen were well liked in Boise. Marko wasn't even in town now, he was in Colorado, but that didn't keep someone from hanging a Spanish flag at the bank. It was flying from the flagpole that normally flew the Stars and Stripes. The damage at the livery was the most severe. The fine carriage that Julen often drove was burned to cinders.

Then one morning just after breakfast, as Julen was leaving for work, he started yelling in anger as he stepped out onto the front porch.

Pia was almost ready to go to work herself when she heard him. "Julen, what is it?"

"Come out here and look!"

Pia stepped out onto the front porch, then felt a wave of fear sweep over her. Painted across the front porch in dripping bloodred paint were the words:

DEATH TO ALL YOU DIRTY BASCOS

"That does it," Bart said when he came down to look at the vandalism. "Keeping this boardinghouse open is not worth getting hurt over or, God forbid, something worse. All of you are going to have to get out of town, at least until some of this hostility blows over."

"We can't leave town. Where would we go?" Pia asked. "Surely it's not just Boise where people are doing these horrible things. Isn't the whole country up in arms against Spain?"

"I think you should go to the home ranch. I know it wouldn't be as comfortable as living here, but with your father and all the herders around, it would be safer."

"The shearing is going on now, and when that is finished, the men will start moving their bands up to the mountains for grazing. There'll only be a couple of men left behind to tend to the rams, so there'd be very few people to protect us out there," Pia said.

"I know where we can go," Floria said. "I have a house in Mountain Home, where I lived before I moved to Boise. It's not very big, but it's roomy enough for four women."

"And what about Mr. Egana?" Pia asked. "If we all leave, what will happen to him? And what about Julen?"

Although that had been spoken in English so Bart could understand, Pia quickly translated the conversation to her mother and sister.

"Yes," Zuriñe said. "I think we should go, and I think we should take Mr. Egana with us."

"The only reason I left was because I was lonely for someone to speak Euskera to, but this time I won't be all alone," Floria said. "We will be comfortable there, I think."

Because they had switched their language to Euskera, Bart couldn't tell what they were saying, but from the tone of the conversation he gathered that his suggestion was amenable to all.

"When should we leave?" Pia asked.

"We'll take the afternoon train," Bart said.

"We?"

"Yes, *we*. I'm going with you. I don't intend to let you out of my sight until I know you're safe. Until you are all safe," he amended. "Pack only the bare essentials. I'll tell my father what is happening, and then I'll be back to get you about one o'clock. Can you be ready?"

"I don't think we have any choice," Pia said dismally.

"I don't know," Frank said. "I'm not sure you should get mixed up in all this."

"It's too late, Pop, I'm already mixed up in it," Bart said.

"I know you feel a sense of obligation to them, but they are just your patients, after all. And I can understand that you might want to see them off safely, but why would you feel it necessary to actually make the trip? Once they get out of Boise, it's unlikely that anything will happen to them."

"Unlikely isn't good enough."

"What do you mean, it isn't good enough? You can't personally guarantee their safety."

"I can, and I will."

"Why? Why do you feel that such involvement is necessary?"

"Because I am going to marry Pia Carranza."

Frank lowered his head and pinched the bridge of his nose. "I was afraid it was something like that."

"I've not tried to hide it."

"No, you certainly haven't. But, Bart, you know how these people are."

"These people, Pop? *These people?* They aren't these people. They are individuals with their own names and personalities."

"I didn't mean it like that. I just meant that . . . well, don't they normally marry inside their own coterie?"

"Yes."

"Then, what hope do you have of marrying a Basque woman?"

"I don't know. Maybe nothing more than hope. But I'm going to hang on to that."

"You are doing all this, and you haven't even asked her?"

"Not yet."

"How do you know she'll even have you?"

"I don't know. But that's not going to stop me from asking."

When Bart returned to the Bizkaia House, he was, once again, wearing his pistol, and he had $427, money left over from the $500 his grandfather had given him six months earlier. He didn't know what he might need it for, but he thought it was a good idea to have it with him, just in case.

Julen already had a wagon backed up to the front porch and was loading the baggage. Bart had carried his own luggage, a suitcase plus two medical bags. Egana was sitting on the front porch with his legs dangling over the edge.

"*Ez dut utzi,*" he said resolutely. Then when he saw Bart, he repeated in English, "I'm not going."

"Why not?" Bart asked. "If everyone is gone, who will cook your meals for you?"

"I am not a coward to run away in the night," Egana insisted.

"Mr. Egana, nobody thinks you're a coward. Did you not go out onto the front porch and face down the mob the night they broke out the windows?"

"I did?"

"You did. You stood right there on that porch and called out to them, challenging them to send up their champion for you to fight. But they didn't do that. Instead, like the cowards they were, they threw rocks." Bart knew that Egana didn't remember a thing about that night, and a little bolstering up right now was exactly what was needed.

"Yes." Egana put his hand to his head. "They threw rocks."

"So you can see, if you defended the ladies then, why I'm counting on you to defend them again. Do you think I would send them to Mountain Home if I didn't think you would be there to take care of them?"

"Yes," Egana said, nodding happily. "Yes, I will go and I will take care of them."

"I knew I could count on you. You are a good man."

All four ladies came out then, each carrying a small valise. When Bart saw that Zuriñe's bag was tied with a rope, he was sure this was what they had brought from Guernica, and he was struck by the enormity of the sacrifices they had made to come to America. Now, through no fault of their own, they were being forced to move again. For many reasons, he hoped that they would not have to stay long in Mountain Home. He hoped that when they did decide to return to Boise, they would still have a house to come home to.

Egana climbed up on the driver's seat beside Julen, while the four women and Bart rode in the back of the wagon with the baggage. When they reached the depot, Julen jumped down and began unloading.

"What are you going to do, Julen?" Bart asked.

"Mr. Moore has said I can come there if I need to, but I think I should stay and watch over the Bizkaia House."

"That's noble, Julen, but don't risk your life to save it. If you need to get away, you know my place is just two blocks down the alley. Run if you have to, do you understand?"

"I do." As Julen's eyes began to water, he extended his hand to Bart. "I thank you for your friendship."

Julen then told the women good-bye, shaking hands with each of them.

"Old man, take care of yourself," he said to Egana, and then climbed into the wagon and rode away.

"Mr. Egana, you stand guard over these while we go inside. Will you do that for me?" Bart asked as he set his medical bags down.

Egana nodded and smiled.

Bart came back outside first. "Mr. Egana, I've got your—" Bart stopped in midsentence because two men were haranguing Egana, shoving him back and forth between them like kicking a ball.

"Where are you goin'? You goin' to sink another American ship?" one of them said, giving him a shove.

"Hey, don't be runnin' into me," the other said, laughing as he grabbed Egana and pushed him back."

"Stop!" Egana said. *"Utzi pakean!"*

"'Oozi pookie'? What does that mean?" one of the two men asked.

"It means look out!" Bart said, grabbing the man by the shoulder, jerking him around, then landing a punch squarely on his jaw, knocking him down.

"Why you son of a—!" the other man shouted, reaching for his gun.

"I don't think you want to do that," Bart said, drawing his pistol before the haranguing cowboy was able to get his pistol even halfway out of the holster.

"This ain't none of your business, mister," one of the cowboys said. "We're just funning with this old Basco. He's a likin' it."

"I don't think so. Mr. Egana, you step over here." Bart cocked his pistol. "Now, which one of you wants to have some fun?"

"We didn't mean nothin' by it," the cowboy said.

"Then I'm going to ask you to pull your pistol out with only your thumb and forefinger," Bart said, "and lay it here on the bench."

Nervously, the cowboy did as he was directed.

"Now reach down there and get your friend's gun."

Again, the young man complied.

By now several other passengers had noticed the commotion, and Mr. McGraw, the stationmaster, came out to see what was going on.

"Abe, would you mind taking these two guns into the depot and holding them there until after the train leaves?" Bart asked. "Otherwise I might have to shoot one or both of them."

"Now, there ain't no need of you worryin' none about that," the nervous cowboy said. "Me 'n' Carney here will just go on our way. We'll come back and get our guns after the train is gone."

Carney, the man Bart had knocked down, was just now getting up, rubbing his chin. "What happened?"

"You fell," Bart said, and a couple of the waiting passengers who had seen the whole incident laughed. He was glad that Pia and the others had not seen this. He hoped that Mountain Home would be better.

"Let's not tell anybody what happened." He put his finger to his lips, and Egana nodded.

A moment later the women came out of the depot.

"We have the tickets," Pia said, smiling.

"Good. We should be there before nightfall."

"Here comes the train!" someone shouted, and looking west, they saw the train backing into the station.

∽∾∽

Once they boarded, they found it was quite crowded. Because Pia and Bart were the last to get on, the only available seats were two at the front of the coach. Pia was glad that their seat was separated from those of the other four; it would give them the opportunity to talk without having to be so guarded. As the train started, she felt Bart's hand on the seat between them, and she reached her own hand down to grasp it.

They rode in silence for some time, then Bart said, "You're awfully quiet. What are you thinking about?"

"How long we're going to have to stay in Mountain Home and how much I'm going to miss you."

"I'm going to miss you, too, and I don't mean just at the office."

Pia's smile was radiant. This was the closest Bart had ever come to telling her he cared for her.

"Would you miss living at the Bizkaia House?" Bart asked.

"Oh, Bart, do you think something will happen to it while we are gone?"

"I have no way of knowing. I hope not, but even if it's still there, would you miss it?"

"Do you think I would miss sleeping in the cellar in the same room with my sister? I don't think so."

"What's going to happen when Marko gets back?"

"We've heard from Father Ignacio, and he's chosen two women to be the brides for Dabi and Luken, but he doesn't have one for Nikola yet."

"Then does that mean you won't have the big wedding with all five men getting married together?"

"Only three will be getting married." Pia held her breath, waiting for Bart's reaction.

"Would you want to get married?"

"Would I want to get married? Bart . . . I . . . I thought . . ."

"What did you think?"

"I thought you'd be happy that I wasn't marrying Marko."

"Who said anything about Marko? I asked you if you would want to get married."

Pia's eyes opened wide as the realization of what Bart was saying penetrated. "Well, now, that depends on who is asking me."

"I'm asking," Bart said, turning in the seat and looking directly into her eyes. "Pia, will you marry me?"

"Before I answer, I have to know—do you love me?"

"I love you with all my heart and soul, Pia. I want you by my side for now and forever." He leaned closer and kissed her without regard to where they were or who saw them."

Pia put her arms around him. "Yes, I will marry you!" And they kissed again.

Zuriñe had been watching Pia and Dr. Wilson from her seat back in the car. She studied the animated expressions on Pia's face, and she realized that this wasn't the first time she had seen that. Anytime Dr. Wilson was around, Pia could hardly take her eyes off him, and he seemed to feel the same way about her.

Obviously there were feelings between them. Zuriñe didn't know a lot about love, but if there was such a thing, was that what Pia and Bart shared?

She had been Sabin's wife for twenty-six years, and she had borne him two children. She had lived in Guernica and he had lived in America for half their married life. When she had first greeted him in Boise, it was like greeting any other boarder, not the man who was her husband.

During the holidays, Sabin had shared her bed, but they had not shared their bodies. She had thought it strange because, at forty-three, many women her age still bore their husband's children.

While she was thinking these thoughts, Zuriñe saw what was happening between Bart and Pia. She saw them kiss, not once but twice, and Pia looked happy. If Pia loved Bart, would it be fair to Marko to make them marry, just because Sabin and Lander had decided that was how it was going to be?

No. If she had any influence over her husband, she would try to get him to change his mind. Her daughter would not have the same kind of marriage that she had.

"Floria," Zuriñe said.

Floria had been looking through the window at the passing countryside. "Yes?"

"I want you to watch Pia and Dr. Wilson."

"What will I see?"

"Nothing that you haven't already seen, if you're honest with yourself," Zuriñe said.

For a long moment, Floria watched Pia and Bart. She saw the smiles, the shining eyes, the vibrancy of their private conversation.

"Yes," she said, nodding. "I've seen it."

"Pia cannot marry Marko. She doesn't love him, and I don't think he loves her."

"What is love? Do you love Sabin? Do I love Lander?"

"Sabin and I have had a comfortable marriage, and you and Lander have had the same. But does your heart leap when you see him?"

Floria was quiet for a moment. "No," she admitted.

"For Pia, and for Dr. Wilson, there is something between them—like a rainbow after a thunderstorm, like flowers in the meadow, something that is different from anything that you or I, or anyone we know, has ever felt. I don't want Pia to lose this. And I don't think you want Marko to lose that either. You have said yourself that Marko is more American than he is *euskaldunak*. Maybe he wants to choose his own wife."

"What you say is true."

"If Dr. Wilson asks Pia to marry him, I think she should say yes."

"What will Sabin say?"

"I don't know," Zuriñe said pensively. "I don't know."

They changed trains in Nampa, taking the eastbound toward Mountain Home. This time the train was less crowded and the six had seats closer to each other, with Bart and Pia being directly across the aisle from the others.

A porter, wearing a starched white jacket, came through the car, striking a three-note chime. "Dinner is now being served in the dining car," he said in a melodious and easily heard voice. He repeated the chimes. "Dinner is now being served in the dining car."

Bart leaned across the aisle to address Floria and the others. "I've been your guest so often at the Bizkaia House, will you be my guests for dinner tonight?"

"To eat in the dining car would be wonderful!" Pia said, then repeated Bart's invitation to the others.

"Do you remember on our trip here how some people ate in the dining car while we had to get off the train and scramble for our meals? Bart wants to buy our dinner in the dining car."

"Yes!" Elixabete said excitedly.

"But won't that cost a lot of money?" Floria asked in English.

"I want to do it," Bart replied with a smile. "And besides, my grandpa will be paying for it. He gave me some money, and I think this would be a good time to use it."

After a quick consultation with Zuriñe, Floria looked back toward Bart and Pia with a big smile. "Yes, we would like that."

Pia was impressed with the dining car. On each side of the car tables were covered with crisp white cloths, and each table had a vase with a fresh flower in it. Glistening silver was already in place.

The center aisle was covered with a rose-colored carpet, and the walls between the windows were of rich mahogany. On each wall between the windows was an electric light with a milk-glass tulip lampshade. They were met by a white-jacketed waiter, who, seeing the six of them, pushed two tables together so that they could all sit together.

"Would you care for some wine?" the waiter asked.

"I think a bottle of red wine would be appropriate," Bart replied.

They decided that Bart should order for the group, and he perused the menu for a moment.

"We'll start with a cup of consommé," Bart said. "Then for our main course we'll have roast sirloin of beef with horseradish, green peas, and baked potato. And for dessert, the bread pudding with brandy sauce looks good."

"Excellent choice, sir," the waiter replied with a broad smile. He soon returned with the bottle of wine and poured each of them a glass.

"What shall we drink to?" Pia asked, picking up her glass. "Perhaps we should drink to a safe journey."

"How about to our friendship?" Bart asked. "And for a safe trip, too."

Their food was delivered more quickly than Pia would have thought, and for the next several minutes the diners enjoyed their meal, saying little more than appreciation and acclaim for the quality of the food.

Then, as dessert was being served, Floria looked across the table at Pia. "Pia, I'm going to speak in English because I don't want your family to know what I am saying."

Pia, disconcerted by Floria's comment, laid her fork down and looked at Mrs. Segura anxiously.

Floria held up her hand. "Don't be alarmed. I want to ask you some questions, and I want you to answer me truthfully."

"All right," Pia answered hesitantly.

"Do you plan to marry Marko?"

Instinctively, Bart reached for Pia's hand.

"Mrs. Segura, I . . ."

"Let me ask it this way. Do you want to marry Marko?"

"No, I don't."

"And what about Marko? Does he want to marry you?"

"He would if he is forced to—but neither of us wants to marry each other."

"He has told me as much," Floria said, "though he has not spoken to his father. Do you intend to marry?"

Pia looked to Bart, who, like Pia, was following Floria's comments, as was Egana, who could speak enough English to understand the gist of the conversation. Zuriñe couldn't understand the words, but she could understand the substance of the conversation. Only Elixabete continued to eat her dessert, unaware of the drama that was being played out.

"Is it Dr. Wilson? Is he the one you want to marry?"

"Yes," Pia said.

"Your father is going to be very much against this. He will say a Basque only marries a Basque."

"I know that." Pia then switched to Euskera so that her mother could follow what she was about to say. "Bart loves me as I love him. He has asked me to marry him, and I have given my word that I will. I know *Aita* will not be pleased with me, just as I know that Marko will give me his best wishes." Pia looked directly at Zuriñe. "It is my wish, *Ama*, that you will give me your blessing."

"It isn't *my* blessing that you need, Pia."

"I know, but I would feel better if I knew that you were not my enemy in this."

"My daughter, I am not your enemy."

Tears came to Pia's eyes, and she reached across the table to take her mother's hand and lifted it to her lips. "Thank you, *Ama*. From the bottom of my heart, I thank you."

"Your mother has given us her blessing?" Bart asked.

"Yes," Pia said. Zuriñe had not specifically given her blessing, but that she had said she was not Pia's enemy was blessing enough.

"Will this stop Gorka from marrying me?" Elixabete asked, her chin trembling.

"Of course not," Floria said. "At least one of my boys is going to marry a Carranza, and Gorka is very pleased to take you as his bride."

A broad smile of happiness spread across Elixabete's face. "Then, my sister, you have my blessing in your marriage as well. I hope that *Aita* will allow it, and that you will be very happy."

"Thank you, Elixabete." What Pia didn't say was that she was now determined to marry Bart, with or without her father's permission.

FIFTEEN

They made it to Mountain Home and Floria's vacant house before dark. Even though the house had not been lived in for the past five years, it had been maintained because men coming and going from the home ranch often stayed there when they came into town for supplies or before making the trip to Boise.

The house was cold, but Bart soon had a fire going in the big potbellied stove. There were only three rooms and a sleeping loft that was open to the one big room that served as the kitchen, dining room, and sitting room. Floria and Zuriñe shared one room, giving the other to Mr. Egana, while Pia and Elixabete were in the loft. Since Bart only planned to stay for one night, he slept on the daybed in the great room.

Bart would have loved to have had a few moments with Pia after their momentous day, but the sleeping arrangements and the circumstances didn't allow it. It was just as well, because everyone was exhausted.

When they awoke the next morning, Bart volunteered to go to the general store to get foodstuffs that would augment the tinned staples that Lander kept on hand. Bart intended to buy bacon, eggs, flour, and coffee, which would get them through breakfast, and then Floria and Zuriñe could stock up on the things they would need for their stay.

When Bart started out toward the store, the first thing he saw was a big sign across the front of a saloon.

SPANIARDS NOT SERVED HERE!

Though this refusal of service in a saloon would have no direct effect on any of the people he had brought to Mountain Home, it indicated that Boise wasn't the only place to be struck with anti-Spanish bias. He wondered if that included Basques as well because in this area sheepherding was important to the local economy.

"Yes, sir, eggs, bacon, flour, and coffee," the storekeeper said, putting all the purchases into a paper sack. "Nine cents for the eggs, ten cents for the bacon, five cents for a pound of flour, and ten cents for a pound of coffee. That'll be thirty-four cents."

"Here you are," Bart said, counting out the money.

"Prices are high enough now, but it looks to me like we're about to get into a war. And if that happens, why, it's Katy bar the door, because prices are more 'n' likely goin' to go sky-high. I wouldn't be surprised if we don't wind up havin' to charge fifteen or maybe twenty cents for eggs, and who knows how much for coffee? Most of the coffee comes from Spain, you know."

"Spain? I thought it came from South America."

"Well, they all speak Spanish down there, don't they? It's the same thing. If you ask me, we should run ever' damn one of them Spanish, Mexicans, and Bascos out of our country."

Bart didn't answer the clerk. Instead, he picked up his sack, bought a newspaper, then walked back to the house.

"Is there any place out at the home ranch where you could stay?" Bart asked Floria when he returned.

"Not really. That's why I was never out there, even when I lived here. Why do you ask, Bart?"

"I got a paper at the store, and the headline says it all." Bart laid the paper on the table.

SPAIN SENDS THREE FLEETS OF WARSHIPS ACROSS THE ATLANTIC

POSSIBILITY OF WAR IS NOW ALL BUT CERTAIN

SENATOR EUGENE HALE OF MAINE SAYS WAR CANNOT BE AVOIDED

Pia read the headlines aloud.

"Oh!" Elixabete said. "Do you think people will find us here, like they did in Boise?"

Pia translated the question.

"It's different here in Mountain Home," Bart said. "Everybody knows the Basques are honest and hardworking, and that they spend their money here. But I think it might be a good idea if they know at the home ranch that you're here. I think I'll hire a wagon and ride out to tell either Sabin or Lander. And besides, I can check on Wilson and see how he's getting along."

"I want to go, too," Pia said. "I want to see Gabina, and I want . . . I want to see *Aita*."

The drive from Mountain Home to the home ranch took half a day. When they arrived, shearing was in full swing, and it seemed like organized chaos. Thousands of sheep were bleating, and scores of men were shouting back and forth . . . mostly in Spanish, as nearly all the shearers were Mexican.

"Harris! Harris!" Dabi was yelling when they arrived. "Take a group down to the south chute! We're going to open that one up!"

"All right," Harris replied. He was the American in charge of the shearers. The shearers weren't employees of Segura's, but were an independent team working for Jim Harris, who had the shearing contract. Dabi, who normally acted as the camp tender to the herders, was now overseeing all the docking of the tails, the castrating of the male lambs, and the branding with paint as well as the shearing.

Dabi looked up just as the spring wagon carrying Bart and Pia drove up and smiled. "Well, look what the cat drug in. You just had to come see how your namesake's getting along."

"That's one of the reasons we're here," Bart said. "How are Gabina and Wilson doing?"

Dabi smiled. "Estebe says his wife is ordering him about. And when the baby is hungry, everyone in the camp knows it. His crying would put a coyote to shame."

"Well, that's a good sign. We'll go see them in a minute."

"Pia, is Marko back?" Dabi asked.

"No, he wasn't there when we left Boise."

"For all the education that boy has, he sure doesn't put it to much use. We haven't heard one word from him since he went to Colorado. But I thought for sure you'd get a letter from him."

"No, nothing," Pia said.

"Is Gabina still in your cabin?" Bart asked, wanting to extricate Pia from the conversation.

"No, they're in Estebe's wagon. It's the third one in the first row," Dabi said, pointing in the direction of the standing sheep wagons.

When they reached the wagon, Bart tapped lightly on the door, and Pia called out in Euskera, "Gabina? It's Pia and Dr. Wilson. May we come in?"

"*Bai!* Come in. Come and see my healthy baby!"

Bart opened the door, then followed Pia into the cramped wagon. Gabina was sitting on the bed holding the baby.

"Here," Bart said, taking little Wilson and cradling him in his arms. He was rewarded with a movement of Wilson's lips that Bart insisted was a smile. "You're a fine, healthy little fellow, and I know someone who wants to hold you." He handed the baby to Pia. "Tell Gabina I want to examine her incision."

Gabina lifted her shirtwaist and lowered the top of her skirt so he could examine the incision. It seemed to be healing well, with no sign of infection. "Tell her I've brought her some more soap, and to use it to make certain she keeps the incision clean, but all looks well."

They spent a few more minutes with Gabina, asking questions about her care and about the baby, and all seemed to be well. Gabina continued to thank both Pia and Bart for delivering her baby, never once realizing how close both of them had come to death.

When they left the wagon, Bart took Pia's hand in his. "Seeing that makes it all worthwhile. Sometimes I wonder why I'm a doctor . . . but then there's something like this."

"You mean a miracle?"

"You could say that, but I've got an even bigger one."

"What's that?"

"That I found you." He squeezed her hand.

They went back to the shearing shed in search of Dabi.

"What are they doing?" Bart asked when he saw him with several other men.

"The raw wool is very dirty when it's first sheared," Pia said. "It's sweaty and it has all kinds of sticks and vegetation caught in it, so it has to be bathed several times. They put soap and soda ash in the water."

When Dabi saw them, he walked over to meet them. "What did you think of the baby? Is he not the loudest baby you have ever heard?"

"He didn't cry for me," Pia said. "I held him, and he was very contented."

"It's because you're a woman," Dabi said.

"We're here to see Sabin. Do you know where he is?" Bart asked.

"You're too late," Dabi said. "Sabin's band was sheared last week and he's already moved them out. Is something wrong?"

"Well, yes and no," Bart said. "Out here you may not know it, but an American ship was sunk in the Havana harbor."

"Let me guess. They're saying the Spaniards did it."

"Yes, and in the paper I bought this morning, they're saying Spain is sending warships."

"I'm glad we're not in Spain. They'd start conscripting the Basques first, just because they know we'd give anything if we could have our own country," Dabi said.

"Unfortunately, there are some people in Boise who don't recognize the difference between a Basque and a Spaniard," Bart said. "So the sentiment against Basques is getting a little intense. There was a—demonstration of sorts—at the Bizkaia House the other day."

"And that's why we're here," Pia said. "We've closed the boardinghouse for a while and we've come to stay at your mother's house in Mountain Home."

"How bad was the demonstration?"

"They threw some rocks, broke out some windows, and spread kerosene on the porch, but Rube got there in time to stop it before they lit their torches. Mr. Egana went out to try and stop it, and they threw rocks at him."

"Was he hurt?" Dabi asked, concerned.

"He had a rough night the first night," Bart said, "but he seems to be fine now. He's in Mountain Home, too."

"I don't understand. We've gotten along so well all the time we've lived in Boise. Do you think it will come to a war?"

"If we're to believe what the papers say, it could well be. At first there were reports that they thought there was an explosion on board the *Maine*, but now everything I read seems to point to a torpedo," Bart said. "I'd really like to tell Sabin. Do you have any idea where his camp is?"

"He left last week, and the snow hasn't melted enough to take his band on up the mountain, so I expect he's holding them in the midlevel range right now. There's water and grass available there."

"If we wanted to find him, about how far would we have to go?"

"He's probably no more than thirty or forty miles away. Go until you get almost to the mountains. Then, when you start going up, you'll see piles of rock about a mile apart. I'd say Sabin is somewhere around the fifth rock boy or so. He'll be easy to find, he's got a band of a thousand freshly shorn sheep and each one's got a baby. If you don't see them, just listen."

"It's a little late in the day to start out now, but if we got an early start, we could probably get out there and back in one day. Is there a place where we can sleep?"

"Yes, Pia can have my cabin," Dabi said, "and you and I can sleep in the cookshack."

They all retired early, not only because Bart and Pia would have a long drive ahead of them the next morning, but also because Dabi and Estebe would have a full and busy day shearing the sheep.

After Pia said good-night to everyone, Bart walked her to Dabi's cabin.

"I wish you could come in," Pia said.

Bart chuckled. "So do I. I thought about telling Dabi our news, but until we talk with your father, I don't think we should tell anyone else. And as long as Dabi thinks he's looking out for Marko's interests, I'd better get back to the cookshack or he'll come looking for me."

"You're right, but that doesn't mean I'm not going to dream about you."

"On the other hand, here in the dark, with nobody to see us, there's no reason I can't kiss you good-night."

"You haven't always been so careful about whether there was light or not. I seem to recall you kissing me under the lamplight on Christmas Eve. You kissed me while the man my father had just told me I was going to marry was being congratulated."

"I did, didn't I? Do you recall, was it a good kiss?"

"Yes."

"Was it as good as this one?"

Bart cupped her cheeks in his hands, then pulled her face toward him. She parted her lips against his, and he felt the hot satin of her tongue darting into his mouth, seeking his. The kiss was hot and slow and long, and it grew until it began to take control of each of them. Bart dropped his hand to her hip. Even through her clothing he could feel the heat of her body and the quivering of her insides, and he knew that her trembling was due only partly to the chill of the night air.

As Pia gave herself up to the depths of the kiss,

she realized that she was totally pliant in his hands, subservient to his will, spinning into a bottomless vortex. When Bart pulled her to him, Pia could feel an intrusive hardness pressing against her. There was no mystery about what it was; she had seen it when she had gone to his room. She pressed herself against it as hard as she could, feeling a charge of excitement, a promise of something more, something much greater than the pleasure she was experiencing now.

Involuntarily, it seemed, Pia reached her hand down to stroke that bulging presence, and though she was feeling it through his trousers, she remembered, with a sensual-laden excitation, how it had felt when nothing was between her bare fingers and that naked, pulsating hot skin.

At last they came up for breath, and when she looked at him, even though it was too dark to see her clearly, Bart had but to call up the picture of her face in his mind—the deep, dark, shining eyes, the long, flowing lashes, the high cheekbones, the perfectly formed nose, and the graceful sweep of her dark brown hair.

"Good night, my love," Bart said.

"I wish we—"

"I know." Bart put his thumb on her lips. "But we don't want Dabi to come look for me, do we?"

"No, not tonight."

"Get some sleep. It will be a long, hard ride tomorrow."

Bart waited until she was inside with the door closed before he started back through the darkness to the cookshack. He walked slowly to give himself time to cool down. It wouldn't do to be seen by anyone at this very moment.

As was normal for him when he was out with his sheep, Sabin Carranza awakened before daybreak. He got dressed, then stepped outside to relieve himself.

"Esti, Bekindi, where are you?" he called. "Why are you not here to tell me good morning?"

It was still cold, and he reached in through the open door of his sheep wagon to grab his coat. The coat, with its sheepskin lining, kept him warm even in the coldest weather.

"Where are my dogs?" he called.

Esti came running up to him.

"Ha! I thought you would come around when it was time to eat. All right, come on."

Esti didn't come to him. Instead she stayed about ten yards away from him.

"Esti, what is it? Where is Bekindi?"

Esti turned and ran for several feet, then stopped and came back toward Sabin.

"What is it? What's wrong? Bekindi!" he called. "Bekindi, where are you?"

He heard Bekindi's bark, then he looked back at Esti. "All right, Esti, if you want me to come with you, I will."

Sabin followed after Esti, who broke into a trot.

"Wait a minute, slow down here," Sabin called. "I'm not a young man; I can't keep up with you when you run so fast. If you want me to follow you, slow down."

Esti did slow down and they continued on, Bekindi's bark getting louder until, about a mile from the wagon, Sabin saw the dog. Bekindi was standing on a precipice looking down into a draw.

"What is it, Bekindi? What's down there?"

Bekindi ran to Sabin, then turned around and ran back to the edge of the draw, barking all the while.

When Sabin got there and looked down, he saw a ewe with its lamb about twenty feet below. The wall was steep, but not sheer, and Sabin was certain the ewe could make it up by herself, but she wouldn't leave her lamb, who couldn't make the climb.

"All right, let me see what I can do," Sabin said. "I think I can help your baby, but you're going to have to get out by yourself."

Sabin got down on his hands and knees to look for a way down. He saw a few ledges, and some protruding junipers that would provide him with handholds.

"All right, dogs, you stay here, both of you," he said. "I'll go down and get the little fellow."

Sabin began climbing down the side of the draw. A few of the ledges were loose dirt and didn't give him as much of a foothold as he'd expected, but slowly, carefully, and grabbing on to the vegetation, he finally made it safely to the bottom.

"All right, let's take a look at you," he said to the lamb. He picked the lamb up gently and ran his hands all over it in examination. "It seems like you're just fine, so let's see what I can do about getting you back to the band."

Holding the lamb under one arm, Sabin began climbing up the side of the draw. It was much more difficult going up than it had been coming down, primarily because he could use only one hand. Then, just as he was almost to the top, he reached out to grab a small juniper. He felt it was strong enough because he had used it on his descent.

This time the juniper uprooted, and Sabin felt the sickening sensation of falling. He let go of the lamb and began flailing against the wall, trying to find something to grab.

He hit the bottom hard, twisting as he came down. He felt a sharp pain shoot through his leg and knew that he had broken it.

"Ahh!" he said, lying on his back in the bottom of the draw, the little lamb bleating beside him.

He lay there for several minutes, feeling the throbbing pain in his leg. Finally he forced himself to move and tried to climb the side of the draw. The pain was too intense, and he lacked the strength to pull himself up with his arms alone.

"What good would it do me if I could make it to the top?" he said, speaking aloud so he could hear a human voice, even if it was only his own. "I couldn't make it back to my wagon."

The lamb continued to bleat, and he drew it to him, hoping to give it comfort.

He was quiet for a long moment and heard both of his dogs whining. Looking up, he saw their anxious heads peering over the edge of the draw, staring down at him.

"You two stay with the flock. Keep them together," he said. "The camp tender will be here in a few days, and he'll take care of you. There's no need for all of us to die."

The dogs continued to whine, but the little lamb lay down beside him.

SIXTEEN

Bart and Pia left at daybreak. The camp tender said that since they were visiting Sabin, they could save him the trip, and he filled the buckboard with supplies.

The bright, sunny day became warmer than they had expected.

"Pia, before we talk to your father, I want you to be absolutely sure you want to marry me," Bart said. "What will you do if he says no?"

"I love you, Bart. What more can I say?"

Bart smiled and lifted her hand to his lips. "To me, nothing could be more important."

They drove for another half hour, then began to hear the clanging of the bells and the bleating of sheep.

"We must be close," Bart said.

"There's his wagon down by the spring," Pia said, pointing. "But I don't see *Aita*. Maybe he's inside fixing a bite to eat."

"Are you nervous?"

Pia nodded. "I won't lie to you. I'm nervous, but

I'm also resolute." She smiled. "Resolute. I remember Father Ignacio making me learn that word, and it says exactly how I feel. I am firmly resolved and determined to marry you, Bart Wilson, whether *Aita* approves or not."

Bart kissed her lightly, then stopped the wagon and set the brake.

"*Aita! Aita*, where are you?" Pia called. Hopping down, she climbed up the three steps, then opened the door to the sheep wagon and looked inside. "He's not here."

"He can't be too far away because the sheep are here," Bart said. "Help me unload and then we'll drive around and look for him. Like as not, he'll see us before we see him."

Before they had the wagon completely unloaded, a dog came running up to them.

"There's Esti," Pia said. "Did *Aita* send you to welcome us?" She bent down to pet Esti, but the dog started barking and then ran away.

"That's funny. I wonder why Esti didn't greet me?"

Esti returned, barked, and ran away again.

"*Aita! Aita*, where are you?" Pia called.

Esti returned.

"I think she wants us to follow her," Bart said.

Pia started out following the dog, but Bart called her back.

"Let's take the wagon. He may be farther away than we think."

Pia climbed in, and Esti barked continuously until they followed. She loped ahead, turning back frequently to make sure they were still behind her.

"Pia, give that call. See if your father answers it."

Pia cupped her hands around her mouth, then gave the high, warbling yodel.

Then they heard it, the *irrintzi* being returned. But it wasn't high and strong, but weak and troubled.

"Something's wrong, Bart!" Pia said, her voice reflecting her fear.

"Yell again."

Again, Pia gave the call, and again it was answered.

"I think it came from that way," Bart said. "On the other side of the flock."

"You drive," Pia said. "I'll get the sheep out of the way."

Pia jumped down and started separating the sheep, sometimes having to physically push them aside. As the buckboard moved through the flock, the curious sheep closed back behind it so that Bart was totally surrounded by bleating animals.

Again Pia yelled, and again she was answered.

Finally they got through the sheep and found the other dog standing at the edge of a ravine. Bekindi was barking.

"Laguntza, jaitsi dut!"

"He has fallen!" Pia said.

Jumping down from the buckboard, Bart followed Pia, and they hurried to where Bekindi was standing. About twenty feet down, they saw Sabin lying on his back with a lamb standing nearby.

"Aita, what happened?"

"I came down to get the lamb, and on the way up I fell. I think I have broken my leg."

"Bart is here with me."

"Dr. Wilson?"

"Yes."

As Bart started down the slope, the rocks began to give way. He stopped his fall by grabbing one of the junipers.

"Bart, be careful!"

When he reached the bottom, Bart did a quick examination of Sabin and could easily tell that he had a compound fracture.

"We've got to get you out of here and back to town," Bart said.

"I don't know how you're going to do that. I can't climb up that wall, and you can't carry me."

"Do you have a rope?"

"Yes, it's on the back of the sheep wagon near Zaldi's oats," Sabin said. "Do you have any water?"

"Yes, we have water, and there's some food. I'll get it down to you."

Bart climbed back up the side of the draw. "He has a compound fracture of the tibia," he said when he got to the top.

"What does that mean?"

"The tibia is the shinbone." Bart pointed it out to Pia. "And it's not only broken, but the end piece is protruding through the skin. We need to get him someplace where I can treat him."

"How are we going to get him out of there?"

"I'm going back to the wagon to get a rope." Bart grabbed the water canteen and the knapsack that still had some bread and cheese from their trip. "I'm going to take this down to him before I go."

"I can do that."

"All right, but be careful. I can see how he fell; those rocks start sliding with the least movement."

Bart stayed until Pia was safely at the bottom with her father, then, with a wave, he left and headed back toward Sabin's wagon with the horse at a rapid trot.

"Here you are," Pia said, handing the water to her father.

Before he took a drink, he cupped his hands. "Pour some of the water for me."

Pia did as she was told, and the lamb drank first. Pia smiled. A herder took care of his sheep first, then himself.

When the lamb had drunk its fill, Sabin took several swallows of water, then started on the bread and cheese.

"What are you doing here?" Sabin asked.

"We came to see you, and to tell you we have closed the Bizkaia House and come to the Segura house in Mountain Home."

"What? Who gave you permission to do that?"

Pia told her father about the mob attack on the Bizkaia House and the sign that had been painted across it. "They are insane, *Aita*. They don't know the difference between the Spanish and the Basque. Bart thinks the United States will go to war with Spain very soon."

Sabin let out a long sigh. "We Basques just can't get away from the Spanish no matter where we go."

"How do you feel?"

"My leg hurts, though not as much as before." He was quiet for a long moment. "I thought I was going to die."

"It's lucky we came when we did. Esti led us to you."

"Esti is a good dog. So is Bekindi. When you're out here, all alone, they are wonderful friends."

They were quiet for a long moment, then Sabin said, "Have you heard from Marko?"

"No."

"Neither has Lander. He's very upset with Marko."

"Why is that?"

"Lander thinks Marko should be in Boise. He should be getting acquainted with you."

"I don't think Marko wants to marry me."

"We have talked, and Lander and I think that, too. Lander says he made a mistake with Marko. He thought giving him an education would be good, but now Marko thinks like an American. We think you should marry Dabi, now."

"*Aita*, I don't want to marry Dabi."

"Daughter, you have to marry someone. You will turn twenty-three on your birthday, and you must bear children soon."

"I want to marry someone else."

"Who? Is it Julen? Julen is a very good man and would make a good husband for you."

"No, *Aita*, it isn't Julen. It is someone else, and I have come to ask your blessing."

"If it isn't Julen, and it isn't one of the Segura brothers, then I know of no other eligible men. How can I give my blessing for a marriage to someone I don't know?"

"You know him, *Aita*. You know him very well."

Sabin was quiet for a long moment, then said, "I don't want to speak of this now. I am in great pain."

"I'm sorry, *Aita*. Of course, we will not speak of it until later. Rest your head on my lap. I think you'll be more comfortable that way."

Pia moved so that she could hold her father's head in her lap, and after a few moments he went to sleep. Pia looked up and saw both Esti and Bekindi looking down anxiously.

"I am with him," Pia said to the dogs. "You need not worry. The best thing you can do for *Aita* is watch the sheep."

Both dogs disappeared, and Pia was alone with her father. She listened to his somewhat labored breathing and hoped that, while he was asleep, the pain would be less. She knew that he knew exactly whom she was talking about when she'd said she wanted to marry someone else. And though he didn't give his blessings, neither did he come out and forbid it. Pia held on to the hope that it was a good sign.

A few minutes later she heard Esti and Bekindi barking. "*Aita*, I think Bart is back."

Sabin opened his eyes.

"How is he doing?" Bart asked when he appeared overhead.

"He's been sleeping."

"That's good."

Bart stepped over to the buckboard and pulled up one of the sideboards that was held in place by stakes and iron collars. When he got the board out, he looked it over. It wasn't as long or as wide as it should be, but it would have to do. He needed a brace for Sabin to pull him up.

When Bart returned to the top of the gully, he had the sideboard tied to the rope. "Pia, I'm going to lower this down to you. When it gets there, untie the rope and then hang on to it while I pull you up."

When Pia reached the top, Bart backed the wagon as close to the edge of the ravine as possible and attached the rope through one of the iron collars where the sideboard stakes had been. Then he slid down the slope, using the rope to help him.

When he reached Sabin, he took a syringe from his shirt pocket.

"Moving you is going to be pretty rough, so I'm going to give you a shot of morphine to help with the pain."

Bart gave the shot, then he moved Sabin onto the sideboard. With the bottom of the board even with the bottom of his foot, it only came up to his shoulders. Bart wished that it came all the way up to Sabin's head, but it braced his back and, most important, his leg. Bart had several smaller pieces of rope, which he used to tie Sabin to the board.

"Pia, start moving the wagon, but do it very slowly. Don't let the horse get away from you. I'm going to have to make certain the board doesn't get hung up on something, so if I yell, stop immediately."

"All right."

Getting Sabin up the side of the ravine took longer than Bart had expected, but Sabin finally reached the top.

"He's up!" Bart called as Pia stopped the wagon. "Mr. Carranza, I'm going to help you stand, but I don't want you to put any weight on your leg. When I get him to the wagon, Pia, put this board upright against the back, and if he can lie against it, I think I can slide him in."

With Pia inside the wagon to help hold her father's head up, Bart got the board with Sabin into the back of the wagon. Fortunately the effects of the morphine had taken hold, so it wasn't as painful an ordeal as it could have been.

"I have to get you back to the home ranch," Bart said.

"Do what you have to do here. I can't leave my sheep," Sabin said.

"*Aita*, you have to go. Bart can't help you out here."

"No. A shepherd does not leave his sheep."

"What if someone stays with the sheep? I have tended sheep, and I can tend them again," Pia said. "I will stay with the sheep until we can get someone else."

"Where is the lamb?" Sabin asked.

"I'll get him," Bart said, so once more he descended into the ravine. "Poor little thing. He's probably a bummer now, so, Pia, you'll probably have to feed him."

"I'll take care of him."

Pia watched the buckboard drive off, then knelt down before the two dogs as the lamb wandered off toward the band. Soon a ewe was running toward the baby, and Pia was pleased that at least one of her problems had been solved.

She began petting both dogs at once, and their tails were wagging ecstatically. "Esti, Bekindi, you were such good dogs taking care of *Aita* and keeping the band together! Now you're going to have to help me for a while. You know I can't do this without you."

Both dogs kissed her, and she smiled. "Let's go back to the wagon and let me find you something to eat. I'm hungry, and I'll bet you are, too."

The dogs followed her back to the wagon, where Pia fried some mutton for them. She knew that sheepdogs could never be given raw meat, lest they develop a taste for it and start to kill the sheep they were supposed to be protecting.

Pia warmed a can of pork and beans for herself. The dogs ate hungrily, and Pia put a lid on the pot of beans, intending to finish them for her supper.

"We'd better get the sheep back together, boys," she said to the dogs. "*Aita* won't be happy if we lose one."

During the time Sabin had lain in the bottom of the gully, the dogs had been so watchful over him that they had abandoned their herding duty, and now Pia saw that several sheep had wandered away from the band. It took Pia and the dogs most of the rest of the day to get them all bunched again. She decided that it would be easier to hitch up the horse and move the sheep wagon to the band, rather than trying to drive the sheep back to the bedding ground they had been using. Leaving the dogs with the sheep, Pia started back toward the wagon.

It was late afternoon and she noticed a dark cloud rising in the west. The cloud moved quickly, and the bright blue sky became gray. A wind came up, and she bent her head as she continued toward the wagon, but then felt a stinging dampness hitting her face.

Sleet!

She turned around to see what the dogs would

do with the sheep. She knew that she should drive them to a sheltered location because the freshly shorn sheep and their lambs could not survive without protection from the storm.

Running back toward the animals, she gave the signal for the dogs to turn the animals and head them to a low mound of hills that might act as a windbreak.

But the instinct of the sheep would not allow the dogs to turn them into the storm, and with the goat's bell jangling, they began running away from Pia. She had no choice but to follow them, running as fast as she could, watching as the sheep got farther and farther ahead of her.

Finally, she saw Toki, the goat, take a sharp turn to the right and head for an arroyo, with the flock following behind her.

By the time Pia caught up with the band, now crowded together in the gulch, the sleet was coming down hard, stinging her face. Though her sheepskin coat had kept her upper body warm, her skirt was cold and wet.

Even though she had tried to turn the band, she was thankful now for the goat, because Toki had found the only shelter in sight. The sheep had all bunched together, and while Pia worried about the young lambs being smothered, or even crushed, she knew that at least the sheep wouldn't freeze to death.

But, what about her? She had no shelter against the storm, no canvas to make a tent, no blankets, only her sheepskin coat. Bekindi ran off.

"Bekindi, no!" she called. "Stay here with us!"

What if Esti left as well? She had run so far away from the sheep wagon, she wasn't sure she could find her way back tomorrow if she didn't have the dogs to lead her. That is, if she didn't freeze to death this night.

Bekindi came running back, barking, then he turned and started away again. By now it was nearly nightfall, and what light there was behind the clouds was so dim that Bekindi was quickly lost in shadow. But he continued to bark, and Pia and Esti moved toward the sound.

Pia saw the dog moving up a hillside and disappearing into an opening that was not facing the wind.

"Good dog!" Pia said excitedly. "You've found us a cave! If only I had blankets and a sheepskin." For a fleeting moment she thought of the night she and Bart had slept under the stars on a sheepskin after Gabina's baby was born.

"And Bart," she added with a chuckle, glad that she could joke in such a situation.

She climbed into the cave, or more properly, she thought, a concave, because she had no idea how far back into the hill it went. In the dark she could not see, and for a moment she thought that this could be the den of some sheltering animal. But then she felt one of the dogs nudging her. Of course, the trusty Bekindi would have checked that for her.

Sitting on the rocks, she was relieved to be out of the wind and the sleet, but she was still quite cold. She slipped out of her wet skirt and laid it out as well as she could, hoping that it would freeze dry by morning. Thankfully the wool had been heavy enough to keep her petticoat dry, and she wrapped it around her as she hugged her legs to her chest. The two dogs were with her, and as if aware of the advantages of shared body heat, they snuggled up to her. Later into the night it got much colder, and even though Pia had matches, with nothing to burn they were of no use to her. She said a prayer of thanksgiving for the two dogs. Their proximity would keep her from freezing. She hoped.

As soon as he got Sabin back to the home ranch, Bart had two men carry him into Dabi's cabin. There, after taking away the makeshift stretcher, he cut the trouser leg off, then cleaned and examined the wound.

"What happened?" Dabi asked when he saw the leg.

"I tried to climb up hill carrying a lamb, and I fell," Sabin said without elaboration.

"It was more than that," Bart said. "But your leg isn't as bad as it looks. I don't see any signs of infection. I think I can reset the bone, splint it, put on a cast, and it will heal. But you won't be able to walk for quite a while."

"I have to get back to the sheep," Sabin said. "Pia can't stay there for long."

"Don't worry about your sheep. Estebe has taken his band out already, and we can join the two together," Dabi said. "He's not up to the midlevel yet, but he can be there in a few days if Pia can hold them."

"I don't know about Pia," Sabin said, "but I know Esti and Bekindi will be waiting for me, so they won't push the sheep too far."

"Well, let's get this leg set first," Bart said.

He opened his bag and began taking out the things he would need. First he got out a bottle of chloroform and some cotton. As he had done with Gabina, he put the cotton into a glass.

"I'm going to put you asleep so you won't feel anything while I do this, and when you wake up, it'll all be done."

Sabin nodded his acceptance.

Bart gave the glass to Dabi. "Hold this over his nose and mouth and count to five. Then, be ready to do it again when I tell you."

"All right."

"Now."

Dabi administered the chloroform as directed, and Sabin went out quickly.

"I want Sabin to go into town when this is over. Can you find someone to take him?"

"You mean to Boise?"

"No, just to Mountain Home. Mrs. Carranza is there, and I think if he's there, she can keep him from trying to do too much. This leg will heal by itself if he'll just let it, but if he stays here, he'll be right back on the mountain."

"I'll take him myself, first thing tomorrow morning," Dabi said.

"Good."

It took two more applications of the chloroform before Bart had the bone set and in a splint. When he was finished, Sabin's left leg was in a plaster-of-paris cast from his knee to his ankle.

"That's all I can do," Bart said, closing up his bag. "Now, I wonder if I might borrow a horse."

"You're going back out to find Pia?"

"Yes."

"You can use Bernat. He's my fastest horse."

"I appreciate that. I'll stay with Pia until Estebe joins the bands."

"I thought you might do that."

"Look, Dabi, before I go, there is something that needs to be said. I know about your culture, and I know that Sabin and your father have said that Marko will marry Pia. But I also believe that Marko doesn't want to marry her." Bart stopped, waiting for Dabi to speak, but when he didn't, Bart continued, "I have asked her to marry me, and she said yes. I intend to marry her as soon as I can get her back to Boise."

Dabi chuckled. "I've known from the beginning that Marko didn't like the idea of two old men picking his wife. I think he considers himself as American as you are."

"Marko is a good man, and a good friend. I consider you a good friend, too, Dabi, and I wouldn't want to see anything disrupt that friendship."

Dabi put his hand on Bart's shoulder. "You marrying Pia isn't going to affect that at all. That is, unless she teaches you how to beat me at *mus*. And for what it's worth, you have my blessing."

Bart chuckled. "That means a lot to me, but what I really need is Sabin's blessing."

"That, I fear, my friend, may be a bit harder to get."

Bart was able to cover the distance to the sheep camp a lot faster on horseback than in the buckboard. But halfway to the wagon, it began to sleet. Bart turned up his collar and rode on. It would nice and warm in the sheep wagon, and he comforted himself with the thought of a warm meal, probably a soup on a night like this. And maybe a hot cup of coffee. But what was most enticing was the thought that he would be sharing the wagon with Pia.

He had the blessings of Pia's mother and Dabi and, no doubt, Marko. He felt reasonably certain that Sabin would come around as well. But what about his own parents? What about Marjane? How would they feel about his marrying Pia?

In the storm, Bart stayed close to the rock boys, thankful that they were mainly in a straight line. When he passed the fifth one, he turned and headed toward the spring where he knew the wagon was sitting. When he found it, he was surprised that no lantern was lit. It didn't seem that late, but in a storm such as this, what would be better than to be warm and cozy in bed? Maybe, warm and cozy in bed with me? He smiled at the thought.

When he reached the wagon, he tied off his horse, then hurried to the door.

"Did you miss me?" he called when he opened the door. But the wagon was cold. He moved to the bed, thinking Pia must be sleeping. Then he felt a chill pass through him that was much colder than the sleet.

Pia wasn't there.

SEVENTEEN

Bart realized that Pia had to be outside, somewhere in this storm. But why had she gone out into weather like this?

Even as he asked himself the question, he knew the answer. No sheep were around, and she was with them. Perhaps she was trying to bring them back and was caught in the storm somewhere. But where? Was she safe? Did she have any shelter?

Bart lit a lantern and looked around the wagon to see what he could find in the way of camping equipment. He knew from listening to the tales the sheepherders told that they would often have to spend the night out with the sheep, away from the wagon. They prepared for that by carrying with them pieces of canvas for making a tent, as well as extra food.

"And dry socks," Dabi had said. "Don't forget socks. I think the worst thing that can possibly happen to you is to have wet socks, especially when it's cold."

It didn't take Bart long to find Sabin's camping

equipment in a compartment under the bed, and that it was all still here made Bart's head spin with worry and fear. Pia was out there with absolutely no camping equipment! She had no shelter, no protection of any kind against the storm!

Bart grabbed the canvas and a rubberized poncho. He was going to find her. He had no idea how he was going to do that in the middle of the night, but he was going to find her!

A few minutes later he was back on his horse.

"Sorry, old fellow," he said, speaking soothingly to Bernat. "But we're going to have to go out into this again. The woman I love is out there, and you have to help me find her."

Bart worried about hypothermia. If Pia was cold and wet and her body temperature dropped too low, it could be fatal. He had to find her.

"Pia!" he shouted over and over until his voice became weak in the wind.

All through the night, the wind howled, and Pia could hear the sleet coming down. She was thankful that Toki had found a degree of shelter for the sheep, and that it was sleet falling and not snow. In the draw, if it was heavy enough, snow would smother the sheep. She worried that she would lose a few, if not many, of the fragile newborn lambs, either from the cold or from being trampled in the press of the animals.

She was less frightened for herself now as she was protected from the sleet and the wind. Flanked by the two dogs close against her, she finally fell into exhausted sleep.

⤬

Bart wandered far into the night, calling Pia's name until his voice was hoarse, but never once getting a response. Then, when he saw one of the rock boys, he realized that he had passed this same spot earlier. He was riding in circles! Worse than that, he now had absolutely no idea where he was.

This was foolish. He wasn't going to find her tonight. He could only hope and pray that she had found some sort of shelter, somewhere, and would survive the night.

Bart found a dry creekbed in a cut about six feet deep, and he led his horse down into it. Here, at least, he was out of the bone-chilling wind. He tied the horse's reins around his arm.

"This is the best I can do," Bart told the horse. "I'm counting on you to get me started at first light."

When Pia awakened, she looked out into the pale-gray wash of early light. The storm had stopped, and when she stepped outside, she saw that the sky was clear. Soon the sun would be up, and she hoped its warming rays would melt the sheen of ice and rejuvenate the band of sheep.

Pia made her way down the slope, going as carefully as she could, all the while thinking of her father's accident. The sheep were beginning to mill, even though they were still crowded together. When she walked among them, she found several lying on the ground, dead, and she felt a keen sense of pity for the poor animals that had succumbed. She also felt a sense of guilt at the economic loss for her father.

That was when she heard the firing of three shots.

At first it frightened her, then a broad smile spread across her face as she realized that it must mean someone was trying to find her.

Raising her hands to cup her mouth, she shouted the *irrintzi* at the top of her lungs. It echoed and reechoed back from the hills.

Bart felt a charge of relief, extreme joy, and a thrill of excitement that exceeded anything he had ever before experienced. Then without consciously thinking of it, he returned the yell, or as close to it as he could get. Shortly thereafter he saw Esti bounding across the ground toward him.

"Esti, good dog! Oh, what a good boy you are! Take me to Pia!"

Esti turned and started running back, and Bart urged the horse into a gallop. Then he saw her, standing on top of a hillock, waving her hand over her head.

The galloping horse closed the distance in less than a minute, and almost before the horse had stopped running, Bart swung out of the saddle. He ran toward Pia, who was running toward him, and when they met, he threw his arms around her and covered her with kisses of unbounded joy.

"You're all right! I was so worried about you!"

"I wasn't worried. I had Esti and Bekindi with me, and I knew you would come."

"How did you know?"

"How do I know the sun will set tonight?"

Bart kissed her again. "I was afraid I'd lost you."

"You asked me to marry you, didn't you?"

"Yes."

Pia smiled at him. "Then, it's going to take more than a little rain to separate us."

Bart chuckled. "I'd say a sleet storm and freezing winds when you're out here with no protection is more than a little rain."

"I had protection. I told you, I had Esti and Bekindi."

"As far as I'm concerned, those two dogs have just made a friend for life. Are you hungry?"

"I'm starved. But so are the poor dogs."

"I brought some food," Bart said. "Some bread, a can of beans, a can of peaches."

"We had some lambs die last night, poor things. If you can carve one of them up, I'll get a fire started and cook some meat for the dogs."

"There's an old pine stump. It will be so full of resin that it should be easy to start, even though it's still a little wet. Just light it and let it burn. It'll give us a good fire."

Pia got the fire started, and a short while later Bart came back with some lamb chops.

"Oh, you did well," Pia said.

"It wasn't cold enough for the carcass to have frozen. I've got a skillet in the camping gear. And salt and pepper. We'll have us a good meal, then we can start back to the wagon."

"I don't think the sheep will go back. There's fresh grass here, and water. We're going to have to bring the wagon up."

"All right. After we eat, I'll go hitch up Zaldi and bring it here."

The smell of the cooking lamb caused Pia's mouth to water with anticipation, and she saw both Esti and Bekinki licking their chops. The dogs got the first meat, devouring it quickly.

"All right, Esti, Bekindi, it's time to get to work. Get the sheep out of here."

The dogs moved to obey her command, then Pia and Bart feasted on lamb and beans.

"You know that meal that we ate in the dining car?" Pia asked.

"Yes."

"This one is much better."

Bart laughed. "I agree."

With their meal eaten, and the utensils as clean as they could get them, Bart got ready to go back to the wagon.

"You'll have to feed Zaldi," Pia said. "The poor thing hasn't eaten in two days now."

"I'll make sure he's fed, and I should be back before supper."

Bart started toward the horse, then stopped and came back to Pia. "I love you," he said, then kissed her.

"And I love you." Pia laughed. "I can't believe that you gave an *irrintzi*."

Bart laughed as well. "Yeah, I did, didn't I? How was it?"

"It was awful." She smiled. "But it was the most beautiful sound I've ever heard."

Bart had the wagon back before six o'clock that evening, and he saw Pia sitting on a rock with one dog lying at her feet. She was watching the sheep, who were now gathered and content.

Pia came to meet him as he stood in the sheep

wagon, driving the horse from the open door. When he came to a stop, she stepped on the bottom step and he leaned down to kiss her.

"How was your day?" he asked.

"It was good, knowing that you were coming. And knowing that I wouldn't have to sleep in a cave tonight."

"What makes you think you're going to sleep tonight?" Bart asked, a twinkle in his eye.

Outside, the wind blew. The wagon shook, but because it was tight and well constructed, the wind didn't come through and the fire in the stove kept things warm. Pia felt as if they were in a cocoon. She found that idea sensual.

"Here's your father's bota bag," Bart said, taking the wine bag down from the hook. "Shall we have a little squirt?"

"I want it in a glass." She added with a smile, "Even if it has to be a jar."

"Pia?"

She looked over at him.

"I like this." He filled two small jars he had found and handed one to her.

Pia was sitting on the bed, with her shoes off, and she pulled her legs up under her. She took a sip from her jar.

Capturing a beam of light from the lantern, the wine seemed to glow. Pia used her hand to brush her hair back, then took a swallow of her wine, and Bart was certain he had never seen a more beautiful picture.

"I love you," Bart said. "I have never felt about anyone, or anything, the way I feel about you."

"It's funny. As a young girl, growing up, I knew that I would get married someday. That's the purpose of being a Basque woman—get married and have babies. But love wasn't something I ever imagined. It wasn't something I ever witnessed, and it was nothing that ever came to mind . . . until I met you. I think I fell in love with you before I even knew what love—what true love—was."

Bart smiled. "You still don't know what love can be." He put his wineglass on the table, then reached over and took Pia's glass from her. "But I promise you, after tonight, you will know." He moved over to sit on the bed beside her.

Pia was well aware that they were but inches apart, inside this cocoon, more than thirty miles from another human being. These were the opening steps in a dance that she had never before danced, and the thought of what might happen—no, what was *going* to happen—here tonight caused her skin to tingle with anticipation.

Bart put his hand to her cheek and held it there for a moment, his fingers burning into her skin. Then he leaned forward to kiss her. As before when he had kissed her, she felt every nerve ending in her body come alive.

Their kiss turned into a sensual duel, Bart's tongue capturing hers, her tongue responding, invading, then withdrawing, until finally she pulled away, awash with what was almost unbearable pleasure.

But Bart didn't stop. He continued to kiss her mouth, her cheeks, her throat, and then he did something he had not done before. He thrust his tongue into her ear. Almost instantly, it seemed, Pia was a helpless, quivering entity, with no control over what was happening to her.

By the touch of his hand, Bart let Pia know that he wanted her to lie back on the bed. It took only the gentlest of pressure because Pia wanted to continue down the path Bart was blazing for them.

That want intensified when Bart unbuttoned her blouse, then continued with his kisses, from the hollow of her throat down to the tops of her breasts. He began removing her blouse, and she lifted her shoulders to allow him to do so. Then he unlaced the front of her camisole, and freeing her breasts, she anticipated the pleasure she was about to experience. That night in the Bizkaia House when she had gone to him, she had presented her breasts to him, and she knew what pleasure his lips and tongue on her breasts could bring.

Then as before, his mouth found her nipple, and she arched toward him in pure and unbridled pleasure. His tongue began describing a circle around her nipples, first one, then the other, starting rings of fire of such intensity that she wondered how Bart's tongue could stand the heat.

She writhed under the assault of his lips and tongue, pulling him closer to her. So pleasurable was his attention to her breasts that she barely noticed that he was undoing the band of her skirt. Again, with the slightest pressure to suggest what he wanted, she arched her body from the bed and he pulled away the skirt. She slipped out of her cami-sole, leaving only her drawers.

His hands slid down across her belly, then to the top of her drawers, and with a gentle tug, and almost without her knowing he was doing it, the drawers were off, and she lay naked before him.

"What a beautiful creature you are," Bart murmured as he ran his hands over her body. "Your skin is shining like a golden statue in the lamplight."

Pia loved Bart. She trusted him, and she knew that she would grant him whatever he asked, whether by word or touch.

Bart's gentle touch reassured her. His fingers moved lightly, sensuously, over her belly, her thighs, and the insides of her legs, causing a pool of damp warmth to welcome Bart's finger. His finger stroked her gently, and as it had happened before, his finger slipped inside. She felt an exquisite pleasure, perhaps an even greater pleasure this time because she knew that here, in their private cocoon, there was no chance of interruption.

She also knew she would learn the secret that had been promised last time, but left unfulfilled. Bart's finger found a sensitive nub, and suddenly a new and much more intense wave of pleasure began to radiate out into larger and larger circles until her entire body was involved.

"Oh, Bart!" she gasped, unable to keep quiet.

Bart smiled at her. "This is only the beginning, the best is yet to come."

Now standing before her, Bart took off his own clothes, and she saw it again, that enormous shaft rising from him. Then, climbing onto the bed, he stretched out over her, supporting himself with his arms and legs.

He once again began kissing her, as his penis stroked where just minutes before his finger had been. When he felt her moisture laving his shaft, he positioned himself over her.

"When I enter the first time, there will be a little pain, but I promise you, it will only be for a moment. Then you will feel the most exquisite pleasure you have ever imagined."

As Bart had warned, Pia felt a sharp pain. But he had also said that the pain would be over instantly, and it was. All she could feel now was the pleasure of being completely filled by him. She engulfed him as he thrust in, then withdrew slowly, thrust again, and withdrew, each thrust sending wave after wave of indescribable pleasure through her.

She couldn't understand it. All the pressure, the fullness, the depth of it, was between her legs, but her entire body, from the tips of her toes to the top of her head, was tingling in sweet agony. She lifted her legs, and holding him tightly, she was unable to stop the moans of ecstasy escaping from her throat. She moved her body with his, matching the rhythm, feeling herself winding up tighter and tighter until it happened! Everything before, all of it, the waves of pleasure and ecstasy, had been nothing compared to this! It was as if she had been struck by a bolt of lightning! Not once, not twice, but three times, before finally she began coasting down, only to hit an eddy and then soar up again.

Then she heard Bart's breath become labored, she felt him tense, then with a groan and a final surge he thrust deep into her, bringing her, with him, one more time.

He collapsed on the bed beside her, breathing hard now, his arm around her, pulling her nude body against his. Outside the wind continued to blow, and the little wagon rocked back and forth gently. In the stove a gas bubble popped in one of the burning logs. Pia reached down to pull the quilt up over them.

"Bart?" Pia said quietly.

"Yes, my love?"

"Nothing. I just wanted to say your name."

Pia's head was on Bart's shoulder, just below his chin. He kissed her on the top of her head. Nothing about the kiss was sensual, it was little more than feeling his lips brush against her . . . but it bespoke a possessiveness, a mutually recognized truth that from this night on they were bonded together.

St. John's Cathedral—Boise

Bart had asked his father to be his best man. He had asked Marko to be his groomsman, and the three of them were waiting in the sacristy.

Alphonse Joseph Glorieux, the bishop of Boise, stepped into the room. "Are you gentlemen ready?" he asked, his Belgian accent still strong, even though he had been in America for over thirty years.

"I've changed my mind," Bart said.

"What?" the bishop gasped.

"You'll have to excuse my son, Bishop. He has a rather strange sense of humor."

"Oh." The bishop laughed. "To be sure."

இ౫ு

Because so many of the Basque community were moving their sheep to the high country, few were in Boise. Bart had asked Pia if she wanted to wait, but she was as anxious as he was to be married.

Zuriñe and Floria were sitting on the front pew on the left, while Bart's mother and his grandfather and Aunt Suzie were sitting in the front pew on the right.

A dozen people, mainly friends of Bart's mother, were scattered throughout the church. Just then Julen pushed Sabin's wheelchair up the aisle and put it next to Zuriñe.

Pia, resplendent in a white wedding gown, was standing in the narthex along with Elixabete and Marjane.

"Oh, my," Marjane said. "You absolutely have to be the most beautiful bride I have ever seen in my life, and I am so happy to have you as my sister." She hugged Pia, almost crushing her flowers.

"Thank you, Marjane."

"I can't wait to help you become an American citizen." Marjane smiled. "That way, you can vote."

Pia smiled. "I want that very much." She meant it.

Mr. Egana came into the narthex with a huge smile on his face. "I've never done this before."

"You've never escorted a bride down the aisle?" Marjane asked.

"No. I've never worn a suit." He held his arms out to show off the suit Sabin had bought for him.

"You look wonderful," Pia said, taking his arm.

The organist began playing "Trumpet Voluntary

in D," and the bishop led Bart, Frank, and Marko into the chancel.

"Oh," Marjane said. "There they are. I've never seen Bart look happier in his life. It's time for me to go." She started up the aisle, followed by Elixabete.

"Are you ready?" Mr. Egana asked as he offered Pia his arm.

"I've been ready a long time," Pia said as they proceeded down the aisle.

When they reached the front of the church, Mr. Egana sat beside Julen, and Pia took her father's hand. When in the ceremony the bishop asked, "Who giveth this woman?" Sabin said a loud "I do," and both Pia and Bart smiled. They knew they had his undeniable blessing.

The reception was held at the Bizkaia House, now sporting a fresh coat of paint and new windows.

"It looks like Pop and Grandpa are talking for the first time in years," Bart said when he saw Eli and Frank sitting beside one another. "It's a miracle."

"There's an even bigger miracle. *Aita* calls you an Amerikanuak now, an American Basque."

"I am pleased to be your husband, and I am pleased to be a Basque."

Just then Eli approached Bart and Pia. "Tell me, darlin'," Eli said, "would you allow an old coot to kiss the bride?"

"I would love to be kissed by an old coot," Pia replied with a lilting laugh.

Eli planted a kiss on her cheek, then reached into his inside jacket pocket and removed an envelope. "I've talked this over with Suzie," Eli said to Bart, and she agrees that this should be your wedding present." Eli handed the envelope to Bart.

"Well, thank you, Grandpa." Bart opened the envelope, then pulled out a folded piece of paper. He looked at it for a second, then gulped. "Grandpa, this is a deed to thirty thousand acres in Owyhee County!"

"They tell me it's not good for much. Except for raising sheep."

"I . . . I don't know what to say. I am overwhelmed."

"Use it in good health, my boy."

EPILOGUE

Ten years later

Thanks to Sabin's guidance and expertise as a ranch manager, Bekindi Ranch became one of the most successful sheep-raising operations in all of southwest Idaho. Bart had given up his medical practice and now lived and worked full-time on the ranch.

The sun was low and the western sky was ablaze with color, red, purple, pink, and gold. Though it wasn't cold, the tops of the Owyhee Mountains were wearing snowcaps.

Bart and Pia were sitting on their porch swing, rocking gently back and forth as they watched the show of color. He had his arm around her, and he pulled her closer to him, though it was symbolic only. She was already as close to him as she could get.

"Bart, is it a sin to be as happy and contented as I am?"

"Why should it be a sin?"

"I don't know, maybe because it just seems too good, somehow."

"The best is yet to come," Bart said.

"You always say that."

"Have I ever been wrong?"

"No," she agreed.

Frank and Sabin were throwing a football back and forth on the front lawn, and the ball hit the oak tree, breaking off a limb.

"Boys," Bart called, "be careful with that tree."

"You're always saying be careful with the tree," Frank said. "What's so special about this tree? It's just another tree."

"Come over here, sit on the porch," Bart said. "I think it's time you let your mother tell you about this tree."

"I planted this tree from the acorn of the Tree of Guernica. Under that tree the noblemen of Biscay and the kings of Castile and Aragon guaranteed the Basque people their liberties," Pia said.

"You're Basque, aren't you, Mama?" Sabin asked.

"Yes."

"Are we Basques, too?"

"We are all Amerikanuak," Bart said. "That means 'Basque, living in America.' And the reason I want you to learn about this tree is because it's always good to know something about your heritage."

Pia continued, "In our hearts we will always remember that among the Basques, each one is the equal of the richest, each one is the equal of the poorest, and no matter where in the world a Basque might go, we will always remember this tree and the promise of freedom."

"You know what, Mama?" Sabin asked. "This tree is like we have our own statue of liberty!"

"Yes," Pia replied with a broad smile, "it's our own Statue of Liberty."

Turn the page
for a look at

MARCI'S DESIRE

another blazingly hot Western romance

BY SARA LUCK

Now available from Pocket Books

ONE

Marci Winters left her dormitory and headed for the gymnasium on the second floor. Wells College was one of only twenty-six schools to receive the wonderful apparatus invented by Dr. Dudley Sargent, a professor of anatomy and physiology at Harvard University, and Marci made use of it daily. When one entered the cavernous room, it looked as if the iron frames and crossing bars were part of the ceiling, but they supported trapezes, horizontal and vertical ladders, and swinging hemp ropes.

She climbed one of the ladders and transferred to one of the bars of a trapeze. Pumping her legs, she got the swing going, then lowered her body so that she supported herself with the bend of her knees. With her arms hanging down, the feeling was exhilarating. She wished Mazie had come with her, so that she could have practiced some of the aerial somersaults she knew.

Just as she was dismounting, dropping down to the mat, which was more than a foot thick, she heard the door open and the distinct click of shoes on the gymnasium floor. Marci adjusted the split skirt of her exercise costume and stood ready to take her reprimand.

It is not becoming for a young woman to take such delight in the toning of her muscular structure.

When you take your place in society, others will look with disdain upon your prideful display of your body.

A Wells girl does not yearn to find her place among the acrobats who perform for Barnum and Bailey.

It is with much distress that I forbid you to use the apparatus for one week.

How many times had she heard Dean Smith tell her this over her three years at college?

"Miss Winters, I thought I might find you here."

Miss Helen Fairchild Smith was the dean of the school. A short woman, she always stood erect, exuding dignity and serenity. She took it upon herself to train the girls to accept their places in society. She embodied Mr. Wells's original philosophy in training every woman that passed through the college to realize that a woman's true and only sphere was her influence on the home and society. It was instilled in every student that the family was the real source of influence, and whether it be for weal or woe, the woman had the most influence over the future of civilization.

"Miss Winters, following the dinner hour, I would like for you to meet with me in the library. I will expect you there by eight o'clock."

"Yes, ma'am." Marci listened as Dean Smith walked the length of the gymnasium, her footfalls once more sounding loudly on the hardwood floor.

Dean Smith had surely known what Marci was

doing on the apparatus, yet the dean had not chastised her. And now she was asked to meet in the library. Was she being expelled?

She could vividly recall the last evaluation the dean had written to her parents: *Marci is one of my most challenging students. She is a natural leader—smart, talented, and personable. If only she weren't so headstrong and opinionated.*

Both her parents had reprimanded her for not conforming to the Wells philosophy, and DeWitt Winters had been particularly critical. He often reminded her of the privilege it was to attend the college where Frances Cleveland, the first lady of the United States, had matriculated. If Marci was being asked to leave school, how would she face her father? How would she face Stanton? Would he still love her if she was expelled?

"Oh, I am sweating so," Marci said a few minutes later, speaking to Georgiana. Marci dabbed at her face with a towel.

"Nonsense, child, Wells women never sweat. They glow, elegantly," Georgiana said, perfectly mimicking Dean Smith.

Marci laughed out loud. "Yes, ma'am."

"I see you got your weekly delivery of flowers." Georgiana walked over to the table, then leaned forward to smell the fragrant pink and white hyacinths. "I didn't read the card, but I can guess what it says. 'With affection, Stanton Caldwell.'" Georgiana exaggerated the words as she said them.

"Well, this time you're wrong. It says, 'With *much* affection, Stanton Caldwell.'"

"Why does he always sign his first and last name? Does he think you'll forget who he is?"

"You just don't understand Stanton. He is a very formal person."

"Ha! You're about the most informal person I know."

"Ahch!" Marci clutched at her chest as she stood in her underwear before her roommate. "You would say that to a Wells girl?"

"Yes, a Wells girl who has no modesty. I still don't understand how you got stuck with a staid, old man like Stanton."

"He's not that old, and besides, I met him at President Cleveland's inaugural ball. No one finds fault with Mrs. Cleveland for marrying a man twenty-eight years older than she is, so who can say anything if Stanton is twelve years older than I am?"

"Oh, yes, how can I forget the budding socialite on the arm of her father, the secretary of the treasury, at the inaugural ball," Georgina said with an affected accent.

"He's not the secretary of the treasury. He's the second comptroller, so that means he's just a glorified accountant, and there are a lot of very boring things he and his family are expected to attend."

"I'm serious. What was there about Stanton that made you attracted to him? He seems so different from you."

"Actually, he chose me, but I don't really know how he did it, because there were about ten thousand people in the Pension Hall for the inauguration. But what really impressed me was how much he already knew about me. He knew my father's position and that we'd moved from Roxbury and that we were now living on V Street."

"Didn't that make you feel a little creepy?"

"Oh, no, not when I saw how handsome he was!

You know, Georgiana, he could be a model for a Norse god—blond hair, deep blue eyes set in a perfect oval face. There's only one thing I don't like and that's his mustache." Marci smiled when she thought of the tickle his mustache caused when his lips brushed against her.

"All right. We accept that he's a good-looking man."

"He is, isn't he? And he's mature. Sometimes I have to pinch myself just to remind me how lucky I am to know someone like Stanton. Last summer we saw each other almost every week. And then when I was home for the holidays, we spent as much time together as we could, but he's always so busy."

"Whatever he did, in my book he's proven himself. What man sends his girlfriend flowers every week of the year?"

"Grover Cleveland," Marci said.

"Oh, yes. It must be something about a Wells girl. I wonder if Mrs. Cleveland's roommate knew she was going to be the wife of the president of the United States when she was getting all her bouquets. Tell me, will you invite me to your wedding?"

"Of course I will. I may even ask you to be a bridesmaid, but it may be a while, because he hasn't even asked me yet." Just then the clock in the hallway chimed seven. "We'd better hurry. I have a conference with Dean Smith right after dinner, and I don't want to be late."

"In the library?"

"Yes, how did you know that?" Marci asked.

"Because she asked me to meet her at eight o'clock."

Marci let out a deep sigh. "Thank goodness. It's

not just me. I thought I'd done something really dreadful this time."

Following dinner, Marci, Georgiana, and six other young ladies gathered in the library.

"What have we done?" Ellen Barker asked the group. "Does anyone know why we're here?"

"For her to ask us to meet at eight o'clock? That's really not characteristic of Dean Smith, especially when she knows we all have examinations tomorrow," Georgiana said.

"No one told about us sneaking out of the dormitory and meeting the boys from Cornell last weekend, did they?" Carrie Frey asked. "Maybe someone heard when they threw rocks on the windows."

"That was nothing," Marci said. "There were ten girls and two boys. If anything, the boys should get in trouble."

"Shh, I hear her coming," Georgiana said.

Everyone grew respectfully quiet waiting for the dean. When she stepped into the library, all eight women looked like soldiers standing at attention.

Dean Smith laughed when she saw them. "Ladies, how did you know what I'm going to ask of you? Please, sit down." She directed them toward a table, where she took the head chair.

"Every year at this time, certain women's institutions are invited to participate in a social engagement"—Dean paused for effect—"at the United States Military Academy."

There were several oohs and aahs as the girls tittered among themselves.

"This year, Wells College has been honored with an invitation to participate in this prestigious event, and it is my distinct pleasure to announce that you girls have been selected to represent us with your presence." Dean Smith lowered her head and clasped her hands before her. "I must say that not all of you met with my wholehearted support, but each of you had multiple advocates from the faculty singing your praises. Therefore, I have put my imprimatur upon each one of you to represent Wells. Do not disappoint me." The dean looked directly at Marci.

"Several of you are very close to Miss Nash in the art department, and I have selected her to act as your chaperone. Remember, ladies, it is an honor to be invited to West Point, for the United States Military Academy represents the pride of our nation."

All the girls reacted excitedly over the prospect of going to the academy, though it was Georgiana who found the courage to ask, "What is this social engagement?"

Dean Smith paused for a moment, then smiled, perhaps as if remembering something from her younger days, when she lived at Annapolis, where her father had taught mathematics at the Naval Academy. "You're going to a hop, my dear. A dance."

"Oh!" Carrie Frey squealed in delight. "Oh, yes, I saw a corps of cadets marching in the Fourth of July parade in Albany. They are all so handsome!"

"When do we get to go?" Ellen asked.

"The event will be this weekend. You will take the train into the city and then travel by boat up the Hudson River. I know that many of your homes are clustered not far from the river, and I might suggest that before boarding the train, you notify your parents should they want to visit with you. We will leave tomorrow as soon as all of you have written the zoology examination."

A general groan of dissent came from the girls.

"Why did you have to remind us of that?" Carrie asked.

"Because first and foremost, you are students. This junket is to be considered a pleasant interlude intended to enforce your academic experience. And now, ladies, I suggest you get a good night's sleep. I've been told by Professor Hart that you will be tested on primates tomorrow. I trust that your venture into the night air a few evenings past was for just such study. Good night."

"That woman knows everything," Ellen whispered as the girls made their way back to the dormitory.

The Wells girls waited on the platform of the Delaware, Lackawanna, and Western Railroad after having been brought by coach to Ithaca. They would change trains at Owego and reach Hoboken, New Jersey, in the early morning.

Many were doing as Dean Smith had suggested— notifying their parents that they would be at West Point for the weekend. Marci sent a telegram to her father and contemplated sending one to Stanton, but she decided against it. She knew he often shuttled back and forth between Washington and New York, and if he was in New York, he could cross the river and meet the train at Hoboken.

But something made her hesitate. She didn't want to see Stanton—not when she had to admit she was looking forward to this trip.

Often when she was a child, her family would travel up the Hudson, going as far north as Catskill to take a road to Roxbury that was at a lower elevation than was the most direct route through the mountains. When the boat passed West Point, she would look up at the gray granite buildings, wondering who lived there. Now, for the first time, she would find out.

West Point

After being dismissed from their morning formation, the cadets checked the chalkboard for orders of the day. One posting drew the most interest.

Those cadets who are not dragging to the hop tomorrow evening will please repair to Mr. Gurney's room, second floor, fourth division, at the close of duty hours today. Drawings for young ladies will begin promptly at 5:30.

That afternoon, John Gurney collected all the names of the arriving female visitors and put them into a box. The cadets who didn't have an invited guest coming to the dance, who weren't *dragging*, as the men called it, gathered in Gurney's room to draw the name of the person they would entertain for the weekend.

"Understand that each of these young ladies will be able to accept or deny any invitations to dance. She will have a dance card, and you will be expected to honor her commitments," the superintendent told them. "If she does not have a commitment, it will be your responsibility to entertain her."

"Excuse me, sir, but what if we find the looks and personality of the young lady whose name we draw to be . . . incompatible with our preference?" one of the cadets asked in an Alabama drawl.

"Cadet Mitchell, not one young lady will be"— Colonel Ernst paused for a moment, then continued—"*incompatible* . . . with your preference. These women have made great personal sacrifices to make the trip to this institution. As gentlemen, I expect each of you to escort the young lady in your charge as if she were a princess."

"Yes, sir."

"Now, I leave Mr. Gurney in charge of the drawing."

Cade McDowell drew just before his best friend and roommate, Casper Conrad.

"Who'd you get, Cade?" Casper asked as he stepped up to draw a name.

Cade read the card. "'Marcia Diane Winters, Wells College, Aurora, New York.'"

"Ooh," Casper said, reading his card.

"What's the matter?"

"Hortense Atkinson. Hortense? And she's from Evelyn College."

"Remember," Cade said, teasing, "no matter what the rumors are about the girls at Evelyn, she's a princess."

After the young ladies were duly checked in to the West Point Hotel, they were summoned by Miss Nash to walk with her out onto a broad open area, which Marci had already learned was the Plain. Marci looked over at the turreted, gray pile buildings on the other side as they walked toward a group of women who were standing at the end of the Plain.

The air was brisk, and the sky was a clear blue, with but a few downy puffs of white clouds floating overhead. Marci felt excited being here, and she wondered what the weekend would bring.

Ahead, they saw a formation of men in gray and white uniforms, standing as still as statues. Some of the girls waved and smiled, but not one of the men looked toward them.

"Well, that's sort of snobbish," one of the girls said.

"They're in formation and they must maintain their military bearing," Miss Nash told her.

"Then, how come one of them is coming toward us?"

"Because he's the one in charge," Miss Nash said. "You can tell because he has stripes on his sleeves."

"Ladies, I am Cadet Captain Edward Schulz, and on behalf of the United States Military Academy, I would like to welcome you. I would hope that while you are here, you have a pleasant stay.

"Each of the cadets that you see in formation has been assigned the pleasure of being your escort for the weekend. When I call the name of a cadet, he will come forward and identify the lady he has chosen from a random drawing, and it will be his responsibility to make certain your visit to West Point is a memorable one."

Marci furrowed her brow when she heard this method of choosing an escort. She wasn't sure how she felt about being handed off in such a way, but as she thought about it, she couldn't think of any method that would be more impartial.

"Cadets, at ease!" Captain Schulz ordered, and as one, the cadets moved their left foot out and clasped their hands behind their back.

One by one the cadets were called from the formation to read off a name. As each girl's name was called, she stepped forward; then the cadet, offering his arm, led her away.

Several names had been called before one cadet stepped forward, looked at the card in his hand, then said loudly, "Miss Marcia Diane Winters!"

"I am Miss Winters," Marci said, responding as had the girls who were previously called.

The cadet smiled broadly.

Marci noticed the man who approached her was taller than most of the others, with wide shoulders and a broad chest. He was quite handsome—not in the classical, almost effete way of Stanton, but in a very masculine way, with dark hair, dark eyes, a square jaw, and a strong chin.

"Miss Winters"—he offered Marci his arm—"I am Cadet Myles Cade McDowell, and I'm pleased to be your escort."

"I am pleased to meet you, Cadet Myles Cade McDowell." Marci took his arm. "And it would please me very much if you would call me Marci."

The smile broadened. "It would be my pleasure, Marci. And, please, I would prefer that you call me Cade. I get to hear my Christian name used so seldom, it would be absolute music to my ears, especially when it comes from the lips of such a beautiful young woman as yourself."

Marci's eyebrows shot up, then she laughed. "If I have to listen to that kind of nonsense all weekend"—she paused for dramatic effect—"I fear . . . I fear the nausea will force me to my bed."

Now Cade laughed. "A woman who speaks her mind. I like you, Marci, and we're going to get along just fine."

And don't forget to look

for the next steamy Western romance

BY SARA LUCK

Available Spring 2014 from Pocket Books

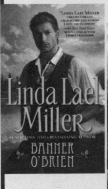
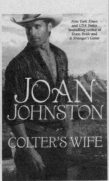
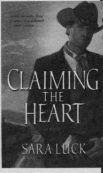